Dangerous Intoxication

"You are different tonight," John said. "Different and rather marvelous." There was a vibration, an electricity between them. Doreen felt it running hotly through her veins. She knew that she was trembling and that John's hand on her bare arm had tightened until the pain of it was almost intolerable. She gave a little gasp and swayed toward him.

Then a voice broke in on them, and the parson from Rangoon was standing beside her.

"I thought you might be able to help us," he said.

And Doreen knew she had been saved from John, only to walk into another trap laid for her by her dead cousin!

Also in Pyramid Books
by
BARBARA CARTLAND

DESIRE OF THE HEART
A HAZARD OF HEARTS
THE COIN OF LOVE
LOVE IN HIDING
THE ENCHANTING EVIL
THE UNPREDICTABLE BRIDE
THE SECRET HEART
A DUEL OF HEARTS
LOVE IS THE ENEMY
THE HIDDEN HEART
LOVE TO THE RESCUE
LOVE HOLDS THE CARDS
LOVE IS CONTRABAND
LOVE ME FOREVER
THE INNOCENT HEIRESS
DEBT OF HONOR
SWEET ADVENTURE
THE ROYAL PLEDGE
THE LITTLE PRETENDER
THE GOLDEN GONDOLA
STARS IN MY HEART
MESSENGER OF LOVE
THE SECRET FEAR
AN INNOCENT IN PARIS
THE WINGS OF LOVE
THE ENCHANTED WALTZ
THE HIDDEN EVIL
ELIZABETHAN LOVER
THE UNKNOWN HEART
A KISS OF SILK
LOVE IS DANGEROUS
THE KISS OF THE DEVIL
LOST LOVE
THE RELUCTANT BRIDE
THE PRETY HORSE-BREAKERS
AGAIN THIS RAPTURE
OPEN WINGS
THE KISS OF PARIS
LOVE UNDER FIRE
THE ENCHANTING EVIL
THE ENCHANTED MOMENT
THE AUDACIOUS ADVENTURESS
NO HEART IS FREE
LOVE IS MINE

STOLEN HALO

Barbara Cartland

PYRAMID BOOKS ◙ NEW YORK

STOLEN HALO

A PYRAMID BOOK

Pyramid edition published January 1973

ISBN O-515-02887-8

Printed in the United States of America

Pyramid Books are published by Pyramid Communications, Inc. Its trademarks, consisting of the word "Pyramid" and the portrayal of a pyramid, are registered in the United States Patent Office.

Pyramid Communications, Inc., 919 Third Avenue, New York, New York 10022

"I want the mask of a saint," he said.
"Mask of a saint, my Lord?"
"Certainly!" said Mr. Aeneas,
briskly. "With or without halo"?

ONE

The hot blazing sun shone through the broken sun-blinds, casting strange variegated shadows on the walls of the room.

From the street below came the penetrating fragrance of coffee, the sound of voices raised in argument and the undeniable and persistent stench of camel, which is an indivisible part of the native streets of Cairo.

Voices rose and fell, sometimes musical, more often parrot-like as they screeched in anger or good-humoured chaff, but the woman lying on the bed was quite unaware of them.

She had grown used to the noises of the city, so used that they irritated her less than the buzz of a mosquito, or the creak of the rusty bed springs each time she turned over fitfully.

She was wearing only a thin cotton nightgown, but it clung to her figure in damp patches and every now and again she wiped beads of perspiration from her forehead with the back of her hand.

After a while she opened her eyes and lay staring at the ceiling, intent on her own thoughts, until a restless movement drew her attention to an open letter lying on the bed.

She took it up and read it once again, while knowing every sentence almost word-perfectly.

It was a short letter, but she took a long time to finish it. Then finally she flung it from her as though it were repugnant.

"What am I to do?" she asked herself out loud. "What the devil am I to do now?"

Slowly, against her will, tears forced their way into her eyes, overflowed and ran gently down her thin cheeks.

She lay still until suddenly, with a convulsive movement, she got off the bed and walked towards the mirror which surmounted the stained wood chest of drawers at the far end of the room.

Here she looked at her reflection, at first vaguely, then intently, leaning her elbows on the chest of drawers and resting her face in her hands.

"What are you going to do?" she asked herself again with a wry movement of her lips.

But the tragedy in the eyes that stared back at her was somehow farcical.

She laughed, a broken, bitter laugh, which seemed quickly stifled into silence in the hot airless atmosphere of the room.

She looked back at the bed. Beside the envelope and the letter was a little collection of green notes—Egyptian pounds, ten of them. She walked across and picking them up, thrust them almost surreptitiously as if she was afraid, into the inner pocket of a red handbag.

Then she threw the bag down on the bed and sat down beside it.

"If only I didn't feel so ill," she thought.

Beads of perspiration were gathering thickly on her forehead from the exertion of walking about.

She wiped her face, this time with the hem of her nightgown, then in sudden weakness, rolled backwards against her pillows, lying limp and inert.

Dengue fever, leaving an aftermath of depression and weakness, had raged through Cairo that summer. Doreen Wallis had at first struggled against the high temperature, the nausea and the delirium which threatened to overcome her.

Then she had succumbed like everyone else and had been taken to hospital, too ill to protest.

She had come out ten days later, cured but with strict instructions from the doctors to do nothing, to stay in bed and rest as much as possible.

She had only been too glad to obey, even though it entailed long lonely hours in her cheap lodgings, with often a lack of meals, when the servant forgot to bring upstairs the food she had ordered.

It was only when she had been back four or five days that she found enough strength to write to Tony.

She had expected so much from him—how much she only dared admit to herself now.

He had taken her out to dinner night after night; they had danced in all the gayest and most expensive places in Cairo; she had watched him play polo at The Gezira Club; had used his car when he was not needing it as though it was her own.

She had been certain that he loved her and certain too that if it was not love that she felt for him, it was indeed a deep affection. But it was easy to love anyone who was rich, who was young and gay and amusing.

She had needed all three things so greatly, and deep down inside herself, had been almost abjectly grateful for them.

Every day it seemed to her there was the likelihood of Tony proposing marriage.

Often she knew indisputably that the words hovered on his lips, and she felt herself grow tense, ready to accept, but prepared because of a last flickering pride, to force that acceptance to come slowly and graciously.

It would not be easy to curb her excitement, or hide her eagerness, for she wanted marriage, wanted it even more passionately than she wanted Tony himself.

Only marriage could bring her security and an escape from the past which threatened her ominously wherever she went.

It had been a continual strain hoping against hope that Tony's friends were as ignorant as he was about her. It was not easy for her to escape notice in Cairo; she was too well known, too notorious.

It was ludicrous perhaps, but that word was not exaggeration. She was known wherever two or three older women were gathered together, ready at the slightest sign of her approach to protect their sons behind the aprons of their respectability.

"That is Doreen Wallis!"

How often she had heard it whispered behind her as she came into a restaurant, or moved among the tea-tables arranged on the marble terrace of The Gezira Club.

She knew what was being said, knew that eyes were staring at her with curiosity, resentment and often dislike.

It made her walk proudly, with her head up, her chin set, and it made her use her lipstick and her mascara with a heavier hand, as though they were an armour and a protection against a world that censored her.

At times the lowered voices and inquisitive glances drove her to a defiance which made her behave stupidly.

How often she had been enjoying an evening of friendship with some quite ordinary decent man, until spurred on by the comments which she sensed were being made around her, she had abandoned herself voluptuously into his arms on the dance floor.

"I will give them something to talk about!" she thought hotly on these occasions, but when she was alone afterwards, she could see how stupid she had been.

Stupid because she was always the loser, and those who stood for respectability, for security, for all the things she had never had and never would have, invariably won.

She had lost now!

They—the chattering mouths, the listening ears, and the prying eyes of Cairo—had taken Tony from her.

She could imagine and could understand so easily, how the moment she was ill, and her hold on him had relaxed, that he had been swept back into the social tide from which he had emerged.

Then he would have been warned, cautioned and told all those things about her which she had prayed he would never hear.

Things which he would never have listened to had she been there by his side, ready to laugh such allegations away, to entice him to indifference to public opposition with the touch of her lips and the gentle pressure of her hands.

With a groan Doreen turned over, lying face downwards, so that not even the empty room should see the bitterness of the tears which could not be controlled.

"He loved me, he loved me," she whispered.

She had been so near to loving him. It had been wonderful to know a decent Englishman after all the foreigners with whom she had come in contact these last years.

He had seemed like someone from another planet, with his fair skin; his cleanness; the cut of his clothes; the surprise in his blue eyes at some of the people and some of the sights of Cairo.

He was so dear, so lovable. But now he was gone!

She would never see him again; never hear the sound of his young voice calling her name; feel the strength of his arms around her shoulder, or the touch of his tender yet eager lips on her mouth.

"You are wonderful!" he said to her the night he had first kissed her.

Conventional words, but still there had been a throb in his voice which had meant so much. She had known then that she wanted him, wanted him for himself, as well as for what he could give her.

And she had been afraid, as though she realised what odds lay against her.

He was three years younger than she was, but that didn't matter. After all, twenty-nine was not so very old nowadays, when women of forty and fifty take their places as the most attractive women in the world.

But he was years, even centuries, younger than she was in knowledge and experience.

The son of rich parents, pampered and adored by his mother, he had come out to Cairo on a holiday.

"I want to see the world," he had told Doreen naïvely, and was surprised when she answered bitterly, "You will certainly see a very unpleasant section of it here."

To him it was all fun—the sunshine, the air of gaiety, the hospitality of the English colony, and the pleasure-seeking which made the sum total of everyone's days and nights.

That was the Cairo Tony saw, and only Doreen knew the sordidness, the heartbreak, the misery and the filth which lay underneath so much of it. Not that she wished to enlighten him.

She was prepared to take with both hands that which the gods sent her. She threw herself whole-heartedly into making Tony's sightseeing tour a really happy one.

It was not difficult for her, save that she had so much to gain by being a success and everything to lose if she was a failure.

Together they saw the Pyramids, the mosques and the recently excavated tombs. Together they danced in the glittering garish hotel ballrooms, or under the moon at the open-air cabarets.

Together they explored The Muski, finding in its labyrinth of shops, presents, not only for Tony's family in England, but also for Doreen—quaint boxes of Persian design, a necklace of carved ivory, a belt ornamented in uncut turquoises.

These were now the only things left to her—that and the Egyptian pounds lying on the bed beside her.

"To buy yourself something to remember our happy times together."

That was what he had said in his letter and somehow he could not have hurt her more, could not have thought out a phrase more bitterly ironic.

Ten pounds with which to write "finale" to the hopes which had risen so unquenchably within her; ten pounds to end a chapter in his life.

She was to remember him with the help of a souvenir, while he would look back on these three weeks together as an episode by which he had gained a little experience of the so-called "world".

How well she could understand the attitude of those who rescued him. They would refer to it as

"a lucky escape for that nice boy".

Or say jovially,

"All's well that ends well—he might have got into worse trouble!"

The very last day before she had been taken ill, Doreen had been so certain that everything would be all right. When it had been time to say good night, he had held her closely in his arms and had whispered:

"Wouldn't it be wonderful if you didn't have to go, if you didn't have to leave me!"

She could hardly answer him because of the beating of her heart.

"Oh, Tony, it would, wouldn't it?"

She had waited breathlessly, but he had only kissed her again before he opened the car door and helped her out.

"How can I make him ask me? How can I make him say the words?" she asked herself that night, walking up and down her room for nearly an hour before she got into bed, too agitated, too anxious to sleep, yet still certain that tomorrow would bring her happiness, would hold all that she wished for so desperately.

Flowers, chocolates, little presents and a look of adoration in his eyes which could not be assumed, were all flags of hope along the road of their association.

It was easy to forget other failures, to let the memory of Pepi slide away into the mists of things best forgotten, to force herself to believe that Tony's loyalty would not permit him to be silent were she attacked by those who mistrusted her.

Oh, it had been a fool's paradise while it lasted!

Now she could only accept the inevitable with a kind of limp misery, and know in an agony of cynicism that she must accept the money, even while she longed to send it back to him.

He had already left Cairo, was on his way back to England, to the sanity of his family, to the companionship of decent girls who did not live as she did, and who knew nothing of what existence might mean where humanity finds no security and must grab, grasp, and steal their needs, whatever the ultimate reckoning.

It was hard to remember what she had planned for herself before Tony came into her life.

Only a little over a month ago, yet that month had been so charged with hope and a kind of ecstatic happiness, that it was agonising now, to force herself to face the future.

From the moment of their meeting they had been indivisible; she went everywhere with him, indeed she had been wise enough to know it was her one safeguard.

Once be evasive, once allow other people to get a hold on him and her power would be gone. Yet underneath her keenness there was also a kind of childlike trust and faith in the luck that had sent him into her life.

For it was luck, luck when she was needing it most, when she had been most depressed, most miserable.

The last two years had not been easy, but at least she had a little money—money it was true which Pepi had given her, but pride is seldom practicable and she had tried to think of it as hers, not as in any way belonging to him.

It had taken her some time to get over the shock of Pepi's death, not only the fact of his dying, but over the discoveries which had come about because of it.

It had been hell to find later that those discoveries were known to many other people. Her first instinct after Pepi's death was to tell no one of the revelations which were disclosed, to let the world go on in blissful ignorance.

But someone, she had no idea who, had known the story almost as soon as she knew it herself, and it had spread over Cairo like a forest fire. It was carried from mouth to mouth.

She had realised at her very first appearance in public that the secret she guarded within her heart was no longer a secret.

Queer side-long glances, whispers, snubs, and the humiliation of being cut by people who, only a few weeks before, had been delighted to dine at her house, had told her only too clearly—the truth.

Then she had known that she could do nothing but assume a bravery she was far from feeling, and pretend neither to herself nor to the world.

It had taken courage, for at times she felt that her only choice lay between being crushed beyond all resurrection, or an almost brazen indecentness, as though she must walk naked through the streets that all might see her.

It seemed ridiculous to find that after four years of being married to Pepi, she had not made one reliable solid friend to whom she could turn in such an emergency for advice or support.

When she reviewed her acquaintances, seeking amongst them for someone she could trust, for just one to whom she could go for support and sanctuary, she realised that she should have known long before the true position of things.

Had they guessed? Had they known? The riff-raff who had come to the house; the decent men who so often made excuses for their wives.

It was a bitter thought now to believe that she was the only one deceived.

Yet in the revelation of the truth, it was easy to condemn her blindness. Pepi was so much older that she had been content to let him run his house the way he liked, to accept his friends and to make them her own.

It was only afterwards that she remembered she had often questioned the reliability of those same friends, wondering why Pepi, who was shrewd and intelligent, could find them congenial.

But she had been content with everything that came her way, simply because after years of insecurity, she had found at last for a little while, a safe anchorage and harbour in Pepi's arms—in the status he offered her as his wife.

"How was I to know?" she asked herself both bitterly and angrily after his death.

And while she reproached Pepi, she despised her own credulity.

It was difficult too, not to wonder if her father and mother had had any suspicions of Pepi's plausibility. Yet they had been so obviously delighted at the marriage, so eager to thrust her into it from the very moment that Pepi loomed on the horizon, that it was happily easier to believe in their innocence.

Neither had she been critical; there had never been a more willing bride. The difference in age—thirty-five years—had been quite unimportant beside the fact that Pepi had both money and the inclination for marriage.

That was what counted after the years of dragging around dirty third-rate hotels, of knowing shoddy, third-rate people and of putting up with her mother's querulousness and her father's drunken affability.

Pepi had seemed a godsend at that moment. She did not blind herself to the fact that he did not come from the same class which her mother still boasted they belonged to.

That it was a boast which could be substantiated by neither the principles nor the pride of gentility, made Doreen value it at exactly what it was worth.

There was no question of being ladies and gentlemen when they were quite prepared to skip from one hotel to another when they owed rent, when they must stave off their creditors with palpable lies and by still more degrading tricks, when they would eat or drink with whoever offered them something free.

No, looking back she believed that her father and mother had no suspicion of Pepi being different from what he pretended.

Only she might have been put on her guard by his desire for secrecy—so easily explained away by the fact that an old man marrying a young girl was always a laughable object in the eyes of the public and of the newpapers—by the fact that none of the Greek colony in Cairo called on them after they set up house together.

Yes, there were a thousand pointers which might have led her to the truth, but instead she lived in blissful ignorance until that day when the Will was opened, and she found that in the eyes of the law she had no legal standing.

Pepi had both a wife and a grown-up family in Athens, waiting to demand his estate and personal effects!

TWO

Looking back, Doreen felt that she could divide her life into definite passages of time, at the end of which there was always some shocking revelation to startle and horrify her.

She could remember now, as vividly as if it had happened yesterday, the first time she had been aware that her father drank and drank to excess.

She was only a child, but she could recall the nausea and the shrinking that she had felt at his voice raised in drunken incoherence, at the shuffle of his unsteady steps, and at her mother's tearful reproaches.

These had finally forced her to rush upstairs to her own room with her fingers in her ears, to bury her face in her pillow in an effort to escape a world that was suddenly bestial and horrible.

Afterwards she had grown immune to her father's weakness.

She had become used to what became almost daily scenes, to the cleaning up of his room when they had no servants, and the occasions when for a brief time they made an effort to keep up appearances before new acquaintances, or in strange hotels.

She grew used also to their unchanging penury, to the sordid conditions in which they lived, from which she was the worst sufferer, and to her mother's continual whining.

At times Doreen felt she preferred her father, who at least in nine cases out of ten was both pleasant and friendly in his drunkenness.

On the tenth occasion he became fighting drunk and it was because of this that the original disaster had overtaken them, for he had struck a superior officer and been cashiered from the army.

Henry Wallis when he married had been a smart, engagingly high-spirited young subaltern and it was easy to understand why Mary Wickham had fallen in love with him.

Why, in spite of the protests of her family, who had hoped for a better match or at least one more financially advantageous, she had insisted on the ceremony taking place before his regiment sailed for foreign service.

Mary Wickham had been quite a beauty in her youth. When she died she had become a withered, prematurely aged woman, with the lines of discontent deep ingrained into what had once been a plump, childlike face.

She had been disillusioned from the very beginning of her marriage, for she had hated their time in India, and it was when her husband was doing his last years of foreign service in Egypt, that the disaster which ended his career occurred.

Henry had been drinking for some time.

Mary had been unable to prevent him, for when she protested either angrily or tearfully, he would merely laugh, kiss her lightly, and rush off to get among "the chaps" again.

Henry Wallis was supremely happy.

He liked the feeling of good-fellowship which he found in his regiment, the lack of initiative or heavy thinking that such a career offered him, and the chances such a life provided of constant sociability at the minimum cost.

He was weak-charactered and amazingly uneducated, for he never read a book and seldom opened a newspaper.

He was content to do his regimental duties almost automatically, to exert himself only to amuse, and never to worry or arouse himself if there was a question of work or responsibility.

His regiment was not a particularly distinguished one. Most of the officers were men of no ambition like himself.

It had therefore the effect of a minor revolution when the colonel retired owing to ill-health, and was replaced by a man who required and expected a great deal both from his officers and men.

He had risen from the ranks, and was instantly condemned by Henry and his like as "not quite a pukka sahib". None of them could see that the new colonel was an exceptional man with exceptional capabilities.

Time was to prove that; he rose higher and higher in his profession, until with the irony of fate which seldom misses a coincidence, in the very week of Henry's death, he was gazetted to one of the highest ranks in the Service.

To Henry and his friends, however, he was only a man who had not been to a public school.

Henry was all the more censorious because an inner feeling of inferiority made him self-sensitive and boastful about his antecedents.

In actual fact, his father had been a small town solicitor in the North of England and his mother the daughter of a country doctor who had married beneath her.

A man of better breeding, or indeed of a higher standard of intelligence, would not have underrated his new commanding officer.

But Henry in his weak, garrulous manner, was quite content to be carried along by the general opinion and to condemn the new colonel, even before he crossed the threshold of the mess.

For the first week or so the newcomer made no move, watching with keen perceptive eyes all that went on around him, learning, no doubt, with many misgivings of the material on which he had to work. Then he started.

Discipline was tightened; routine and formality were introduced; things which had been allowed to lapse for years were brought sharply back to the conventional.

The effect on the regiment itself was excellent; on many of the officers it was catastrophic.

Perhaps for Henry alone such a change was humanely impossible. He had always managed, somehow or other, to drift through life, doing not only the minimum amount required of him, but immeasurably less than anyone else.

It was too late now to teach him new tricks. He was both resentful and afraid.

He hated the colonel with all the spiteful impotence of a cowardly nature which is too limp to stand up to anything stronger than itself.

He ran him down behind his back and made obscene jokes about him. He drank to his damnation every time he had a drink—which was pretty often. He veered between being a naughty, petulant schoolboy and a sullen, discontented man.

Both are difficult to deal with, especially when there is no common bond, no human touch which can be ignited to save what sooner or later must be an explosive conflagration.

It came on guest night. Henry had introduced one of his pet cronies—a man whose reputation was too well known to be ignored. The colonel was curt to him; Henry resented the slight.

His resentment took the form of drinking more than usual and when dinner came to an end, he staggered drunkenly to his feet, and demanded from his senior officer an explanation.

The colonel, ready to leave the mess, waved him to one side, but Henry's blood was up and in a fit of bravado, which he certainly would never have experienced in his more sober moments, he rushed at the colonel.

He knocked him down, and before he could be prevented by the surrounding company, who were too astonished and surprised to move for quite a considerable time, hit him again and again.

It was inevitable that a court martial followed and that Henry was cashiered.

At first he could hardly believe that it had happened to him, but when finally he found himself a free man, it took all the natural elasticity of his nature to bring him back to his normal cheerfulness.

"Something will turn up," he told his wife, but unfortunately nothing did.

Their immediate concern was, of course, money, a concern which from the moment his army career was finished, was never to leave him. He himself had a hundred and fifty pounds a year which had been left him by his mother.

Mary had another hundred pounds, hers under a rather extraordinary trust made by her grandfather, in which on her death, the money reverted not to her dependants, but to some obscure charity in the East End of London.

Two hundred and fifty pounds a year and a small child to look after was by no means riches, especially as they elected to stay in Cairo—a city where money runs through the fingers like the proverbial grains of sand.

It was Mary's fault that they did not return to England.

She was abjectly ashamed of what had occurred, making perhaps more fuss about it than was necessary and forcing her own feelings upon her husband to such an extent, that he also would not risk the humility of seeing his friends and relations again.

"You will find something here," Mary told him, "after all, they ought to be glad to employ an Englishman."

At first Henry made a few attempts at getting a job but he soon fell into the position of being a general tout, a hanger-on round bars and a habitué of the racecourse.

There were always foreigners to be plucked in Cairo, and tourists who found a good fellow an asset and who were prepared to pay for it.

Henry was in and out of funds a hundred times a year, but somehow they lived, even in the black periods, in the most expensive city in the world, three people without roots, without even plans save for the immediate present.

Henry undoubtedly enjoyed himself from the moment he discovered the congeniality of the cosmopolitan bars.

It took Mary some time to adjust herself, but when finally she found that if she didn't go out she must sit at home alone and be nothing more or less than a nursemaid in the dingy lodgings or hotels, where they were often the only white visitors.

She decided that Henry was not going to have it all his own way, and she joined him.

A good part of her allowance had to be spent on clothes and the real sufferer in this precarious existence was the child Doreen.

Henry and Mary, once they started to link up as a team and while they were still young, had an exceedingly gay time.

There were always people who were willing to pay for them, and who found them amusing companions, ready and willing for any frivolity, however unconventional.

There were champagne suppers, dances every night, racing, picnics and expeditions, while Doreen was left in charge of some native girl who did as little as possible for the paltry handful of piastres that she received, and who, as often as not, forgot to feed the child.

Perhaps she wouldn't have known how different her life was from that of the ordinary girl of her age had not Henry, in an unexpected moment of affluence, arranged when she was ten, for her to go back to England to stay for three months with her grandmother.

Doreen had been horrified at the idea; she had cried and pleaded with her father and her mother, begging them to let her stay with them, making every possible childish plea and promise to alter their decision.

They were adamant. It was for her good they assured her.

Their sudden interest in the child's well-being was not disinterested: a rich American had offered to take them down the Nile in his boat—a trip which would last for several months—and they had been at their wits' end to know what to do with Doreen.

Mary still kept up with her family spasmodically.

When her mother, Mrs. Wickham, mentioned her grand-daughter in a letter and asked for a photograph, the idea had been born that it would certainly be to Doreen's advantage, as well as their own, if she could go back to England for the summer.

So Doreen had gone, crying up to the very last moment. A skinny, not very attractive child, with eyes too big for her small face, and fair hair, which showed no natural tendency to curl, frizzed fussily under a hat that was too big for her, and which had once been her mother's, but had been discarded as unfashionable.

She had returned to Cairo a very different being.

She spoke very little about her holiday in England and because she kept her thoughts to herself, neither Mary nor Henry had the slightest idea how often she thought about it, or how much it had meant to her.

But it was from that moment she started to live in some ways a life of her own.

She complained, generally with reason, about her treatment from the hotel servants; she kept her own room—even though at times it was nothing more than a cupboard—tidy and comparatively clean. She had ideas about what she should and should not wear and was often openly critical of her mother's appearance.

More experienced parents might have questioned this new attitude and have attributed it to the right cause, but neither Mary nor Henry had much time to spend either looking after or speculating about Doreen.

They accepted her merely as part and parcel of themselves, and an extra expense that they could ill afford.

Also they had enjoyed their trip up the Nile and were so busy talking about that and about the amount of "perks" they had managed to acquire during the voyage, that they had little time for their daughter's reminiscences.

Mary, it is true, did ask after her old home with a wistful expression in her tired eyes, but that was when Henry was not present; when he was, she declared,

"The last thing I wanted to do is to see rain and mud again! At least we were free from that in Egypt."

At sixteen and a half when other girls were still being kept in the schoolroom, Doreen was allowed to go to night clubs, to spend her time with all sorts and conditions of young men, and to make a life for herself, as long as she did not interfere with her parents.

Yet, though she was not aware of it, her growing up had a definite psychological effect on Mary and Henry.

They were both conscious, although they did not express it even to themselves, that they were failures. There was something in Doreen's eager demands of life, in her youth and vitality, which affected them far more surely than any words or sermons could ever have done.

The cost of those dissipated years was there waiting for a settlement, however much they tried to avoid the truth.

It made Henry drink deeper and more often; it made Mary more querulous every day and more bitterly discontented with her life.

They were seldom together without bickering and quarrelling, and although Henry would drop the easy arm of good-fellowship round his daughter and press a kiss on her cheek, she was aware, although she did not understand the reason, that he was a little uncomfortable in her presence and ill at ease.

Mary found fault with her incessantly: her appearance, her clothes, her behaviour—they were invariably called to account on every possible occasion.

But Doreen who had heard the same exasperated note in her mother's voice since childhood, took up the same attitude towards it as she did to the discomforts and privations of their daily life.

They were things to be dealt with as they appeared—superficially irritating perhaps, but certainly nothing which could affect one emotionally or fundamentally.

At twenty Doreen was well known as "that fast Wallis girl".

The epithet was far less deserved than anyone had any idea; her parents' behaviour, her own rather spectacular appearance and the fact that she was prepared to spend an evening with anyone who would pay for her dinner and entertainment, was quite enough to make her a scarlet woman, as far as the more respectable side of Cairo society was concerned.

Actually there was very little harm in what she did, for she had grown too accustomed, since the very beginning of her adolescence, to repulsing unwelcome advances for them to mean very much to her, or for her to give them more than a passing thought.

She liked dancing; she liked a gay time, just as much as any girl of her age, and if she was completely unchaperoned, it was not her fault.

Her appearance, of course, was definitely against her. She made up far too much, and this was due to her mother's stupidity, for instead of encouraging the girl to look her best, while curbing the extravagance of youthful vanity.

Mary never missed an opportunity of telling Doreen how plain she was.

"Heaven knows where we will find a husband for you," she would add, not realising that her daughter took her words to heart.

For Doreen was strangely sensitive about her looks and was desperately anxious to be a success. Optimistically she believed that a generous use of rouge, lipstick and mascara, would transform her rather nondescript attractions into a spectacular loveliness.

Her efforts certainly made her spectacular, but not in the way that she herself would have wished, had she been able to think logically and impersonally about herself.

Mary nagged at her daughter for "looking a tart" but made no serious effort to instil good taste. She herself had for years tried to disguise the inevitable ravages of a hot climate.

But no creams or powders could hide the yellow tinge left by the tropical sun, or the deep lines of irritability, discontent and heavy living, which had taken their toll from her once pink and white prettiness.

Perhaps, too, it was jealousy which made her never offer her daughter an encouraging word, and Doreen became both defiant and secretive towards her mother, donning too, a youthful reserve which is all the more pitiable, because it inevitably hides both uncertainty and humility.

She little knew what envy she aroused in the breasts

of other girls of her own age in Cairo, if she had, it would have been a great consolation to her.

They longed to be able to go about freely as she did; to laugh and joke with whatever man took their fancy; to escape from the strict surveyance of mothers, aunts and chaperones, who were always ready to crush the slightest suspicion of license or easy going.

To the debutantes doing the season conventionally, Doreen lived an ideal life. They would hear her accept easily an invitation to dance at some rakish haunt, or watch her scramble unexpectedly through the inviting open door of a car, while they must ask permission, or remain uninvited because a refusal was almost inevitable.

They did not guess that Doreen was jealous of them.

She longed for a mother who would sometimes say "No!" of whom one could be proud, and who would look normal and unobtrusive.

It was not always easy to explain to a new acquaintance that the flashily dressed man, who had obviously lunched well, and who was now talking too noisily and with far too much emphasis at the bar or in the paddock at the races, was her father.

Or that the woman dancing with the sallow-faced young man, young enough to be her son, whose laugh was too shrill and whose dress was cut too low, was her mother.

As she grew older, Doreen was well aware that nearly every young man with whom she came into contact, expected far more from her than she was willing to give.

Before seeking an introduction they had listened to the talk of the town, and she did not need to be told that a few kisses in the car going home, or to be allowed to hold her hand in the shadow of the Pyramids, was not what they had expected from her reputation.

She was cynical enough to guess that while chance acquaintances were astonished, her father and mother would also be surprised if they knew how fiercely she prized her virtue.

She felt with an innermost conviction, almost religious in its strength, that if she surrendered herself lightly she would drown in the rottenness of the maelstrom which whirled around her.

Then, when she was twenty-three and growing afraid of facing her twenty-fourth birthday, Pepi came into her life.

She would always remember her first meeting with him. Her mother had one of her attacks of pain and fainted—one of the many signals which were to prepare them, in a year's time, for the fact that Mary was suffering from an incurable cancer.

They were at the races, the inevitable rendezvous at which they could be found every Sunday afternoon. Doreen helped Mary to the cloak-room, then went in search of brandy.

At the door of the bar she paused; it was not difficult to distinguish her father, for his face was as crimson as the carnation he wore in his buttonhole and he was the centre of a noisy circle of friends at the far end of the room.

She was wondering whether to interrupt him or get the brandy herself, when a voice beside her asked:

"Can I help you?"

She looked round to see a short, dark little man with a kindly expression on his face.

"I would be grateful if you would get me some brandy," Doreen said quietly. "My mother has fainted."

"Wait here," he commanded, and elbowing his way through the throng round the bar, came back to her in a few moments with a glass in his hand.

"Thank you so much," Doreen said, holding out her hand, but he shook his head.

"I will carry it for you. Where to?"

"The ladies' cloak-room," Doreen answered and they walked down the sun-drenched path.

When they reached the cloak-room it was to find Mary standing outside. She was very pale and held out her hand for the brandy without comment.

"Oughtn't you to sit down?" Doreen asked.

"I couldn't stand the heat inside," she answered tersely.

Doreen took the empty glass from her and gave it back to the stranger.

"Thank you very much," she said. "If you will tell me how much it was . . ."

"Allow me to have the pleasure," he answered, "and if your mother is still feeling bad, perhaps I could take her home."

Doreen was about to refuse, but he added:

"I am leaving anyway. I only came to see a certain horse run and that was in the last race."

Before Doreen could say more, Mary obviously annoyed at her hesitation, accepted the offer of a lift.

They moved towards the car park and found a large luxurious limousine awaiting them.

He put the two women in behind but sat in front beside the chauffeur. The communicating glass was down and Mary could only mouth with raised eyebrows:

"Who is he?"

Doreen shook her head and made a gesture of ignorance. They drove in silence and Mary lay back with closed eyes.

"How ill she looks," Doreen thought. "It is this senseless, ridiculous life. No one can do as much as she does at her age."

Calculating to herself, she realised with surprise that her mother was only forty-seven—too young to be so tired, so utterly worn out!

"In a few years," Doreen told herself, "I shall be the same."

She turned away with a shudder. She was afraid of the future, so afraid that it was seldom she permitted herself to dwell on it, or to allow her thoughts to carry her where they would.

It was only too obvious what was happening to her. There had been many men in her life, men who had been prepared to spend pleasurable hours at her side, who found her amusing and lovable, but not one of them had offered her anything tangible where the future was concerned.

At the mere talk of marriage, she would see that wary

look come into their eyes, a look, she told herself, that was like an animal frightened of capture.

The car drew up at their hotel in one of the sordid, squalid side streets which led off the more fashionable quarters of the city. Their host opened the car door himself and helped them out.

"Thank you," Mary said, "it was so kind of you. I hope we meet again."

He shook hands with her and turned to Doreen.

"It has been a great pleasure," he said, "and I would like so much to see you again, if I may."

"That would be lovely," Doreen answered, more from force of habit than from anything else. She followed her mother into the hall.

As she climbed limply and laboriously up the stairs, Mary asked:

"Who is he? What is his name?"

"I haven't the slightest idea," her daughter answered slowly.

"Didn't he tell you?"

Doreen shook her head.

"No."

"How ridiculous of you not to find out!" Mary ejaculated. "After all, he is obviously rich. The car was a good one and the chauffeur's livery was expensive. I thought you had more sense than to let him go without arranging a date. I felt too ill to make the effort, or I'd have done it myself."

"Oh well," Doreen said wearily. "He knows where to find us."

"Let's hope he remembers to use the information," Mary replied. "He's a Greek, I think, and the Greeks always have money."

She relapsed into silence because her breathing was laboured, the steepness of the stairs being almost too much for her strength. Doreen helped her into the bedroom.

"I must lie down," Mary said. "I have got to be fresh for tonight. I am dining at Shepheard's."

"Must you go?" Doreen asked anxiously.

"Of course!" There was exasperation in Mary's voice, as though she thought the question too foolish to really require a reply.

Mary threw the thin crêpe de chine dress she had worn at the races on to the floor, and wrapping a torn and faded cotton kimono about her, sank down on the bed and closed her eyes.

"Is there anything you want?" Doreen asked.

"Yes," she replied. "Give me three of those tablets out of my dressing-table drawer, they are in the left hand corner."

Doreen found them and looked at the label on the bottle.

"Three?" she questioned. "It's a very strong dose."

The tablets were a drug which one could buy at any chemist but which were labelled as "Not to be taken under any circumstances except under doctor's orders."

"And a glass of water."

Doreen did as she was told. As she bent over Mary she thought how desperately ill she looked.

With a sudden compassion for the mother with whom she had little in common, she arranged the pillows more comfortably behind her head and started to tidy up the room.

She hung Mary's dress in the wardrobe, folded and replaced a miscellaneous collection of underclothes into the chest of drawers.

As she finished and turned towards the door, Mary's voice already a little drowsy said:

"Greeks always have money. Don't forget to find out who he is."

THREE

Pepi Altini was known among his business acquaintances as a hard man.

He could drive a shrewd bargain with even the most formidable opponents, but in private life he was in some ways an idealist, and was still, at the age of fifty-eight, seeking a happiness which had eluded him all his life.

He had a yearning for youth. Privately, in his thoughts, he would imagine himself young and strong, seeking out some lovely girl and finding in her his true mate.

Only when he looked in the glass and saw his ageing body, plump and soft from too good living, did he feel despondent and unhappy, but never in any way ridiculous.

One sultry afternoon Pepi at the age of nineteen, had been walking along a hot, dusty road when he had encountered the laughing glance of a pretty dark girl sitting on top of a wall eating ripe figs.

It had not needed much encouragement for him to join her and their first chance meeting was the beginning of many more. On her seventeenth birthday he seduced her.

After that their roads lay apart, for she was sent away from Athens to stay in the country and he never saw her again.

She remained in his mind, however, all his life and became the personification of all that he had missed of youth, of love and the quick, easily fired passion of adventurous romance.

He had married later, sanely and sensibly, the daughter of a business associate of his father. His wife brought him a useful dowry and gave him two sons, both of whom as they grew up, showed a somewhat insolent contempt for their father.

Madame Altini grew fat and gross with age. She was a lazy woman who found connubial passion a bore but took child-bearing in her stride, believing it to be the only important interest of a normal wife.

At forty she was an old woman, content to stay at home looking after her children, eating profusely of the sweet cakes and oil-cooked food, which are characteristic of Greek cooking.

When Pepi told her he was going to Cairo to open a new branch of the business, she received the information placidly and took it for granted that he did not wish her to accompany him.

With a wistfulness he seldom showed, he asked her once if she would miss him and her reply had been characteristic.

"I have my children."

Pepi at forty-two came to Cairo feeling, for the first time since he was a boy, that he was a free man. He enjoyed his bachelor existence and the knowledge that he could indulge his love of gaiety and his penchant for young women, without the unspoken, but nevertheless very obvious, criticism of his sons.

Gradually, so gradually that in the beginning he was unaware of its happening, he began to speak of himself as though he had no dependants.

At first when people referred to his bachelorhood, he took it as a joke, smiling secretly to himself, but thinking it a compliment and prepared, as long as it did not interfere with his business, to let them think as they pleased.

Eventually he realised in all honesty that being a bachelor in Cairo was an asset.

He liked too, to pretend to young women that he was eligible from the marriage standpoint and found it an exquisite joke that more than one unattached blonde was anxiously waiting for the word which would give her a legal hold over him.

What began first as a game, in time became deadly

serious. Pepi was terrified in case the little world that he had built for himself should crumble about his ears.

When acquaintances from Greece arrived to see him he did his best to keep them from too close an association with his newly made friends.

Luckily the interchange of business did not necessitate many personal contacts, and his fears were not aroused more often than two or three times in a year.

He got a reputation in Cairo for being something of a roué. He was known for having discreet, but very entertaining, parties at which the ladies were all young and all beautiful and in most cases, not too virtuous.

He bought racehorses which assured him a place among the more sporting set and he grew used to hearing himself referred to as "a good fellow".

Yet always underneath his superficial happiness, he was haunted by that desire for romance, for a repetition of the passion which had been aroused in him so long ago on that dusty Athens road.

He was well aware that the women he bought offered him their bodies as carelessly as a man might stand him a drink or proffer a cigarette case.

He was rich—that was what mattered to them, and because he was an idealist, Pepi hungered for more, for something which seemed to elude him, even though he firmly believed that one day he would find the fulfilment of his dreams.

When he saw Doreen he fell in love.

There was no particular reason why. She was not nearly as pretty as many of the girls who graced his dinner table night after night; she had none of the allure, or the sparkling sophistication which he had grown to expect from any women whom he patronised.

But he saw, as perhaps no one else could ever see, the raw youth of Doreen, which had not yet completely vanished under the paint and powder of her defiance.

Pepi knew in the first few seconds of their meeting, with a certainty of instinct which was unshakable, that Doreen's detractors lied about her; she was neither wanton nor promiscuous.

He sensed the virginity of her—something in the way she walked, in the way she turned her head and often in a quiet unsteadied gesture, reminded him of a colt that had been worked too soon and too hard, but which, underneath its harness, still retained its untamed spontaneity.

He liked her; he pitied her and against his inclination he loved her.

It began in the usual way with him telephoning her every day and inviting her to the inevitable round of entertainments. Doreen was only too glad to accept.

She liked Pepi, he interested her, and she was clever enough to treat him as a contemporary and not as a man older than her father.

She enjoyed too the luxury of being with somebody really wealthy. The subalterns, junior officials and the young bank clerks who had hitherto been among the majority of her admirers, could not offer her the same value in entertainment that Pepi could.

His car and chauffeur were always at her door; his big, comfortable house with its shady green garden sloping down to the Nile, its well-trained servants and excellent food, was a background she had not hitherto experienced where a man who was interested in her was concerned.

Pepi did not make the mistake of offering her too much too quickly—flowers, chocolates, magazines, these were, of course, at her command, and where before she had received roses and carnations, she now had orchids on her shoulder.

But he would not insult her by gifts of jewellery, furs and expensive dresses such as he had given so often and so carelessly to other women.

Long before Doreen was consciously aware that Pepi was serious in his intentions, he himself had made up his mind that whatever happened, she must be his. The question was how?

He was by no means a fool; he listened to all the stories which were repeated to him glibly about Doreen's parents, of her own fastness and easy going ways with young men, of their general mode of gaining a livelihood.

He believed some of the tales; others he knew to be untrue and to be typical of the tittle-tattle of the town in which they lived. But in his own mind he was certain that any offer he made to Doreen had every probability of being turned down unless it was a legal one.

Because he genuinely loved her, he was afraid of losing her confidence and her friendship by making a false step.

If Pepi growing old and finding disillusionment in his married life was an idealist, Pepi in love was Romeo, Dante and Sir Lancelot rolled into one.

The whole smouldering fire of a frustrated temperament began to blaze and his desire for Doreen grew until he felt that without her, life would be unlivable and that everything he had achieved was without value.

"I love you—I can't live without you," he said passionately and meant it.

It was really so long since he had been home to Athens that there was an excuse for his indifference to those ties across the sea.

At Christmas he usually received a letter from his wife enclosing snapshots or photographs of his sons. One of them had recently been married and the next letter Pepi received would undoubtedly tell him that he was in the proud position of being a grandfather. It meant absolutely nothing to him.

He read the letters mechanically and burnt them, because he was afraid of his servants spying into his secrets.

He was a man of method, and because of it, he had made himself not only indispensable to the business in Cairo, but had also managed to carry off the immense bluff of his independent state for seventeen years.

At least he believed he had. He was not to know that occasionally there were whispers about him, and that sometimes doubts were expressed among his own countrymen.

These doubts, however, were quite unimportant until

he married Doreen. The wedding took place with the utmost secrecy, and it was only after they had been married a fortnight, that Pepi appeared with her at the races and introduced her as his wife.

Then indeed several of the Greek colony began to chatter, but by that time Pepi was beyond warning and, indeed, beyond any sense of danger.

He was like a man who hesitates so long on the brink that when he takes the final plunge, he does it gladly, triumphantly, and rejoicingly. He was deaf and blind to all the signs which a few years before would have made him sweat with fear and anxiety.

He was happy, ridiculously happy, with his bride who was thirty-six years younger than himself.

"You are all I've ever dreamt of in a wife," he told her. "Beautiful, perfect—young."

If Doreen could not reciprocate even in a small degree her husband's ecstacy, she at least was able to give him a deep affection.

She was immeasurably grateful to him for taking her away from her home, although she despised her parents for showing so obviously their joy at the advantageous catch which she had made.

It took her a long time to get used to the feeling of peace in her new home, to the knowledge that there was no wrathful landlord or landlady waiting downstairs to present an overdue bill with angry threats.

It was heaven to know she could lie in her bath, soaking in the warm, scented water, without listening for the rat-tat at the door, which meant another bather was impatiently awaiting her exit.

There was money in her purse; there were exquisite clothes bought at the most expensive shops in which to dress herself. She wallowed in it all, and like a child turned loose in the candy shop, she gorged herself with it.

She hardly had time to think of anything but the sensuous pleasure of being enveloped in luxury, or to feel anything but the sensation of sinking, as it were, deeper and deeper into a feather bed.

Pepi made few demands on her. He was content to

love her. He was neither arrogant nor over-possessive, as a younger man might have been.

He wanted her to be happy and with a humility which was pathetic, he in his turn was grateful to her for bringing him what he had sighed for all his life.

"What can I give you for all you give me?" he asked. "I'm happy beyond words—my dear, my sweet wonderful wife."

Looking back over those four years of married life, it seemed to Doreen later that she lived in a haze.

People came and went; there were parties; there were dances; there were cocktail shakers which appeared to clink unceasingly with the sound of fresh ice; there were days at the races; there were week-ends spent sailing up the Nile, and over everything was the laughter and chatter of many voices.

But for herself there was a kind of immunity from reality which made her feel as though she were but a shadow seen upon a screen.

The one thing she appreciated more than anything else was that she need not pretend with Pepi. He knew the worst about her, and if he was prepared only to see the best, that was his business, so she was not ashamed when her parents came round begging for what they could get, and seldom going away empty-handed.

She could even laugh with her husband about them, neither humiliated nor ashamed, but amused and glad that she at least had escaped from such an existence.

In the summer they went down to Alexandria where Pepi rented a villa, and where they were followed by the same gay, chattering throng, which filled their house in Cairo in the winter.

When he could take a holiday, they went up to Luxor or to Assouan and she accepted his arrangements placidly, enjoying it with that queer detachment, which only broke down when occasionally she would hide her face against her husband's shoulder and whisper:

"I can't believe it is true."

It was only when Pepi's Will was read that she realised what a gamble it had all been. He could not possibly afford the way he had lived.

She had never questioned his business ability, or even interested herself enough to understand exactly his position in the firm. She imagined from the way they spent money that he was a very rich man.

When her whole world crashed about her ears, she found that too was an illusion, as false as her belief that she was his wife.

Pepi left her a letter in which he tried to explain how he had loved her, and how he had believed that marriage was the only way he could gratify that love. He left a Will in which she received a lump sum of a thousand pounds before the rest of his possessions were sold and the proceeds sent to his family in Athens.

"When his bills are paid, there will be practically nothing left," the solicitors told Doreen. "If he had not died when he did, the crash must surely have come."

She did not believe them. It was an absurdity to think that Pepi could have courted disaster or known it had he lived. He was so lucky; if he bought shares they went up; if he backed a horse it came in first. But a gambler seldom finds security in his old age. Pepi, sooner or later, must by all the laws of average, have had to face reverses, but before that moment came, lucky even in his span of life, he died quietly and without either scenes or good-byes.

He made no explanations other than the letter he left Doreen; the only instruction he had given his solicitors was that his Will was to be kept as secret as possible.

But somehow, in the mysterious manner of the East, the full contents of it and of the letter he left for Doreen, were known by the whole town, twenty-four hours after his death.

Taking with her only her clothes and jewellery, Doreen on leaving the house where they had lived, looked for the last time at the windows glittering in the autumn sun, at the flowers bordering the constantly watered lawn, at the palms and shrubs growing to the water's edge, and she wondered that her eyes were dry.

This had been not only her home for four years, but a haven of rest and peace, an anchorage from the tempestuous, precarious existence which once again awaited her.

She could not cry. Pepi's death and all that it entailed had been too tremendous for tears. She could only feel amazed, astonished, and desperately afraid.

She felt at times as though she had always known this must happen, that even when she was married to Pepi she had known that her security was not a permanent one.

She must go back to what was her true milieu, but now she was utterly alone, for both her father and mother were dead.

Mary had died about a year after she had married Pepi. When finally Henry and Doreen forced her to go to a doctor for examination, it was discovered that she had cancer of the chest, so long neglected that it had become a virulent growth, infecting the entire side of her body.

Any operation was out of the question and they could only make her last months of life as easy as possible, by increasing the doses of morphia.

Henry followed her two years later, but his death was a surprise to no one, most people had expected him to collapse sooner than he did.

He missed Mary more than even he, or anyone else, expected, and he sought consolation in a manner which for him was inevitable. He drank until he was seldom, if ever, sober.

His liver was not capable of the strain, and when finally he walked home from a party one evening without a coat and caught a feverish cold, it was only a question of days.

Pepi saw that he had the best doctors, but there was not a chance of saving him. He died quite cheerfully, with a joke on his lips. "Never say die" he grinned when she asked him how he was.

He had got more and more down-at-heel the last years, in spite of the frequent loans from his son-in-law. He had always been dapper in his early days, despite the amount he drank.

After Mary's death he grew slovenly and the servants in the cheap lodgings stole his shirts, so that often he would appear at the races in linen which should have gone to the washtub a week before, and in suits which badly needed cleaning and pressing.

No amount of money made any difference to him towards the end. Doreen would say to Pepi that she could not bear to see her father so disreputable.

Ever generous where his wife was concerned, Pepi would insist on Henry accepting yet another loan, in the hopes that he would appear better dressed and better groomed the next time they saw him.

It was all quite hopeless. The status of his friends and acquaintances had changed.

He frequented, not the better-class bars where he had been an habitué for so long, but the commoner ones where his companions were mixed breeds of every description, amused by the degradation of a white man, and ready to encourage him to sink to their level.

It was all rather horrible and Doreen could not help the sense of relief which came over her when Henry was buried next to her mother in the beautiful cemetery outside Cairo.

She had no idea then that it would be but a year before she would follow another coffin to its last resting-place.

Following the revelations of his Will, Pepi's funeral was held as quietly and as unobtrusively as possible, and yet up to the last moment Doreen could not make up her mind whether to be present or not.

She waited to see whether any of his relations would come forward, or perhaps a representative of the family. However, in the end, she and Pepi's solicitor were the only mourners.

He was buried one glorious spring morning, a morning worthy of the youth and gladness that he had sought so assiduously all his life and found, at least partially, in the last four years before his death.

"You made me the happiest man in the world!" Doreen heard him say, and knew it was the truth.

FOUR

It was four o'clock. Doreen heard a clock strike somewhere far away.

She got to her feet and picking up Tony's letter from off the bed, she tore it into a thousand small pieces. In doing so she believed that she was tearing up the memory of him.

At the same time her instinct told her that things would not be so easy as that; she would remember, and go on remembering, those weeks of happiness and of hope, none the less poignant because they held a permanent anxiety.

She felt too ill to dress and go out, but she knew that sooner or later she must make the effort.

She would have to make it known that she was well again, ready to be asked out to meals, and to be included in the parties which took place night after night.

The old wearisome round would start again, the treadmill of enjoyment galvanised by the hope that sooner or later she would meet some man who would take an interest in her, a man who would find her necessary to him, and who might fill the place that Tony had left vacant.

She knew it was horrible, beastly, a degradation the more painful because it had happened before, yet already while the pieces of Tony's letter fell from her fingers, she was suffering agonies of introspection, she was asking herself whether she could have captivated him by better means than the ones she had chosen?

But Tony had been different. Doreen had known, though no one had ever told her so, that his type of Englishman requires a woman, if she is to hold the position of wife and mother, to be both pure and proud.

It had not been difficult to be aloof, to let their passion for each other go no further than kisses, for Tony employed none of the tiger tactics which Doreen had grown used to expect from the varied and international collection of men she had known in the past two years.

He treated her with the respect and gentleness he would have accorded a debutante and she had lived up to what he expected of her.

Without knowing it she had acquired a new dignity, and indeed a new grace, during their short relationship.

But now she felt that she had been at fault.

Perhaps if she had been his mistress he would have said the words which she had so longed to hear, while chivalry, if nothing else, might have prevented him leaving her while she was still ill.

For the first week she had been in hospital huge bunches of flowers had arrived from him daily.

Generally a tender note was enclosed, and although he had been unable to see her owing to infection, she had been secure in the belief that he was waiting for her, and that the moment she was well again, he would be there, holding out his arms to greet her.

Then had come silence.

For three days she had lain waiting, miserable and apprehensive, for flowers or for a note which never came.

Then a large present of fruit, but with only a card enclosed had raised her hopes. That really had been the end.

She might have guessed that Tony of all people would not send a conventional card, unless something desperate had occurred, something which had severed the bond between them.

But she had been too weak to analyse her feelings at that particular moment, she had only lain with closed eyes, holding the card to her breast, telling herself again and again without conviction, that all was well.

She had written to him when she left the hospital, to tell him that she had gone back to her old address.

The day after she had sent the letter was one of sheer agony, when every sound on the stairs, every voice in the street outside, would find her alert, waiting, hoping, and at last, praying.

It was awful to lie there knowing that she was not strong enough to get up and seek the truth, that she could only wait, tied by her own inability to leave her bed.

There was no telephone in the building, but the drug store next door would take messages for a small charge, and every one of her friends knew of this arrangement and took advantage of it.

At every possible opportunity she sent over to ask if there was anything for her, but always the answer was the same—"nothing".

The next day and the day after had passed in the same manner, yet still some lingering, unquenchable spark within her mind refused to accept the inevitable.

Only today, when in black and white she read Tony's farewell written as he left Port Said, did she know that she was defeated and that there was no longer any hope left to her.

"Oh God it can't be true," she whispered to herself.

She wondered, as she had often wondered before, if she had met Tony two years ago, when she was still affluent, still wearing the luxurious and beautiful clothes which had been bought with Pepi's money, if things would have been different.

She knew, without being cynical, that a woman's background meant so much. Men, the ones that she met, rated her, not at her own value, but from the standpoint of social opinion.

Money, however it was come by, meant something, and Doreen believed that had Pepi left her a fortune, it would have been easy for Cairo to forget a little illegality as regards her marriage lines.

But penniless and with a damaged reputation, there was no possible excuse for her.

She reverted to her own name because she dared not face the humiliation of being challenged should she use the one to which she was not entitled. It was difficult at first to remember.

The words "Madame Altini" would tremble on her lips whenever she was ordering things at a shop, or introducing herself to a stranger.

But gradually her hesitation vanished, even as the memory of Pepi was vanishing into a past which seemed more and more fantastic, because it was in such utter contrast to her present circumstances.

She walked to the washstand and sponged her face with tepid water. She had been too tired all day even to make-up, but now, as though to give herself moral fortitude, she splashed scarlet lipstick across her mouth and powdered her nose.

She noticed with distaste the yellow tinge of her skin, and the way her hair hung lank and lifeless over her ears. The brightening rinses which gave it at other times a look of sheer gold, had faded, and the brittle condition which comes with fever, made the peroxide streaks look sordid and dingy.

Even if it meant that she must be without food, Doreen knew that she must do something to her appearance—it was indeed her only stock in trade, nothing else was imprtant.

A knock at the door startled her. Hastily she picked up a pink embroidered dressing-gown which was laid over the bed, and wrapped it round her.

"Come in," she said.

"Are you better?"

It was the girl from the floor below who stood in the doorway. She was showily dressed in a white crêpe de chine dress, the frock strained across her prominent breasts, and cut far too tight over the posterior.

A wide red patent leather belt matched the jaunty little hat on the side of her head, and her scarlet toenails peeped through white suède sandals.

"Oh, it is you, Alma!" Doreen exclaimed.

When she had first come to the building, she had scorned with a fastidious disdain the gushing overtures of the only other white girl in the building. Alma's profession was very obvious.

But it was difficult to live alone in solitary pride and Doreen had gradually allowed herself to become friendly.

Since she had been ill, she eagerly welcomed the

chance of a talk, when Alma was not too busy to come upstairs.

Indeed, the loneliness would have been almost insupportable without her, for Alma was the only person who bothered to find out whether Doreen had any food, or whether the slovenly native servants had remembered to do her room or make her bed.

"How are you feeling?" she asked, now coming into the room, her broad generous mouth smiling a welcome.

"Rather lousy," Doreen replied.

"You will be for at least three weeks," Alma said. "I had a go of the same fever once myself. I can't tell you what I felt like. The only thing I wanted to do was to die quickly and to get it over. Been crying too, haven't you?" she added with a shrewd glance at Doreen's swollen eyes.

Doreen nodded, not trusting her voice to answer.

"Bad news?" Alma queried.

Doreen felt a sudden rise in her throat.

"Yes," she choked.

"It is that young man of yours, I bet," Alma said. "Tony what's his name. You've heard that he has gone away."

Doreen stared at her and as if in explanation, Alma went on.

"Yes, I knew he had gone. I heard it—you know how one does hear these things—somebody told me at the Continental one evening, but I wasn't hurrying to carry the bad news. I hoped you would get a bit stronger before you knew for certain."

"I suppose I was a fool to expect anything else," Doreen said bitterly.

She could not keep up any pretence with Alma. In a way it was almost a relief to know someone whose walk of life was so completely different to her own, so that she could talk quite frankly about her friends without any feeling of disloyalty.

"It's tough," Alma said. "I know that, you poor kid. At the same time, you didn't have a real chance. When you're down, you're down, and don't I know it!

"You're either going up on the wave, or coming down on it, and when one thing goes wrong, the whole ruddy lot do. You are in the middle of a rotten streak, and the most you can do is to hope for the best and be quite certain you'll get the worst."

That was Alma's philosophy in a nutshell and Doreen had heard it before. But somehow, now, it was vaguely comforting to know it was not her fault, to blame everything that had happened to luck, that mythical wheel of chance which in turning elevates or grinds down indiscriminately.

"Well, what are you going to do now?" Alma asked. "When you're better, I mean."

"Go back to the usual crowd, I suppose," Doreen answered despondently.

"That's the chicken!" Alma ejaculated. "You have got to learn to take it on the chin. Just rest for a few more days and you will be on your feet as right as rain."

She looked at her wrist-watch, set with false diamonds.

"Glory! But I must be getting along," she said. "I have got an appointment at half-past four. I have only met him once before, and he might turn up trumps, although I doubt it. Well, cheer-oh, and, by the way, I have brought you some magazines to amuse yourself with."

She threw on to the bed a small bundle which she had held under her arm.

"Oh, thank you," Doreen said gratefully.

"Don't thank me," Alma said, "thank the lad who gave them to me last night. Just come off his train and he was going to leave them behind in the bar, if I hadn't stopped him.

'Hold hard,' I said to him as we walked away, 'you've left your papers behind.'

'I've read them,' he replied.

'Oh, have you,' I answered, 'well, I haven't, and you are surely not depriving a girl of getting a bit of education on the cheap.'

"He laughed and fetched them for me. I knew you'd enjoy them."

"I shall," Doreen promised, "and thank you for coming up to see me. You always make me feel better."

"I will pop in again this evening," Alma said, "if I am not too late. If I don't, expect me tomorrow when you see me. Tootle-oo."

With a wave of her hand she left, shutting the door noisily behind her and Doreen heard the clatter of her pointed heels going down the uncarpeted stairs.

She left two things: a strong smell of cheap scent and an atmosphere of good-fellowship which it was hard to criticise.

Doreen got back on to the bed and picked up the magazines. One of them was full of cheap illustrated jokes, of the type which just evade the censor and pander to the lowest instincts possible of the reading public.

The other was an American paper filled with pictures of glamorous film stars, posed in so-called unconventional attitudes in their Hollywood homes. As she picked up the second magazine the thin sheets of an evening paper fell from between its covers.

Casually Doreen picked it up, smoothed out its crumpled pages, so that she could read the headlines.

There were the usual sensational international talks. Hitler was precipitating another crisis, this time over Poland. The Australians had won a Test match! Then a large paragraph, half-way down the page attracted her attention.

"BRITISH GIRL'S HEROISM," it read. "MISSIONARY'S DAUGHTER NURSES CANNIBAL TRIBE WHO HAVE MURDERED HER PARENTS."

A name caught Doreen's eye; hastily she folded the paper so as to be able to read it more easily.

"In the annals of history a place will certainly be found for Miss Anne Marston, only daughter of Dr. and Mrs. Marston, the well-known missionaries, who was rescued only five days ago from the ruins of the mission settlement in the Bahrel Ghazel district of the Sudan, commonly known as 'The Bog'.

"Here, just over a fortnight ago, there was a rising among the Jurde tribe, following an outbreak of tropical

fever, which overtook them in large numbers and finally carried off their chief and his family, who had been under treatment from Dr. Marston at the Mission Hospital. Led by their Witch Doctor, who laid the whole blame for the spreading of the disease on the white inhabitants, they murdered the missionary, his wife and several of their faithful servants, choosing Sunday morning when Dr. Marston was holding a service in the little thatched church he and his wife had built with their own hands.

"That Miss Marston is alive, is to the fortunate fact that she had taken several of the mission children for a trip down the river and they had started at dawn, not expecting to return until night had fallen. Darkness was their salvation, for as they neared the mission settlement, they saw flames springing up from the demolished house and church and heard the natives dancing a wild war dance round the conflagration they had kindled.

"For two days Miss Marston and the children hid in the jungle without food until news came to them that the Witch Doctor himself was ill with the fever and the natives, now horror-stricken at what they had done, were awaiting punishment in fear and trepidation.

"Anne Marston boldly walked back to the smouldering ruins of what had been her home and what was now the grave of her parents. There and then she started to minister to the sick and dying who came pleading for her help as though their madness of the past two days had never been.

"Choosing a boy she could trust, she sent him off for help. As the nearest white man was over a hundred miles away and the messenger was delayed, it was nearly ten days before help arrived in the shape of the District Commissioner and several native policemen. By this time Miss Marston was in a state of exhaustion, but was able to give a coherent account of how she had carried on.

"She was taken by boat to Khartoum where she has been in hospital, but has now decided to take a holiday in England while she recovers from the effects of her heroic ordeal and the untimely death of her parents.

"Miss Anne Marston will pass through Cairo on her way to England and a special welcome will be given to her by Dr. and Mrs. Garston, who are the local representatives of the Missionary Society in the near East. And there are many others who will wish to cheer this brave young English girl whose heroism will place her name beside those of Nurse Cavell, Grace Darling and Florence Nightingale."

Doreen read the full paragraph. Then she smiled. She thought of Anne Marston as she last remembered her, a fat, plump child, with two pigtails screwed back behind her ears, saying in tones of unalloyed horror,

"But Granny has forbidden us to eat raspberries!"

Anne would always do the right thing at the right moment, Doreen thought, but even while she admired the courage of her first cousin, she could not help but think that it was inevitable, that sooner or later, she should behave heroically.

"I would have expected it of her," she thought.

She remembered the sanctimonious, self-righteousness of the twelve-year-old child who had bossed her about from the moment she had arrived at her grandmother's, until the moment she left.

No one would have guessed what agonies of shyness Doreen had suffered long ago on that brief visit to England.

She had been afraid of her grandmother; she had been even more afraid of what seemed to her the incredibly grand house, which had been her mother's home.

She hated the smug superiority of Anne, from the very moment that they had been introduced, and told that as they were first cousins they must play together and be great friends.

Although Anne had made it quite clear from the very beginning that she thought Doreen a very inferior companion, this had never been obvious, Doreen knew, to any of the grown-ups.

To them Anne would describe in clear ringing tones at meal-times all the things she had done with her cousin.

"I took Doreen to see the cows, this morning, Granny," she would say and was rewarded with a smile, or a word of praise.

She did not add that she had taunted Doreen with the fear of them and had even pushed her, a frightened child, nurtured in cities, into the path of one particularly ferocious-looking heifer.

Doreen had retaliated on more than one occasion by pulling Anne's pigtails as hard as she could and until she cried in pain. Even now it gave her pleasure to remember it.

When Doreen had left England to return to her parents, she had promised Anne, in front of her grandmother and aunts, that she would write to her.

It had been one of those promises which are so easily extracted from a child when they are too nervous to say "no".

"You will write to each other, darlings, won't you? It would be nice for Anne, while she is at school here, to know what you are doing in the East, and Anne will write and tell you about England, won't you, Anne?"

"But of course," Anne had answered. "And I will pick some English flowers and when they have been pressed in my Bible, send them to Doreen in my letters."

"That's a good girl. And what will you send to Anne, Doreen?"

Doreen shuffled from one leg to the other.

"Well, dear, can't you think of anything?" she had been asked.

"A scorpion," she had answered rudely.

She knew even as she said it, that she only disgraced herself and that Anne came out best from the encounter.

Doreen's mother, Mary Wickham, had been a twin. Her sister had been christened Martha and it was an ironical coincidence that Martha, as if to refute her name, had sought always the spiritual things while Mary had preferred the material.

Martha had married the local curate, who was certain that he had had a call to teach the heathen, and she had been perfectly prepared to follow him to the farthest corners of the world.

A year after they had been married and their first child had been born, they left England for what had hitherto been a virtually unexplored part of the Sudan.

That several better men had failed to make any headway with the Jurde tribe, was no deterrent to David Marston. He was a fanatic in his own way and yet strangely practical when it came to anything unconnected with his religion.

He had originally studied for the medical profession, and the knowledge he had thus gained, was to stand him in good stead when he found himself in a most unhealthy part of the country, with disease of all sorts rampant.

Disease was by no means the worst of their difficulties. They had to overcome suspicion, resentment and even hatred, before they could get any firm foothold among the natives.

Also, while they were not in any way prevented from doing the work of God, missionaries were not particularly encouraged in those regions.

Their presence meant extra anxieties on the part of those responsible for the government, and there had been occasions in the past when police protection had had to be provided.

However, Dr. Marston and his wife gradually made themselves a power in the land, and when they felt they were sufficiently settled, they sent for their daughter Anne from England.

Unlike most twins, Martha and Mary had drifted away from each other after their marriages.

Mary married soon after her sister and at first she would write her long glowing accounts of her life in India, hoping quite obviously to raise a feeling of jealousy in Martha's heart, because she had chosen a life of service and unselfishness.

Anne was born a year and a half before Doreen and Mary had hoped for a son, feeling that in that way she would be "one up" on her twin sister.

When things began to go wrong some years later, she gradually ceased to write at all. She often spoke of Martha, but it was always with a certain resentment, a kind of grudging carpingness.

It was only when her mother was dead and Doreen found among her possessions every letter that Martha had ever written, that she realised that unbeknown to them all, Mary might have felt the separation deeply.

It seemed extraordinary that the two sisters were in the same continent for over twenty years yet never met.

Once or twice, when there had been a congress of missionaries in Cairo, Mary would remark:

"One day I shall meet Martha walking down the street. I wonder if I shall recognise her." Or else, when Henry came home particularly drunk and noisy, she would say sarcastically, "At least, I haven't married a missionary."

It was as though she hated the life Martha had chosen, for she would laugh and sneer continually at "goody-goody people like my sister".

Only sometimes her mood would change with lightning rapidity and she would follow such remarks by an attack on Henry, bemoaning her fate at being tied to a man who had destroyed her self-respect, her pride and sense of decency.

After her mother's funeral, Doreen had burned the treasured letters without reading them. Now she was sorry. She felt she would have liked an insight into her aunt's mind.

Were twins never quite complete without the other? she wondered.

Superficially it was impossible to imagine two more diverse lives than Mary's and Martha's, or for that matter, Doreen thought, than her own and Anne's. Lucky Anne to be going back to England, to know that a home was waiting for her there.

Doreen supposed that their grandmother was still alive and Anne would be going to Brookavon.

How well she could remember the Manor. Mary had dropped all contact with her home the last years of her life, but when she died, Henry had written to Mrs. Wickham and they had received in reply a long letter asking for further news of Doreen.

It had gone unanswered. Henry had lost it in his usual slovenly way and Doreen, content in her marriage, had seen no reason to renew acquaintance with relatives she had not seen since she was ten years old.

Now she was sorry. She wondered if there would still be a welcome for her should she go back. She doubted it—she was hardly likely to fit in with the Wickham family as she remembered them.

Granny, austere, frightening, but a person who commanded respect; Aunt Edith, the unmarried sister of the family, a spinster with a sweet gentle nature, which was quite out of tradition for an "old maid".

Her kindness had frightened Doreen in the past; now she wondered why she had been such a fool and not taken advantage of it.

There was an uncle too, her mother's only living brother, but he had made little impression on her, as he was an invalid.

Old people and good people—yes, Doreen thought, unless Anne had altered very considerably, she would be in her element amongst them.

A sudden longing for the England she had known came back to her. She saw again the Manor House of gracious grey stone set against a background of green trees, orchards and flower-filled gardens.

She smelt the fragrance of grass damp from rain, of the hay ripening in the fields, of the honeysuckle which climbed untamed over the porch—yes, strangely enough, it was all stored up in her memory.

Other things in the past were forgotten or had become but shadowy figments of a fading picture.

But the three months when she had learnt of English country life, when her fear of it had gradually turned to joy, were vivid still, as fresh and as lovely as when the thought of them was a secret solace to a lonely neglected child.

Suddenly an idea came to her. She would see Anne. She would ask Anne to help her. Why not?

"She will help me," she told herself. "She must help me."

FIVE

The newspapers always on the look-out for sensational stories and tired of the war of nerves, decided, for as long as they could boost the public into taking an interest in her, to run Anne Marston as a kind of superheroine No. 1.

Stories, many of them untrue, of the life on the Mission Settlement where she had lived with her father, pictures of her arrival on a stretcher at Khartoum, and of the most ferocious-looking natives of every tribe kept the public interest alive. Combined with articles by many eminent people on "Is Cannibalism Extinct?" "Are Missionaries Necessary?" and "Is Native Man Happier than his Civilised Brother?"

There were several days before Anne's arrival in Cairo for Doreen to plan what she would say to her cousin and how she could best prevail upon her for help.

The newspapers made her aware that she would not have much time to plead her case, for Anne was only to stay two nights before going down to Port Said to catch a ship home to England.

More than once Doreen wondered how her efforts to renew an acquaintanceship made nineteen years ago, was likely to be received.

She knew that in the quiet countryside home in England and in the Mission Settlement run by the Marstons there must have been considerable disapproval expressed about her mother's and father's lives.

What the missionaries had heard was likely to prove the most detrimental, for news in the East travels swiftly and any bit of scandal, however fictitious, is told, retold, and elaborated simply because people are starved for more interesting outlets for their curiosity.

Perhaps the isolation of the Marston Settlement might have helped to keep them in ignorance, but it was only to be expected that from time to time in the past years, Mrs. Marston would have enquired of everyone who came down from the North, as to whether they had seen her twin sister.

Whatever the outcome, however cold her reception, the chance of obtaining help from Anne was not to be despised, and accordingly Doreen wrote her a letter and marking it "Urgent", sent it round to the quiet hotel where she was to stay on her arrival.

It was not an easy letter, in fact Doreen tore up many sheets of paper before finally she compiled a draft which she felt was both adequate and appealing.

She told Anne that she was in desperate trouble and that she must see her; it was a matter of the utmost urgency. She also added that she had been ill and, therefore, could not leave her room.

The decision not to call in person was made after much consideration. She felt that she would be at her worst in the atmosphere of religious respectability, which Anne was certain to have around her at the hotel where she was lodging.

It was likely that various other members of the Missionary Association would be present, and it would be quite impossible to state her case, or indeed to plead with Anne, unless they were alone.

If Anne came to her she could insist on seeing her in private, especially if she was in bed.

Clothes, and the fact that if she was up she must use cosmetics on her face or feel unnatural, all decided her to stay where she was and receive Anne as an invalid.

The conviction that her one hope was to go back to England grew stronger in the days while she waited for Anne to arrive.

There she could make a new start, find a job with the help and influence that her grandmother must be able to exercise and forget the miseries and cruelties of the past.

She was sick of Cairo, sick of her so-called friends, her environment and mode of life. Cairo, too, was a town of memories, and with the fatalism of a sick person, she imagined that the whole city was unlucky for her.

Her parents' death, Pepi, Tony's desertion and the thousand and one little barbed insults and humilities that she had endured, all accumulated now to show her how impossible it was for her to stay on.

She must get away; she must try again! Reconstruct a new life on new lines and, perhaps, who knows, eventually find a happiness greater and more perfect than her most optimistic dreams.

"I have been a fool," Doreen admitted to herself.

Then she wondered if in fact she had, or whether she was the victim of circumstances. It was so difficult, looking back on her life, to know what else she could have done, how else she could have behaved.

She imagined that people said now that she must have known about Pepi all the time; even the most tolerant would blame her lack of curiosity, and suggest that she might have delved deeper into his past, have enquired more earnestly about his antecedents.

Yet why should she? She had been content, and although that was no excuse, she could see the justification of everything that was said about her, and it was a consolation, if a poor one, to know that she had been completely innocent.

She was twenty-nine and so much had happened to her, so much that the sum total of it all might easily have been on the credit side instead of the debit.

But she was honest enough with herself to know that she was an utter failure, and that only something drastic could save her from sinking lower and lower.

She could not go on, she must make a break, and like a rainbow after the storm, came the hope that Anne might prove the means of her salvation.

The newspapers on the morning after Anne's arrival carried front page stories of the heroine leaving Khartoum by aeroplane at dawn the day before.

It was a twelve-hour journey to Cairo, but a flashlight picture showed her being helped through the crowd after landing at the aerodrome late that evening.

She had been in hospital for several days and it was stated that while she was not really well enough to travel and some anxiety was felt by the doctors, Miss Marston herself was so anxious to get back to England that it was decided to take the risk, and catch the ship that had been originally decided upon.

"Oh hell," Doreen thought. "It would be just my luck if she is too ill to come and see me and if she does come, under such circumstances, she is certain to bring some old trout with her. If I don't hear by tonight, I shall get up and go to the hotel myself."

Then the idea came to her that perhaps Anne would not be too pleased to claim relationship. If she had heard half as much about the Wallis family as Doreen suspected, she might wish to keep a discreet silence about her first cousin's letter.

In Doreen's bedroom the hours seemed to crawl by. By luncheon time there was no news. Doreen had tidied the room and lay hot and sticky under the thin covering on her bed, trying to keep tidy by being as still as possible and listening all the time, with tense anxiety, for the sound of voices or footsteps on the stairs.

It was nearly five o'clock before her patience was rewarded. Her heart leapt with anxiety. There came a knock on her door.

"Come in," she said.

The door opened slowly and a voice asked:

"Can you tell me if Miss Wallis is here?"

"Come in, Anne," Doreen said joyfully.

She was so glad to see her cousin, so relieved that her waiting had not been in vain, that her voice was strong and triumphant, so much so that she realised it was inappropriate and she chided herself inwardly.

Anne Marston walked into the room. She was alone.

"I could find no one to tell me if you were here," she said reproachfully. "The front door was open but there was no one in attendance. I have knocked on nearly every door in the building."

"I am sorry," Doreen answered, "but at this time of day the servants go off duty and my landlady disappears to drink coffee until sundown."

Anne drew nearer to the bed and Doreen stared at her with interest. Her cousin was wearing dark sun glasses, but even without them she would never have recognised her.

She was so terribly thin, thinner than she was herself and there were deep lines of fatigue on either side of her mouth.

"How thin you have got!" Doreen said involuntarily.

"I have been ill," Anne answered, "and anyway, the climate in the Sudan is not conducive to fat as you can imagine, and we have had to work very hard these past years."

She sat down on the chair which Doreen had placed by the bedside.

"How awful she looks!" Doreen thought.

She felt too, it was typical of Anne to wear, in spite of the heat, a most unbecoming black dress of thick linen and a black straw hat with such a wide brim that it accentuated the sharpened outlines of her pale cheeks.

"I was so sorry to read of what happened to you and to your father and mother," she said gently.

"I can hardly speak about it," Anne answered in a low voice. "Indeed, it is difficult to believe that it is true—the work of twenty-seven years destroyed in a few hours."

"You were so brave."

"I only did what anyone else would have done in the same circumstances," Anne replied primly and Doreen had the idea that she had used this phrase before and found it effective.

In spite of the importance of this meeting, she felt the old antagonism creeping over her at the proximity of her cousin. She could not help it; there was a self-satisfaction and smugness about Anne which destroyed even the sympathy Doreen wanted to offer her in all sincerity.

Although she looked desperately ill, there was no softening fraility about her, but rather an added severity, as though she would even defy her own body and dare it to offend her.

"Tell me about yourself," Doreen suggested, fighting against a rising animosity, but Anne replied sharply:

"I have come to hear about you. I got your letter. I didn't mention it to those I was with."

"But how did you explain that you were coming out to see me then?" Doreen asked mischievously.

It was faintly amusing to find that she had been right in her supposition that Anne was not proud of her connection with the disreputable Wallis's.

"Under doctors' orders I am resting until seven o'clock," Anne answered frigidly, as if she resented the question. "I am then receiving several of the missionaries in Cairo. They wish to hear my version as to what happened at our settlement. I think, also, they will make me a small presentation."

"Money?" Doreen questioned.

"I believe so," Anne answered. "There is already some idea, and I may say I am very much in favour of it, of raising a sum of money to rebuild the Mission and send out someone to take my father's place—not that they could hope to do what he did, for the majority of the natives had great confidence in him. Nevertheless, we cannot let his work remain unfinished."

"She is already rehearsing her speech for tonight," Doreen thought.

"It is a good thing then," she said aloud, "that you are seeing me now. I had thought that perhaps you would be too ill to come to me and that I must make an effort, however difficult it might be, to come to you."

She could not help noticing an expression of consternation on Anne's face.

"I think that would have been very unwise," her cousin said hastily. "If you have been ill, you must stay in bed, and anyway, as you see, I have come to you."

"Thank you," Doreen said. "I am grateful because I want to talk to you, Anne. It seems strange to think that we haven't met for nearly nineteen years—not since we were together at grandmother's, my first and last visit to England."

"I was there eight years ago," Anne said.

"Eight years!" Doreen ejaculated. "Why, I imagined that you went home for a holiday every year."

"That would have been a ridiculous extravagance," Anne answered. "We were doing God's work, we could not take frequent holidays for our own gratification."

Doreen felt she had been rebuked, but curbing the frivolous retort which rose instinctively to her lips, she said quietly:

"Wouldn't you be more comfortable if you took off your hat and your glasses?"

After a moment's hesitation, Anne did as was suggested, but with an air as though she felt the removal of any garment constituted an unnecessary intimacy.

"My eyes have been very painful," she said. "I can't bear the light, but I think it is dim enough in here."

"Fever always has that effect," Doreen said. Then she looked at her cousin with interest. "Why Anne," she exclaimed, "how extraordinary, but now you have got thin, we really are very alike."

Anne looked at her with the utmost distaste.

"Do you think so?" she said. "I'm afraid I cannot see any resemblance at all. But then, I never study myself closely."

"I am sorry if it annoys you," Doreen insisted, "but I do think so. I suppose it is because our mothers were twins. They were exactly like each other, but my memory of you was as a very plump little girl with pigtails. Now I see that we are both Wickhams in features and in colouring. You are not like your father, or I like mine."

Anne bowed her head.

"I should have been very proud to resemble mine," she said.

Doreen resisted an ardent desire to be rude. She couldn't help her surprise at the way in which Anne had altered since childhood. She could see so many characteristics of Mary and as she knew that it had been almost impossible to know the twin sisters apart, they must have been characteristic of Anne's mother too.

But Anne's face was also an echo of her own; the high cheekbones, the well-moulded jaw, and the eyes set far apart under a square forehead, were almost a frightening reflection of the image which stared back at her from her mirror.

"She has got a mean mouth though," Doreen thought, for Anne's lips were tight and pursed slightly together. "I don't think even lipstick would make her lips attractive."

Unlike her cousin, Anne used no aids to beauty. Her eyelashes were as colourless as her hair, which she wore parted in the centre and scraped back from her temples and she make no effort to disguise the yellow hardened texture of her skin.

"She looks much older than I do," Doreen thought, also with a certain amount of satisfaction, "far more than the twelve months between us."

Then with a sinking in her heart, feeling that she had not opened her case so far very successfully, she said:

"Anne, will you help me?"

"I have got no money," Anne answered quickly.

As she spoke she glanced about the room, so that Doreen knew she took in the poverty of her surroundings and knew without being told, that her cousin was in pretty desperate circumstances.

"I don't want money," Doreen replied. "I want you to take me to England with you."

Anne looked at her, too startled to answer.

"I have got some money towards my passage," Doreen went on. "You would have to augment it a little, but I believe that grandmother would refund it to you once I got back. Anyway, I will travel third-class, or steerage, I will come as your maid, if it would give you any pleasure, just as long as you will take me with you."

"You must be crazy!" Anne ejaculated, obviously before she had time to choose her words. Then having spoken, she realised that her tone had been too sharp. "I mean," she added hesitatingly, "that I don't think it is at all practicable. You see, I am going back, not only in my own interests, but because of the Mission. You understand?"

"No, I am afraid I don't," Doreen said. "Anne, don't be hard about this. You don't know how important it is to me, it means everything in my life. I must get away from here, I must. I have been ill, I have come to the end of my resources.

"I have had terribly bad luck, as I expect you know, and my father and mother are both dead. I have got no one to whom I can turn, no one who will help me. I can't write out of the blue to grandmother, just to ask her for my return fare home.

"Anyway, that all takes too long. I want to go now, to go with you. Give me the chance, Anne, you will never regret it, I swear you won't."

Doreen had sat up in bed as she spoke, her fingers were clasped together pleadingly but she felt, even as the words tumbled from her lips, that they were in vain. Anne's antagonism was obvious.

She had stiffened in her chair, and was looking away from her cousin, but with an expression of undisguised dislike on her face.

"I can't," she said tersely. "Don't you understand, I can't possibly do it. There are deputations, there's the press. This is very embarrassing for me, Doreen, but your common sense must tell you that it is impossible."

"You mean my presence might endanger your reputation," Doreen answered.

"Well," said Anne deprecatingly, "there have been many and varied stories about you, you know, and about your father and mother."

"Some may have been true," Doreen said, "most have undoubtedly been exaggerated. Oh, Anne, can't you understand that I would never have sent for you, never have asked you for this, if I hadn't been desperate."

"I can quite understand that," Anne said coolly. "I will do my best to let you have a little money, I am afraid I can't spare much, but as to your coming with me, that is a question that cannot even be considered."

"It must be, it must," Doreen cried.

She felt as though she must force her will upon her cousin. It was as if Anne was closing the gates of the future against her, barring her out. She was desperate and she had only one person to convince of her desperation; surely she could do that, surely Anne's determination was not stronger than her own?

"Please," she pleaded, "please, please listen. Couldn't you let me come with you, if I don't claim any relationship until we get to England? Say I am a fallen woman, say I am someone you are helping out of your charity. You would even get some kudos out of it."

"The papers would be certain to find out," Anne replied. "I can't risk it, it wouldn't be fair to myself . . . or to the cause I represent."

Doreen lost her patience.

"The papers!" she echoed. "That is all you think about, getting your name in the papers! Publicity! Public approval! The excitement of being a heroine! You are afraid of helping me because your pose of a saint and a Christian martyr might be damaged. You won't see that it is all superficial, so superficial that you dare not hold out one helping hand to someone who really needs it."

Anne took up her glasses.

"I think this conversation is quite profitless," she said in a cold voice.

"You can't leave me like this," Doreen said weakly. "You have got to do something for me, Anne, you have got to."

She saw refusal on her cousin's face. It drove her wild.

"If you don't," she cried, "I will get even with you somehow. I will give interviews to the press, I will tell them stories of your childhood, and I will show you up as the heartless, publicity-seeking hypocrite that you are in reality."

Anne got to her feet.

"You wouldn't dare!" she said.

"Dare?" Doreen echoed. "What have I got to fear? But you've got a lot to lose, and you know it. You are frightened of knowing me now; you will be a damned sight more frightened of knowing me in the future, that I promise you.

"What I have asked of you is perfectly reasonable, and you have refused me, not because it is impossible, but simply and solely because you are flattered by the publicity of a few cheap papers!"

"You daren't do it, you daren't!" Anne said defiantly.

But she was afraid, Doreen knew that, and it pleased her to see how she furtively wetted her lips and that one of her thin hands clutched at her chest.

"Wait and see," she said ominously, "just wait and see, Cousin Anne."

Even as she spoke Anne collapsed.

In a kind of horror Doreen saw her body sag suddenly, watched her crumple up by the chair, and fall half across its seat, her knees on the floor, her hands outstretched, as though to clutch the bed. She was so startled that it was several seconds before she threw back the bedclothes and went to her assistance.

Anne was breathing in an extraordinary way, gasping and half-choking. She was dead weight and Doreen had to use every ounce of strength to drag her up and on to the bed.

When finally she got here there, she saw that her mouth was open, her eyes flicking, as though in pain.

Quickly she rushed to the washstand, poured out a glass of water and brought it over. She tried to force it between Anne's lips, but most of it spilled and ran down her neck on to the pillow.

"Anne," she said, "Anne. I'm sorry! I didn't mean it. Speak to me if you can."

Anne only went on breathing in the same strange manner and it seemed to Doreen that though there was recognition in her eyes, she was unable to speak.

She rubbed her hands, then started to loosen her dress. Her heart was beating, there was no doubt about that. It was thumping violently against the side of her breast, as if it would try to escape.

Thoroughly frightened, Doreen pulled off Anne's shoes and tried to make her more comfortable.

"What am I to do?" she asked out loud.

She looked at Anne's face and saw that it was almost transparent in its pallor. The whiteness of her lips was terrifying and the laboured breathing seemed to be getting more difficult.

"I must get a doctor," Doreen thought.

Hastily she rushed to the cupboard and took out a coat which she put on over her nightgown. She slipped her feet into a pair of shoes, then with a last look at the girl on the bed, opened the door and ran hurriedly down the stairs.

SIX

The drug store was empty. Flies buzzed over the untidy counter and round the bottles on the shelves. Doreen knocked and shouted until slowly, eating a large cake, a small Arab boy appeared.

"What is the name of the nearest doctor?" she said, then realized that he did not understand and added in Arabic, "Get Master—quick!"

He disappeared and after what seemed to her an unconscionable time, the chemist's daughter, a lackadaisical young Egyptian whom Doreen had often seen behind the counter, came languidly into the shop.

She had obviously just got out of bed, for her hair was still in curling papers and she was buttoning her blouse.

"What is it?" she asked none too graciously.

"I want a doctor," Doreen answered. "It is very urgent. A friend of mine has been taken ill in my room."

"Well, if you are in a hurry," the girl said, "you had better ring Dr. Malasque, he's only a couple of streets away. Here's his telephone number."

She held out a card and not waiting for thanks, she left the shop, doubtless to continue her interrupted siesta. Doreen picked up the telephone.

It was with a deep sense of relief that she ran back across the street a minute or two later. She had the doctor's promise to be with her as quickly as he could.

She rushed up the stairs and burst into her room to

find Anne exactly as she had left her, moving her head restlessly, but apparently unconscious to what was going on around her.

Her dress, tumbled and creased in front where Doreen had hastily unbuttoned it, looked frowsy and untidy. To make things easier for the doctor, Doreen undid the belt which enclosed her waist, then noticed that the dress itself unbuttoned down the front. It was not difficult to slip it off.

"You will be cooler," she said to Anne, talking to her, although she had no idea whether her words would be heard or understood.

Under her dress Anne wore a petticoat of coarse cotton. Doreen looked at it with distaste and after raising her cousin's head still further on the pillows to make her as comfortable as possible, she covered her with the light counterpane.

There was nothing more she could do but wait, and she opened the door so that from the top of the stairs she could hear the doctor's car drive up and hail him the moment he entered the house.

The house itself was very quiet. As she had told Anne, this was the hour of day when the proprietress disappeared to drink coffee, or sip sherbert in the cafés near the Muski.

At this time also, the servants went to their homes or to the mosques and Doreen would often be the only person in the whole building.

The front door was left wide open, yet they were not afraid of thieves, perhaps because there was so little to steal, as all the occupants were poverty-stricken in the very extreme.

Doreen walked backwards and forwards from the bed to the head of the stairs, until finally, when she was beginning to be afraid that her summons was to pass unheeded, she heard a footstep in the hall below and saw a man enter.

"Is that Dr. Malasque?" she asked over the stairs. "Will you come up?"

He started to mount the uncarpeted stairs and as he drew near enough for her to see him closely, it was a shock to discover that he was an Arab. She had expected, quite without reason, for him to be English or Greek, but she concealed her surprise.

"My friend," she explained as he reached the top flight, "has suddenly been taken ill. I don't know what is wrong. But she has been laid up with fever for the past few days."

"Let me see her," the doctor said.

He drew out his stethoscope and listened to Anne's heart. Then, having taken her pulse, he pulled down her lower eye-lid to look at the whites of her eye.

"It is her heart, I think. You say she has had fever?"

"Yes, badly, I believe," Doreen answered. "She has just arrived from the Sudan."

"Ah, that will explain it," the doctor said. "I must get her to the hospital. I will go and make arrangements."

"Thank you," Doreen said.

"And the name?" he asked, taking a pencil and paper from his pocket.

"Miss Wallis—Miss Doreen Wallis," Doreen replied.

"I will be back as soon as I can manage it," he answered, walking towards the door. "I think she had better have an ambulance."

"But can't you give her anything in the meantime?" Doreen asked.

"I would not like to take responsibility," the doctor said. "My partner is away. I would like a second opinion."

"Good heavens!" Doreen thought to herself. "He doesn't sound very confident! Perhaps he isn't even fully qualified."

The doctor picked up his bag.

"I will hurry," he said. "In the meantime, don't let anyone move Miss Wallis."

He was gone, hurrying down the stairs before Doreen could explain that she had misunderstood his question and had given him the wrong name. She had thought that it was her name he was asking, not that of the patient.

"Oh well," she thought with a little grimace, "I will explain later, but Anne won't be pleased if she finds herself mistaken for me. I suppose I had better dress before he comes back."

She took off her overcoat and slipping out of her nightgown, searched in the drawer for a suspender belt and some clean underclothes.

She was just putting on her stockings when a sudden sound from the bed made her start to her feet and rush across the room.

To her horror Anne was making a kind of groaning noise, as if she was in an agony of pain which she could not express, and a thin stream of saliva was oozing out of her mouth and running down her chin.

As Doreen watched, powerless to do anything, her head moved from side to side, then with a sudden convulsion, her whole body seemed to arch, her knees bend. Her face was tense and agonised, her hands clenched.

"Anne!" Doreen called desperately. "Anne! Anne! Oh God, what can I do?"

Anne gave a kind of throttled choke and relaxed. Her body went limp, her legs straightened themselves, and as her head fell back, a gaping mouth and open eyes gave an expression of idiocy to her face.

"Anne," Doreen whispered. "Anne."

She knew in an awe-stricken certainty that Anne had died. For a moment she was too frightened to move, too terrified to do anything but stand looking down on her cousin.

Then in an agony of fear, she went to the top of the stairs and looking down into the hall below, she called "Help!"

She heard her voice echo back at her down the hollow of the stairs.

"Help! Help!" There was no other sound.

She came back to the bedside. She touched one of Anne's hands, felt her forehead and then, determinedly, her heart. She was clammy, warm, but utterly still.

"She is dead!" Doreen said below her breath. "She is dead."

Suddenly she felt faint and sick. She sat down in the nearest chair. After a moment, because she could not bear the sight of that open mouth and eyes, she went to the other end of the room and hid her face in her hands.

"It is horrible," she thought, "horrible."

She had seen Pepi die, but it had not been like this. Then there had been nurses and doctors in attendance, an air of hushed efficiency over the whole house, and only the doctors had known the exact moment when he had passed away.

His heart had ceased to beat, and the sleep into which he had fallen three or four hours before, remained unbroken. Doreen had been at his bedside, she had cried, but in peace and tenderness.

This was very different; it was horrible, sordid and beastly. She felt herself tremble.

"I have got to face it," she thought. "I must pull myself together and be ready for the doctor when he comes back."

She looked at the watch on her dressing-table. It was only five minutes since he had left.

Picking up the stocking she had dropped but a moment before and putting it on her other foot, she felt a chill come over her and she knew that in spite of the overwhelming heat, she was shaking with cold.

"Shock," she told herself, fighting for self-control.

She went to the wardrobe. She opened the door of it and looked at the row of hanging dresses and coats, white, red, blue and yellow. She stared at them wondering what was wrong.

Then she realised that subconsciously within herself she was looking for something black. Anne was dead, she ought to wear a black dress. Half stupidly she looked through them again, searching for the frock that she did not possess. The only black garment she owned was an evening cloak.

Then, out of the corner of her eye, she caught sight of Anne's dress where she had thrown it over the chair beside the bed. Nearby on a small table were her hat and sun glasses. Doreen stared at them.

In that moment, slowly but surely, like the pieces of a jig-saw puzzle gradually sorting themselves into the right places, the idea was formed within her. Why shouldn't she put them on?

Why shouldn't she wear the dress, the wide-brimmed hat, and those dark sun glasses? And if she did she would look exactly like Anne—she might be Anne—she would be Anne!

What was to stop her?

She felt dazed and stupid, yet the idea persisted in her head, ringing there like a bell which would not be quietened.

"It would be funny," she murmued to herself, "so terribly funny, to be Anne."

She felt her faintness and sickness leave her. It was as if some vivifying spirit crept into her, urging her forward.

"You have got to do it," it seemed to say. "This is the chance you asked for, the opportunity is at your door."

It seemed as though she were divided into two people, one said,

"No, it is ridiculous, absurd, how could you?"

And the other urged,

"Why not? Who is to know? Why should it be discovered? Anne hasn't been to England for eight years, she said so. People change in eight years, and anyway, you are both so very alike! Why not? Why not?"

"I won't listen, I can't hear," the other self said. "I would be afraid. How could I explain? How could I pretend to have lived Anne's life? Her work at the Mission Settlement—the shock of finding her parents murdered—her bravery among the sick natives."

As if in answer she seemed to hear Anne's voice saying,

"I can't bear to speak about it."

She could see the whole thing planning itself out. She could hear herself murmur that the shock and her recent illness would make it impossible for her to say much of what had occurred.

She would assume a quiet, reticent manner, a modesty and shyness, far more effective than Anne's self-satisfied platitudes.

"I daren't, it is too risky," Doreen protested, but even so, she knew the die was cast. She would do it.

Slowly, as if mesmerised, she crept nearer to the black dress hanging over the chair.

She touched it and looked at Anne in fear, as though she expected to see her eyes move accusingly. . . . Quickly, hurriedly, she slipped on the dress and buttoned it down the front.

She hated the feel of it, and the faint smell which came from the thick cotton.

For a moment she hesitated, she had an impulse to tear the frock off, to fling it from her, then the sound of a car in the street outside galvanised her into a frantic haste.

She looked down at Anne's shoes on the floor—low-heeled and sensible—and slipping them on, found that they fitted her, a fraction large perhaps, but nevertheless they were wearable. Her brain was now working feverishly.

If she was to carry this through, she must leave no traces which might betray her and she must eliminate completely her own personality, under the disguise of being Anne.

She went to the glass, wiped her face clean of powder and rubbed her lips to take away the last traces of lipstick.

She parted her hair in the centre, screwed it behind her head in imitation of Anne's severe style. It was so short and scanty that two hairpins were enough to hold it in place.

She hardly recognised herself when she had finished, but she had no time for reflection.

She turned towards the bed. There was something horrible in that open mouth and thrown-back head.

"It might be me," Doreen murmured to herself, then added out loud, "It is me. I am dead. From this moment I am dead."

She picked up Anne's hat, pulled it on and fixed the dark glasses behind her ears. Not one of her friends would know her now! She looked round the room, and noticed her red handbag.

Should she take her own money with her? Instinct

answered that it was unwise, a note might be traced. No, she must face the fact that she herself was dead.

Nothing in the room belonged to the new Anne Marston.

Trembling, half from weakness and half from a breathless fear which gripped her even as it drove her forward, Doreen walked down the stairs.

The blinding sunlight in the street was almost overwhelming.

She walked a little way then hailed a taxi. She gave the name of the hotel and sank back against the back seat as if to hide herself.

"I have done it now," she thought. "I cannot go back."

A million problems immediately presented themselves to her mind: she would not know where her room was in the hotel—she was not certain of Anne's engagements, she would not know the missionaries!

Another question was money.

Even as she thought about it she was conscious of something hard in the pocket of her cotton dress. Putting in her hand she drew out first a linen handkerchief, then a small zip-fastened purse containing two neatly folded notes and some Egyptian silver.

"How like Anne not to carry a bag," was Doreen's first thought, then she corrected herself. "I mustn't think like that, I must remember that I am Anne. I don't carry a bag."

It was not a long drive to the hotel. As the taxi drew up and the door was opened by a commissionaire, she felt a sudden panic which made her want to run wildly in the opposite direction.

Then a will-power she did not know she possessed, forced her to walk up the steps and through the revolving door. She was standing inside the doorway, uncertain what to do, when the reception clerk called out to her.

"There are two notes here for you, Miss Marston."

Automatically Doreen went forward and accepted the envelopes with a smile.

"Thank you," she said.

"You are welcome," he answered, handing her the key of her room.

She felt it cold in her hand. She clutched it with a sudden feeling of relief. This was easy, easier than she had anticipated.

She turned away from the desk and walked towards the lift. There was a small boy in attendance. She heard the gates clang behind her, then they shot upwards.

It was done now, there was no going back: Doreen Wallis was dead!

SEVEN

Alone inside the bedroom Doreen felt the almost unbearable tension of her body relax.

She leant back against the door which she bolted behind her with trembling fingers, as if she were pursued.

For two or three seconds she believed she was going to faint; an utter weakness made her limbs tremble and sweat broke out on her forehead. She groped her way from the door and sat down on the nearest chair.

She pulled off the dark glasses and looked around her. She was in the usual characterless hotel bedroom, so tidy, so devoid of individuality, that for a startled moment she felt that she had come to the wrong room and that this one had never been occupied.

Then she noticed by the bed a morocco-bound volume. It was undoubtedly a Bible.

Before she looked around further, Doreen read the notes she held in her hand. She ripped open the envelopes.

The first contained nothing more exciting than a request to visit a shop where antiques of all descriptions would be displayed to her.

The other was signed "Ella Garston." Doreen read it through.

"Dear Miss Marston,

"My husband has made arrangements with the manager for the use of a small private sitting-room for our reception this evening. There will be no extra charge for this. We will arrive at about a quarter to seven and I will come up to your bedroom, in case there is anything you would like to ask me before we proceed downstairs. I feel that you may be glad of our support, as well as sympathy, which, as you know, is yours. Your affectionate sister in Christ,

"Ella Garston."

Instinctively as she finished reading the letter, Doreen glanced round for the time. An electric clock over the mantelpiece told her it was ten past six.

She had thirty-five minutes' grace—thirty-five minutes in which to prepare herself for the greatest ordeal she had ever experienced in her life.

She started to her feet and made a systematic search of the room. It was almost pitiable how little she found. There was a coat hanging up in the wardrobe and two or three severely plain cotton underclothes in the chest of drawers, otherwise apparently Anne had no possessions save the Bible by her bedside, which Doreen was amused to find contained several press cuttings.

"Of course," she thought to herself. "Everything of hers must have been burnt at the Mission. I suppose she bought or was given these few things in Khartoum."

She went to the dressing-table and looked at herself in the mirror. On close examination doubts began to assail her. Did she really look like Anne? Would she deceive the Garstons who had seen her before?

Would she be able to brave the more penetrating investigation of the relations and friends Anne had made in England, even though it was eight years since they had seen her?

"It is too late to go back now," she told herself.

Then horror-stricken she looked at her hair. It was quite obvious, even to the most amateur eye, that at one time peroxide had been used. What was she to do?

It was obviously impossible to go down to the reception wearing a large straw hat, which in itself was an ample disguise. She opened the drawers hastily. There was nothing, not a piece of chiffon or ribbon with which she could bind up her hair, could disguise the tell-tale golden streaks.

The only black thing she could find was a clean pair of black stockings, apparently the only pair Anne possessed besides that which she had been wearing.

Instinctively, with a sudden jump of the heart, Doreen looked down at her own legs. She had forgotten, when she had put on Anne's shoes, that the stockings she was wearing were her own.

They were a deep sunburn tone of thin silk, quite ordinary in themselves, but dashing, to say the least of it, on someone of Ann's character, who was supposed to be in deep mourning.

Hastily she slipped them off and put on the pair of coarse lisle thread that she found in the drawer. Once again she looked desperately round the room for something to hide her hair.

She found it in the three-quarter length cheap silk slip of the overcoat which was hanging in the wardrobe. She tore it out, heedless of the damage she did to the coat, and bound it round her head, leaving only a suspicion of hair showing in the front, nothing over the ears.

Had she been made-up, she knew a turban effect would have been rather smart and sophisticated, but as it was, it gave her the effect of a housewife who, about to clean out her rooms, had bound up her head to protect it from the dust.

All this had taken time, yet at twenty minutes to seven, Doreen realised that her nails were too long and pointed.

She hated to cut them with the cheap pair of nail scissors she discovered on the dressing-table, but by this time she was shaking with fear that she would forget some small detail, which would betray her more effectively even than her ignorance of the Jurde Tribe.

She was now ready and she had only to adjust the darkened glasses to her eyes, when a knock came to the door.

For a moment she could not move, feeling her voice die in her throat as she tried to speak.

Then forcing herself to act, she crossed the room, drew back the bolt on the door and said, "Come in." The outside key turned in the lock and Mrs. Garston entered.

"Are you ready, my dear?" she asked.

Her answer, Doreen felt, was in the nature of a test. Supposing she noticed a dissimilarity in the voice? Supposing—but her fears were cut short by her visitor.

"Yes, I can see you are," she said briskly without waiting for Doreen to reply. "That is good. We have lots of time, but I think we might go downstairs. I expect you are feeling nervous. Well, try to leave everything on our shoulders, or rather, I should say, on those of my dear husband. He is used to taking up all sorts of burdens, I assure you.

"He won't let you down this evening. There are only to be about ten or twelve of us after all. We have just heard that the Matthews cannot get back in time from Ismailia, and I regret to say that Professor and Mrs. Brown are both laid up with fever. Well now, if you are ready . . ."

She stopped.

"No, wait, there was something I had forgotten. . . . My husband made me promise to give it to you . . . the money."

"For the Mission?" Doreen asked. It was the first words she had spoken.

"No, no, of course not," Mrs. Garston answered. "What we were speaking about this morning, the little advance my husband promised you, out of what the Association owes your father. I am sorry it couldn't be more, but I think you will find it enough for some clothes.

"Of course you will need things on the voyage and for the few gratuities you will have to give on board ship. Don't over tip, my dear, there's no reason for it and it won't be expected of you. Your ticket is being got today. Dr. Garston will bring it to the station."

She took an envelope out of her bag and opened it.

"There now," she said. "There's fifteen pounds—you had better count it to make sure there is no mistake."

"I don't think there's any need for that," Doreen said with a nervous laugh.

"Well, put it away safely," Mrs. Garston said. "One can't be too careful, you know. Have you got a bag?"

"I don't think—no I haven't," Doreen said.

"Well then, in your pocket, dear child, and pin it to your dress. It is what I always do myself. There's nothing so safe as a good safety-pin where notes are concerned."

She looked at the dressing-table and added:

"No safety-pins? Dear, dear! Isn't it terrible the amount of small trivial things one has to buy on occasions like this? I have often said to my dear husband that he has no idea how difficult it is for women to do without the little details of life—pins, tape, buttons, they are such an essential part of our existence, aren't they?

"Well, let me look. I may have one in my bag. Yes, here it is, a black one. That's fortunate, isn't it?"

Meekly Doreen stood while Mrs. Garston pressed the pin through the notes she held in her hand, then pushing them into her pocket, steered the point through the black cotton lining.

"When you go to bed tonight," Mrs. Garston said, "slip them under your pillow. This is a very respectable hotel, but of course, all the floor servants are natives and one can't trust them, not with anything, although I expect there's no need for me to tell you that."

"I will remember your advice," Doreen murmured.

"There now! We are ready!" Mrs. Garston exclaimed.

She walked to the door.

"I suppose you must wear those dark glasses my dear? It seems such a pity to hide one's eyes when one has to speak to people. So much expression is lost, isn't it? As I always say to my husband, 'eyes are the windows of our souls'."

"I am afraid I cannot take them off," Doreen said hastily.

"No, no, I understand, you must obey the doctor's orders, however irksome! Never mind, we shan't expect too much of you this evening, and the moment our little ceremony is over, you can slip up and go straight to bed. Have a little supper on a tray with a nice hot cup of tea and you will soon drop off to sleep. After all, you have got a busy day in front of you tomorrow, we mustn't forget that."

"What time does my train leave?" Doreen asked as they were waiting for the lift.

"Half-past four, I think," Mrs. Garston replied. "That will give you time to shop in the morning. Would you like me to come with you, dear? I had promised to take a reading at our women's club, but I dare say I could persuade someone else to deputise for me."

"No, no, of course not," Doreen said hastily. "I shouldn't think of interfering with your plans. Besides, I can manage quite well, there are only a few things that I want to get."

"If you are quite certain that you will be all right," Mrs. Garston said reluctantly.

Doreen felt she would rather have enjoyed a morning shopping.

"Quite certain," she replied firmly.

With what was almost a sigh, the good lady stepped into the lift as the small boy flung open the gates.

Dr. Garston was tall, with a hearty voice and a jovial manner, which struck one immediately as being assumed, and quite foreign to his inner nature.

"Well, how are we this evening?" he asked Doreen, hodling out a large bony hand, and taking hers in a firm clasp that gave her the impression of being deliberate, as though he told himself that a forceful grip showed both a strong mind and a strong faith.

"I am very tired," Doreen replied, "and I am hoping very much, Dr. Garston, that you will excuse me from saying anything. I feel, under the circumstances, it would be quite impossible for me to make any sort of speech."

She dropped her head for a moment, lowered her voice.

"I don't want to break down," she whispered.

It was a good bit of acting and it had its instantaneous effect on the Garstons.

"But my dear child, of course we understand," Mrs. Garston said, putting a hand on her arm. "You must just leave everything to my husband as I suggested to you. I see no reason why you should say anything except 'thank you' when they present you with the small sum we have already collected, and give you our promise of further contributions."

"That is so kind," Doreen murmured. "I feel I could not do more."

She intercepted a glance between husband and wife which seemed to her one of approval. It crossed her mind that perhaps Anne had not shown such a depth of feeling, but had been quite ready to take a business-like and efficient interest in all the arrangements.

"I entirely sympathise, entirely, of course," Dr. Garston said, clearing his throat. "As my wife suggests, if you will leave it to me, I feel sure I can very adequately convey to the company your true feelings in the matter. Excuse me a moment." Someone had appeared at the door and beckoned in his direction.

"Sit down, dear," Mrs. Garston said.

Doreen did as she was bid, only too glad to obey any suggestion which prevented her making any further effort. Apart from her fear, she was genuinely as weak as Anne might have been.

This was the first time she had been out since she left the hospital, and the strain of events had made her feel curiously dizzy and faint.

"Do you think I could have a drink?" she asked Mrs. Garston, then added, "Of water, I mean."

"Of course. I will get one," Mrs. Garston replied.

She went towards the door, but before she could get there, Dr. Garston came back accompanied by three men with cameras.

"These gentlemen of the Press, Miss Marston," he said, "are very anxious for photographs. I feel sure that you will not mind obliging them."

"Not alone," said Doreen hastily. "I don't wish to be photographed alone. If you and Mrs. Garston were with me . . ."

She did not know why, she only felt that there was less danger in a group. There was no likelihood of her being recognised, yet never for a moment could she escape the fear that the door might open and someone call out her real name.

The Garstons were only too willing to oblige, and obviously gratified at her request.

"Naturally, if you want us," Mrs. Garston said. "We are proud to support you."

They were grouped together by the window and by the time the photographs were taken, guests were arriving, and there was no further chance of Doreen procuring the drink she so urgently needed.

"I ought to have asked for brandy," she told herself and nearly laughed out loud at the idea.

How shocked the Garstons would have been! She was quite certain that they were both teetotallers, and the rest of the guests invited to meet her undoubtedly looked as if they were lifelong abstainers.

"This indeed," Doreen thought to herself, "is a very different strata of society to what I have known in the past."

Most of the men assumed the same hail-fellow-well-met manner as Dr. Garston. The women were usually soft-voiced, self-effacing and incredibly badly dressed.

It was unbelievable, Doreen thought, that they could want to look like that, or that they could buy such badly cut dresses and in such needlessly hideous material. The wonder was that they had procured for themselves husbands.

Each one with her strained-back hair, shiny face and grotesque garments, might have been a stage parody of the unwanted spinster, yet by some miracle they had all, somehow or other, managed to get married, and, in most cases, to produce children.

And what was more, they were perfectly satisfied with themselves and their lives, or at least they appeared to be.

They certainly radiated self-satisfaction, and one thing which struck Doreen, was that they seemed almost to glory in the fact that the Marstons had been murdered.

Did it, she wondered, give them each a personal feeling of adventure and danger, or was a martyr's crown the only ultimate glorification they could expect in their drab lives?

Dr. Garston spoke, as he explained, "on behalf of Miss Anne Marston, who feels unable, after such a very recent bereavement, to bring herself to address you personally."

He told them the tragic details of what had occurred, with many elaborations, and spoke warmly of the wonderful work which had been carried out by Dr. and Mrs. Marston for the last twenty-seven years.

"We have all been encouraged, at different times," Dr. Garston said, "by the glowing reports sent to us from this outlying post on our great battlefield. I refer, of course, to our fight under the banner of Christ.

"Dr. Marston was that rare thing, an idealist who, to a great extent, attains his ideal. I think Miss Marston will forgive if I say that in some ways I am glad that he did not live to see what might have appeared to him to be a great setback.

"His wife, too, was one of those helpmates who do so much in their own quiet way to spread the Gospel of our Lord. Together they have laboured; together they have found their rest with God, and if they have left us a legacy of inspiration, they have also left us a responsibility which none of us can shirk.

"We must carry on; we must continue the work which Dr. Marston began so nobly and for which he died so heroically. We can suffer no defeatist ideas where the faith of God is concerned, and at the place, where Dr. Marston was forced to lay down his arms, we will take them up and carry them forward.

"Ladies and gentlemen, I ask you to work for the continuation of the Marston Settlement and to remember in your prayers that dear brother and sister of ours who have passed the great barrier into the peace of God."

There was hardly a dry eye in the room when he sat down. Handkerchiefs were hastily put to one side for prolonged applause.

When it ended another missionary rose and after speaking for nearly ten minutes on exactly the same lines as Dr. Garston, he carried up to Doreen a tray on which there was a bag of money.

"On behalf of my colleagues and myself," he said in funereal tones, "I wish to present to the new Marston Mission Settlement the sum of eight pounds, twelve shilling and sixpence, which we have collected in the past few days. We also wish to express our deep sympathy for Miss Marston, and our entire accordance with the sentiments so ably expressed by Dr. Garston."

There was more applause and Doreen bent forward to take the bag of money, acknowledging it with a quiet little "thank you."

"Let us pray," Dr. Garston said.

They all sank to their knees for two long extemporary prayers, which were followed by the singing of a mission hymn without accompaniment and a final blessing.

The ceremonial proceedings were then over and everyone pressed forward for a few words with the guest of honour. Doreen managed, however, by keeping near Mrs. Garston and by answering all questions in a quiet hushed voice, to avoid any uncomfortable moments.

Mrs. Garston was invaluable, for while chattering away to someone on her left, she always had one ear alert for what was being said to her distinguished protégée, and she managed, in nine cases out of ten, to get in an answer long before Doreen could even open her lips to speak.

At last the party began to disperse, and after the final handshakes had been given, Mrs. Garston turned to Doreen.

"You must slip off to bed, dear child. You mustn't tax your strength, whatever you do. Oh, and about the money," she added hastily, seeing that Doreen was still holding it in her hand, "I think it would be wise if you gave it to my husband. Of course, there is no need for you to take it to England. We will have it placed in the bank here, and we will make this the headquarters of the fund. Any contributions you manage to raise at home can be sent direct to us."

"Do you think that is best?" Doreen asked.

"Much the best," Mrs. Garston said firmly. "I know you would not like the responsibility of looking after such a special fund, my dear, any more than I should. Much better leave it to my husband. He's drawing up an appeal to be inserted in the newspapers which I am sure will be immensely effective. We hope the money will come rolling in. He will be treasurer, of course."

Doreen had a strong desire to say that she would like to be treasurer, but she knew instinctively that it would be an unpopular move, so meekly she handed the money over to Dr. Garston, who slipped it into the spacious pocket of his black alpaca coat.

"Don't you worry your head about finance," he said. "I will attend to all that, I am used to it. My wife always chaffs me and says she never sees me without a ready reckoner in one hand and an account book in the other.

"Well, perhaps she is right. This means another little file for the pigeon-holes in my desk, but a very precious one it will be."

"Both in spirit and in fact, we hope," Mrs. Garston added. "You will work hard in England, won't you, dear Miss Marston, and try to get lots of notices in the newpapers about our appeal.

"Newpapers are such a help. I remember once we got contributions from all over the world for our orphanage, just because one of the papers ran a story about a crocodile climbing up the river bank and eating one of the orphans. It wasn't quite true.

"What happened was one of the children fell into the river and we think he was eaten by a crocodile. But anyway, it did us an enormous amount of good. Hundreds of pounds came in by every post, in fact Dr. Garston was quite snowed under, weren't you, dear?"

"My wife is not suggesting that you seek publicity, Miss Marston," Dr. Garston said severely, "but at the same time, if it is God's will that we can turn such things to His use, the opportunity will come."

"I am sure it will," Doreen said faintly, holding out her hand. "Good night and thank you."

They walked with her to the lift and it was with a sigh of relief that she saw the last of their up-turned faces as she sped upwards.

She kept her composure until she was within the confines of her own room.

Then at last she began to laugh, at first quietly, then hysterically, until the tears were rolling down her cheeks and she was forced to bury her face in the pillows on the bed to prevent people passing down the passage being surprised at the sounds.

EIGHT

It was such a relief to arrive on board the ship waiting at Port Said and to find that she had a cabin to herself, that Doreen could have embraced the red-faced, jovial purser who said to her:

"I have managed to wangle it, Miss Marston. I felt, under the circumstances, that you would so much prefer to be alone."

The tension of the journey itself, the ordeal of interviewing several press reporters on the landing-stage before she went aboard, faded into the background like an unpleasant nightmare.

All that mattered was that she was alone and could relax in the small, but well-fitted-up cabin, to which she was escorted by a smiling stewardess.

Doreen pulled off her hat and the dark glasses, which she had grown to dislike, even while she welcomed the protection they gave her, and after holding her handkerchief under a tap in the basin, wrung it out and put it against her aching head.

It had been insufferably hot all day and even now that darkness had fallen, the cabin was airless and stifling.

She was very tired. The anxiety and the intense fear of discovery which never left her, had brought her a restless night, bathed in the perspiration of weakness, and more than once she had wondered if her fever was returning and that morning would find her unable to travel.

At half-past seven when her breakfast had been brought to her bedside, she had been limp and utterly fatigued. But she had not been able to stay in bed and rest, and before nine she had been up and dressed and starting off to visit the cheaper shops.

No one knew better than Doreen how to make a pound go farther than anyone else.

She had managed, while expending the least possible amount of money, to get herself several frocks, a coat and two pair of shoes and, if less serviceable, some more attractive underclothes than those which had been chosen by Anne.

She had kept to black, partly because she felt that the deepest mourning would be expected of her, and secondly because it was far more economical in the long run to have everything to match.

"I shall look like a crow," she told herself, "but it can't be helped."

It was difficult to subdue her taste for smarter and more sophisticated styles and choose only the plainest and most unobtrusive garments.

"I must risk nothing," she kept repeating over and over again in her mind.

The only concession she allowed herself was the purchase of a box of powder and a powder-puff and a very pale, hardly discernible lipstick.

These she would not dare to use until she was far away from Cairo, but at the same time she refused to arrive in England with the complexion that she had now.

A good face cream she felt was a necessity, and she

did not grudge the extra shillings which procured her one of really good quality.

Then came the problem of her hair. A small bottle of hairdresser's blue was not difficult to get and by eleven o'clock Doreen, back at the hotel, had been washing her hair in the basin in her bedroom, intent on dimming the pseudo-gold which glittered defiantly through rinse after rinse.

The final result was so subdued that only a very experienced eye would have guessed that her hair had ever been tinted, but until the last streak of peroxide grew out, Doreen was comforted by the knowledge that among the other things she had brought back from the shops were several yards of black chiffon which could be wound round her head at night.

Although her train had left Cairo during the hottest part of the afternoon, she had been touched to find quite a company gathered to say good-bye to her on the platform.

Most of the missionaries who had been present the night before had come to wish her God-speed. Dr. and Mrs. Garston were, of course, very busy hurrying up and down giving her advice, seeing to her luggage, and making themselves a general nuisance to all the officials on the train.

A small bouquet was presented by a reluctant child, and she was photographed at least a dozen times, standing among groups of missionaries and at the door of her carriage.

As the train had moved out of the station, she had leant out of the window and waved, and there had been a genuine lump in her throat, not for that little group of eager pioneers of the Gospel, but for all that she was leaving behind her.

It was only then that it had come to her that this was the moment of rebirth. Doreen Wallis was dead and it was the new Anne Marston who had waved a tearful farewell to everything that was familiar.

It had been impossible, during the night, for Doreen not to think of Anne lying still and cold in the hospital mortuary, not to wonder what was being done about her, to long with a desperate and insane desire to go back to her own room. She wanted to touch, to feel, to know if only for one moment, something which was her own.

Then, as the train had gathered speed, she knew that her last chance was gone. She was parting from her old life for ever.

From the dingy little hotels where she had lived for so many years with her father and mother, from the house by the river where she had acted as Pepi's wife, from those graves in the distant cemetery where Pepi and her parents lay, and from all the streets and places which now, as she was leaving them, became beloved monuments.

Monuments to her childhood, to Pepi, to Tony and to all those other men who had come into her life and passed out of it again, meaning sometimes so little, sometimes so much.

Would she ever forget, ever be free of those ghosts which accompanied her waking or sleeping?

Once again Doreen said to herself, "I have died. I have got to remember that only Anne is alive."

She had sat down in her seat and tried to study the large heavy magazines that Dr. Garston had given her at the last moment.

She had telephoned him at luncheon time and asked him to be kind enough to bring with him to the station all the literature that had been published in the past about the Mission Settlement and about her father and mother.

"I want to be so very certain of my facts," she had explained easily on the telephone, "and sometimes my memory is at fault."

"But of course," he said. "I understand, my dear child. I will look them out for you. I think we have the back copies."

He had not forgotten and when Doreen looked at the large pile of reading matter, she felt slightly dismayed. Nevertheless, it was imperative she should be cognisant of the life she was supposed to have led.

It was almost terrifying to realise how little she did

know about missionaries, about their work, or about the tribes in Africa.

The only natives with whom Doreen had had any contact were those in Cairo and Alexandria, and although she could speak a few words of Arabic, enough to give orders to the servants, she was frightened lest someone really knowledgeable should question her and that she would break down and find herself utterly at a loss.

One thing she was quite certain of in her new position: that whatever happened she must not return. This, indeed, was her last glimpse of the dark continent.

"I can have a breakdown, or I can make some excuse when the moment comes," she told herself confidently.

She did not dare question the future too closely. In her heart she felt, coiled like a snake, a cold agonising fear of it.

But for the moment she forced herself to concentrate, almost fiercely, on the actual present, determined not to slip up, not to overlook anything which might by any possible means jeopardise her security.

The ship began to move about midnight. Doreen, who had been unpacking in her cabin, came up on deck and finding a quiet spot, leant over the rail to say her last good-bye to Egypt.

She looked down on the quay at the crowds of upturned faces, on heads covered with the conventional red tarboosh, on the ragged urchins, screaming shrill, unintelligible remarks.

Behind were the dark unlit buildings and the streets, glittering and garish with lights, the coffee shops packed with Arab customers in spite of the lateness of the hour.

The ship was moving, steaming slowly out of the Canal under a sky brilliant with stars.

"They never seem to go to bed in this place," a voice said.

Instinctively Doreen put her dark glasses up to her eyes—she had been holding them in her hand while she said her silent farewell. She saw a big broad-shouldered man leaning on the rail beside her.

He must have come up so quietly that she had not heard him.

"It is a long time since I have been here," she said.

"I would hate to tell you how many times I have seen the old joint fading away," he said. "Yet it has a fascination. I always come up on deck to watch us pull out. Well, thank heaven we shall shortly be free of this ghastly heat. You have come from Cairo?"

"Today, yes," Doreen answered.

"So have I," he answered. "Full of fun as usual—it's the paradise of the tired business man. Did you see that new show at the Kit-Cat—jolly good, wasn't it?"

"I was only there one night," Doreen said primly.

Inwardly she smiled. She knew the show to which he referred, an exotic, semi-naked act which had packed the cabaret night after night. She glanced at the stranger and wondered who he was.

His voice had a roughness and edge to it which she could not quite place. Yet she rather liked what she could see of him. His face and profile showed sharp-cut features and a strong chin.

Nevertheless, she was not prepared to be confidential about herself, and as the ship moved slowly over the dark water, she turned away from the rail.

"Good night," she said.

"Good night," he answered. "See you tomorrow, I hope. My name is Dale—John Dale, and the bar is a permanent address for me this trip."

He smiled at her and irrepressibly she smiled back. There was some kind of underlying gaiety about him to which she could not help but respond. Sharply she galvanised herself into action.

"Good night," she said again, hoping her voice sounded cool and distant.

In her cabin Doreen gave herself a good talking to.

"You will have to be very careful," she said, looking at herself in the glass. "The slightest flirtation, or even familiarity, with a member of the opposite sex, is likely to be quite a sensation where Anne Marston is concerned. This is a very different thing to being Doreen Wallis. Now pull yourself together, my girl, and cut out the sex appeal."

She looked at her reflection and laughed; it seemed almost impossible that anyone could find her attractive at the moment.

She loosened her tightly dragged-back hair and wondered if she dared to wear it in a style slightly less severe. Then there were the glasses; must she go on wearing them? They ensured her safety.

Yet, having studied all those neatly cut-out press notices at the back of Anne's Bible, there were no recent photographs, as far as she could see, of Anne without them. Dare she leave them off? she questioned.

She would certainly look less depressing.

Once again she chided herself angrily. Why should she worry about her looks? That indeed was the least important part of her new self. For Doreen Wallis they had been all important, her face had been her fortune, but for Anne Marston it was different—her reputation was what mattered.

"It is hard to part with the convictions of twenty-nine years when it comes to vanity," Doreen thought.

She got into her bunk, her face and neck greased in the belief that such treatment would gradually improve the texture of her skin.

To her surprise she slept peacefully and with an abandon she would not have thought possible. Physically she had been utterly exhausted, but mentally she had felt so keyed up that she had expected another night of restless tossing, of fears and imaginations.

However, she did not move until nearly eight o'clock and woke to find the reflection of sunlit waves flickering from her porthole on to the white ceiling of her cabin. She climbed up in her bunk and looked out.

The ship was right out at sea, there was no land in sight.

As though the very sight of the water gave her a sense of escape and imbued her with new strength, she stretched and smiled in the sunlight.

There were not many people in the dining saloon and the chief steward, on hearing her name, led her to a table at which there were only two other people, but which he told her was the chief engineer's.

"I will see that you are looked after, Miss Marston," he said, and Doreen thanked him.

There was a kind of deference in his voice which pleased her. It was nice, for once, to feel that she was well known but in the right way.

She had grown used in the past to a too familiar attitude from head waiters, who had a horrible confidential air as they led her to some obscure table with a new, and perhaps too ardent, young man by her side.

She had known exactly what they thought of her and of her life, and although she had told herself that it was completely unimportant and not worthy of a moment's consideration, she resented the insolence they so skilfully implied, without at any time laying themselves open to rebuke.

She ordered a large breakfast and when she had finished her coffee, went up on deck.

It was a glorious morning with a promise of heat later in the day, but, as always out at sea, there was a cool breeze. She felt it gave her new life and strength.

She longed for the rain, the rough boisterous wind she had known only once, nearly nineteen years ago when she had stayed in England.

How cold she had been at first—she could feel herself now, small and shivering under a pile of blankets in the big room where she had slept at her grandmother's.

How strange it had been to watch for one long day the rain teeming down over the garden, battering down the flowers, drenching the shrubs, making even the trees themselves bow to its force. She had been half afraid of it, yet fascinated.

Then, when in the evening the storm had stopped and the evening sun had come creeping out for a short hour before sunset, gleaming through the clouds, making every raindrop glisten and sparkle like a diamond, it seemed to Doreen as though a miracle had occurred.

She could smell now the lush damp fragrance of it.

For a long time after she had gone home she used to recall it, especially when she lay in some airless, cramped bedroom, unable to sleep for the heat, stifling under a mosquito net, naked because she could not bear the touch of anything on her body, but finding a mental relief and a healing solace in her memories of England.

She wondered now if her father and mother ever had the craving for their native land that she had experienced.

It seemed extraordinary that Mary, who had been brought up in the countryside, could have tolerated the East for all those long years. There had, of course, been Alexandria in the summer, when they were prosperous enough to go there.

Then they could bathe and enjoy the long lazy hours lying on the beach. But surely nothing could compensate her for England, for the home she had known and loved in childhood and adolescence.

Yet familiarity was a strong tie; at this very moment, illogically and unreasonably, Doreen felt homesick for all that she was leaving behind.

She might hate Cairo, dislike the many associations it held in her mind, but at least it was familiar, and there was an extraordinary comfort in that very familiarity.

"Why am I here?" she asked herself fiercely as a quick change of mood shook her tempestuously. "I must be crazy. I have thrown away everything, all that I know and all to which I have ever belonged. I want to go back."

In a panic she would have sought the sanctuary of her own cabin, but as she turned, she came face to face with John Dale.

"Well, if it isn't my little friend of last night," he said, and held out his hand. "How are you feeling this morning? It's easier to breathe now the land of Egypt is left behind us, isn't it? I see you're an early bird," he went on. "I never sleep the first night at sea, so I said to myself 'A breath of air for you, my boy,' but once I find a few congenial friends, you won't be seeing me until luncheon time."

"I slept amazingly well," Doreen said, feeling that some sort of remark was required of her.

"That's the ticket," John Dale answered. "Perhaps you do a lot of travelling?"

Doreen shook her head.

"Very little," she answered.

"Well, if it isn't experience which makes you settle down so quickly, it must be an easy conscience," he said, laughing. "What about a chair," he suggested, "or shall we walk?"

"Oh, let's walk," Doreen replied.

"Good!" he ejaculated. "A constitutional is just the thing for me. I am beginning to get on the fat side. Fifteen years ago I was as thin as a lath, but in those days I was working down the mine . . . and do they make you work? I'll say they do!"

"What sort of mine?" Doreen questioned.

"Diamond—that little stone which makes the girls' eyes sparkle! Still, that was long ago and it is a long story. I was just doing it to show my old dad that I could and would! He's the sort of guy who doesn't appreciate his son unless he can prove himself a chip off the old block! Well, I showed him that I was no sapling and once the old boy believed it, he turned trumps! You know him by name, of course—Joseph Dale is the man and I'm proud to be his offspring."

"Yes, of course," Doreen said politely.

"Joseph Dale," she repeated to herself.

She imagined that she should know the name, but somehow, while it was vaguely familiar, it conveyed nothing to her. Luckily, there was no need for her to make many comments, for her companion was quite prepared to ramble on.

"Just come up from Johannesburg this trip," he said. "Went down to see the old boy and find out what he wanted to do about the market. I am a stockbroker now—seems tame after all the things I have done, but it gives me employment and that is as difficult to find as most things these days. I'd loathe to be one of the leisured classes, wouldn't you?"

"I am afraid that I never had a job of any sort . . ." Doreen answered, then remembering that her work in the Mission Settlement would most certainly be considered one, added ". . . that is a paying one."

"Ah! Now you're talking," John Dale laughed.

"Employment and paying employment are two very different things, as a great many people find out."

They had walked once round the deck and he stopped at the entrance to the smoking lounge.

"What about a drink?" he asked. "Too early for you? There's no closing time aboard ship, you know!"

"I would like a glass of milk," Doreen said demurely.

When she left hospital the doctor had ordered her to drink at least a pint a day and she felt that now was the moment to obey him.

"My goodness! But that's a change," John Dale exclaimed. "I've never met a woman aboard ship yet who didn't say yes to a champagne cocktail and make the excuse that she was getting her sea legs. Steward!" he shouted at the top of his voice.

The steward who was busy at the other end of the smoking-room, turned disdainfully at the sound, but when he saw who it was commanding him, he came across with a smile.

"Good morning, Mr. Dale. I thought we should have the pleasure of seeing you before long."

"And you weren't far wrong, my boy, because here I am and this lady and I are thirsty. We have been up with the lark and have done a morning's constitutional worthy of any Anglo-Indian colonel! What more can you ask of your passengers?"

"You'll have the usual, Mr. Dale?" the steward asked.

"Wait a minute, not so fast," John Dale replied. "This lady is asking for an unknown beverage, in fact, I hardly think you would keep such a drink aboard ship. What was it you said?" he asked Doreen in pretended ignorance.

"Milk," Doreen replied, "just ordinary milk, from the cow, if possible."

"Do you hear that, steward?" John Dale said with a roar of laughter. " 'From the cow, if possible,' and mind it is none of your fancy tinned stuff."

Doreen regretted her choice when the thin, rather watery-looking glass of milk was brought to her.

"It was taken on board last night, miss," the steward

explained apologetically. "But it is poor stuff we get from those gippies."

John Dale had a huge glass of what he called "black velvet"—stout and champagne mixed together—and though she was sorely tempted to join him, Doreen felt that she must stick to her guns and behave as she believed Anne would have done in the same circumstances.

The smoking-room began to fill up; John Dale's large voice hailed several acquaintances, who waved to him or came across for a few words before settling down at another table.

It seemed to Doreen that more than one person glanced curiously at her, and after a while she had the uncomfortable suspicion that she had, perhaps, not been particularly wise in her choice of a companion.

Had she been travelling as Doreen Wallis she would have shrugged her shoulders and not giving public opinion a second thought, but as things were, she must be on her guard and avoid anything which might be wrongly constructed, or which could cause gossip.

So about ten minutes later, in spite of John Dale's protests, she made her excuses, and having thanked him for her glass of milk, left him and went below to her cabin.

"Perhaps I am making a mountain out of a molehill," she told herself regretfully when she found herself alone again with nothing more entertaining to do than read the magazines with which Dr. Garston had provided her. "Why should there be anything wrong with John Dale? And who is his father? I ought to know but I don't!"

She speculated about him a good deal that day. In the evening she was to learn a lot more.

NINE

Doreen dressed for dinner with care, more care, she felt, than she should have taken.

Because already she was well aware that while her dress was plain, practical and of cheap inferior stuff, she herself had a knack of wearing clothes which made anything she put on, provided that it fitted her, look, to a certain degree, smart and interesting.

And she knew, from what she could see of her reflection in the small high mirror of her cabin, that she had, in her black dress, a look of distinction.

The dress was entirely without trimming of any sort, save for a puritanical collar of white muslin the long points of which reached half-way down the bodice.

It was by no means an evening dress. Doreen had been wise enough to realise that someone of Anne's type would not care for evening clothes, but the skirt touched the ground and in it she knew that she would look as would be expected of her—demure, appealing and impeccably respectable.

The day had not passed without incident. At luncheon she had come down a little late, to find her table companions assembled before her. The Chief Engineer got to his feet, shook her by the hand, and introduced her.

When they had seated themselves, he said:

"The Captain asked me, Miss Marston, to express his regret that there was not a place at his table. We have been full up since we left Bombay, but, if I may say so, what is his loss is my gain."

The people surrounding her were mostly old and in ordinary circumstances she would have thought them exceedingly dull, but there was something rather fascinating in finding that they treated her with a respect and interest that she had never in her life experienced before.

"What it is to be a celebrity!" she told herself a little cynically, but at the same time she enjoyed the novel sensation.

When luncheon was over, one of the women at the table invited her to coffee in the lounge. She was the type of old woman who, in Cairo, had been Doreen's most bitter enemy.

The wife of a retired tea planter, she spent every winter abroad revisiting India and Ceylon to keep in touch with old friends and acquaintances. She was full of gossip and a fund of knowledge and scandal about the majority of people with whom she came in contact.

Three weeks aboard ship was, to her, a real enjoyment, for she could delve into hundreds of other people's lives, prying out their innermost secrets with the relentlessness of a sportsman after his prey, using the material she collected for making the maximum amount of trouble for those concerned.

Had she not learnt during the meal that Mrs. Waverton Watson had not been to Cairo for many years, but expected to visit it next year when her son was stationed there on his way home from India, Doreen would have been frightened of her.

"You will be in your element there," Doreen thought, listening to the old woman's well educated and carefully modulated voice repeating a cruel scandal about someone to whom she had taken a dislike.

Such maliciousness would have been alarming, had not Doreen sensed that for the moment, at any rate, Mrs. Waverton Watson was most anxious to be pleasant to her.

"I must be far more important than I thought," she murmured to herself as they walked briskly into the lounge and Mrs. Watson dispensed with a withering glance some unfortunate new-comer, who was about to take her favourite sofa.

"Really," she said loudly to Doreen as they settled themselves, "people who get on at Port Said have absolutely no consideration for those who are making the whole voyage. I have always told the steward that places should be reserved in this lounge, but he says it is against the rules of the company. I must get my husband to write to the Head Office when we return. He knows several of the directors and doubtless if he made a complaint, it would carry weight."

"I am sure it would," Doreen said agreeably.

"I presume you are travelling alone?" Mrs. Watson asked.

"I am afraid I am," Doreen replied. "There was no one, you see, to come with me."

She spoke in a subdued voice and had the pleasure of seeing Mrs. Watson assume that expression of lugubrious gloom which is traditional when speaking of the dead.

"Of course, of course. A terrible loss for you—terrible," she murmured. "And I am going to suggest that should you feel in need of a chaperone on this voyage, I shall only be too happy to offer you any assistance within my power."

"That is very kind of you," Doreen murmured.

"It will be a pleasure because I was much impressed," Mrs. Watson said patronisingly, "by the report of the way you behaved under such extraordinarily difficult circumstances. You are going to relations in England, I presume?"

"To my grandmother," Doreen answered.

"I wonder if I know her! Is her name Marston?"

"No," Doreen replied. "It is Wickham. She is my mother's mother and she lives at Brookavon, a tiny village in Gloucestershire."

"Wickham. I seem to know the name," Mrs. Watson said. "I think I have heard my son mention it. There may have been a brother officer of that name in his regiment."

"I am afraid they are quite ordinary people," Doreen said mischievously.

"But I am sure they will be very proud of you," Mrs. Watson answered generously. "You have done well, my dear. And what are you thinking of doing when you get back to England?"

"I haven't really decided," Doreen replied.

"You will be careful, I hope, not to let newspaper publicity and all that ridiculous fuss turn your head," Mrs. Watson said. "I am afraid, from what I have read in the papers, you will find some kind of ovation waiting for you at the end of our journey. I know how painful it will be for you in the circumstances."

"And how you would enjoy it yourself," Doreen thought to herself.

But out loud she murmured something deprecating, and Mrs. Watson was delighted with her quiet manner and modest bearing.

August approval was not content with giving Doreen coffee after luncheon; she invited her to the same ceremony after dinner. Doreen was rather bored with Mrs. Watson by this time, but not knowing how to refuse her, meekly followed her once again into the lounge.

During the course of the evening the only parson on board made her acquaintance. He was travelling from Rangoon and when introduced, he recited a set speech of commendation and commiseration, which she felt he must have been preparing ever since he heard she was on board.

Seeing her in the lounge with Mrs. Watson, he had come across and asked if he might join them. Mrs. Watson had acquiesced to his request, but none too gracefully, and Doreen had been amused to realise that she considered he should not have pushed himself forward, but have waited until she condescended to invite him.

"We are very full for the time of year," the parson remarked.

"I have seldom been on this trip without finding it packed," Mrs. Watson said with the air of an experienced traveller, to whom nothing could possibly be new or informative.

"And we have got a quieter lot than usual," the parson continued, "although an old friend got on at Port Said, who ought to make things hum a bit."

"Whom do you mean?" Mrs. Watson asked, curiosity overcoming her frigidity.

"John Dale," the parson answered. "You know who I mean, of course. The only son of Joseph Dale the South African millionaire."

With the greatest difficulty Doreen prevented herself from showing a too obvious interest. She sat still and listened quietly hoping that she would hear more.

"Of course I know John Dale!" Mrs. Watson said. "A dreadful young man! I remember the last time I was coming back from Calcutta, he and several of his friends were sleeping on my deck. They used to come to bed in the early hours of the morning, singing and shouting as if there was no one on board but themselves.

"They were drunk, of course. I complained to the purser and I told him that if it ever happened again, I should write to the Head Office in London."

"Disgraceful! Disgraceful!" the parson said. "Yes, I am afraid John Dale is well known on this line. The funny thing is that they all like him. Even the Captain has a good word for him, although he has had to speak to him pretty severely before now, if I am not mistaken."

"I suppose people will always make excuses for people with money," Mrs. Watson said bitterly.

"Well, there may be something in that," the parson replied. "At the same time he is a good-natured chap. Three years ago when several stokers got injured in the fire which broke out in the hold—you remember there was a great deal of talk about it at the time. . . ."

"I was on board," Mrs. Watson said icily. "I very often travel by this line, you know."

"Oh, were you?" the parson exclaimed, quite unaware that he was giving offence. "I had forgotten. Well, anyway, John Dale got up a subscription for the fellows, contributed at least three-quarters of it himself, and arranged that they should be taken off at Marseilles to be sent the whole way back to England in an ambulance coach.

"It saved one fellow's leg, I am told. The doctor on

board wasn't capable of dealing with a really complicated case of that sort."

"I'm quite sure he wasn't," Mrs. Watson said. "I have asked him to attend to me on several occasions and I have always found him most incompetent. I have told the purser, it is disgraceful we can't have better medical attention on a ship of this size."

This, Doreen realised, was an old grievance and Mrs. Watson and the parson anecdoted about the doctor until the poor man's character was torn to shreds. Doreen realised regretfully that she was not going to hear any more about John Dale.

She had, however, at last remembered why his father's name had seemed familiar. Of course she had heard him talked about, and he had even been pointed out to her many years ago on the race-course, a self-made man who, besides being immensely rich, was undoubtedly a political power in South Africa.

Vaguely the conversation about him came back to her now, but she had no idea he had a son. A millionaire—that word sounded pleasant in her ears, but at the same time she realised she would have to be very careful not to get herself talked about with anyone so notorious.

"I needn't worry myself unduly," she thought. "It's unlikely he will find me what he calls 'congenial'."

Because John Dale was friendly and chatty his first hours on board, it didn't follow that he would wish to continue the acquaintance once he had found his feet.

Nevertheless, she wondered what he was doing. She had not seen him at dinner, but that was understandable, the saloon was very packed and it was only possible, from the position in which she sat, to inspect half the room.

She drank down her coffee and got to her feet.

"I think I will get a breath of air before I go to bed."

"It is much too cold for me," Mrs. Watson replied.

"Well, I will come back and say good night later," Doreen answered.

"There will be dancing in a few moments," the parson said. "Are you going to dance, Miss Marston?"

A shocked ejaculation from Mrs. Watson made him recall the tactlessness of his words.

"No, no, of course not," he added hastily. "I am sorry, I forgot."

Doreen smiled at his embarrassment and walking out of the lounge, found her way on to the deck.

It was a lovely night, calm and still. The sea was smooth, phosphorus shining on the waves as the ship ploughed them apart. One end of the deck, canvassed in, was bright with lights and already the ship's band was starting to tune up.

"I would like to dance," Doreen thought to herself and knew that was an impossible aspiration.

So she turned her back on temptation and walked to a quieter part of the deck. As she did so, John Dale, accompanied by two other men, came towards her.

"Well, if it isn't my little friend!" hc exclaimed heartily. "And where are you off to all by yourself?"

"I was taking the air," she answered, "before going to bed."

"To bed!" he said. "I have never heard such nonsense. You come along and dance with me. We have lots of time for a turn before these johnnies try to take my money off me. And what a hope they've got!"

"I am not dancing, thank you," Doreen said.

John Dale would have started to expostulate, but one of the men with him interrupted.

"This is Miss Marston," he said, "in case you don't know. Miss Anne Marston—you know who I mean."

"By jove, isn't that like me!" John Dale shouted. "Gave her my name and never asked for hers. Well, I am proud to meet you, Miss Marston. I have read about you and I think you are a damned plucky girl. I can't say fairer than that, can I?"

"Of course not," Doreen answered.

"Then come and have a drink to show there's no ill-feeling," he suggested.

"Thank you, but I don't drink," Doreen replied. "You know that."

"Only milk," he roared. "Yes, I know, that's all right, but still, this is after sundown, and after sundown on board ship even T.T.'s throw away their blue ribbons. Isn't that true, old boy?"

He turned to the man who had already spoken, and as he clumsily put a heavy hand on his shoulder, Doreen realised that he had had more than enough to drink.

"I am tired tonight," she said quietly. "If you will forgive me I will go below. Good night."

She was gone almost before he realised it. As she hurried down the companion way she could hear his great voice shouting after her, but she could not hear what he said.

"Damnation!" she thought in her cabin. "And I would have liked to have joined them."

But it was a risk she dared not take. So miserably, at nine o'clock when every other young person aboard was drifting on to the deck to dance under a star-strewn sky, Doreen undressed, and went to bed.

If she felt resentful overnight, the next day she blessed her good sense for at luncheon-time the whole ship was buzzing with the story of how John Dale had given a party in the bar and having invited all the most rowdy personages on board to join him, they kept the band playing all night and only staggered noisily to bed when dawn was breaking.

"It is a good thing Mr. Dale has plenty of money," the parson said sourly. "The breakages last night must have come to a considerable sum. The money could have been expended in many more profitable ways."

Doreen hid a smile. How well she knew the sort of party where the company's idea of amusement and entertainment was to drink as much as possible and then break up the premises.

The more things broken, the more money needlessly expended, only added to the joviality of the evening.

A week ago she knew she would have been amongst the very first to enjoy last night's party; and it was more than likely she would have been among the ringleaders of noise and damage.

"So this is the way they used to talk about me," she thought as she heard everyone round her discussing in tones of horror last night's festivities.

There was one red-headed girl with an impudent tip-tilted nose and a very good figure, who came in for most of the criticism. Doreen learnt that she was a divorcée and that everyone on the ship had expected she would set her cap at John Dale.

Apparently they had not been disappointed, for the party last night had been given in her honour.

"She has been looking for another rich husband for some years now," Mrs. Watson said, "and from what I have heard about both of them, it would doubtless be a very suitable match."

Doreen saw nothing of John Dale that day but next morning, when she was sitting on deck reading a book, he walked up to her unexpectedly and sat down in the next chair.

"Where have you been hiding?" he asked.

"Nowhere," Doreen replied. "I might ask you the same question."

"Oh, I have been about the place," he answered.

"So I hear," she said with a smile.

"And that hasn't been to my credit, eh?" he asked. "All right, I'll come clean! I had the hell of a hangover all yesterday. Just couldn't see out of my eyes. However, I bucked up after dinner and several of us gathered in the bar. Why didn't you come and join us? Cheer you up, you know. No use moping about the place, is it?"

"I'm not," Doreen assured him.

"Well, I suppose it is a bit difficult for you," he said. "By jove, you know, I'm not certain you don't get the best of it. If one drinks too much, one feels damned ill afterwards."

"Does one?" Doreen questioned with a faint smile.

"I'll tell the world!" John Dale replied.

Then hitching his chair nearer to Doreen, he said in a confidential voice,

"I wish you would help me, Miss Marston. I hate drinking, I do really, but it has got me, you know. You would think a man of my type ought to have too much will-power to get drunk, yet I can't help it."

"The remorseful type," Doreen thought to herself. "I have met this before."

She could hear her father speaking almost identical words, enjoying his hour of repentance, ready to make a thousand good resolutions, because in some inexplicable manner, it gave him pleasure to break them.

It was startling to discover the same weakness in this big broad-minded man with his cheery good humour and general air of strength and determination.

She looked up at John Dale and almost without thinking, took off her glasses, so that she could see him better. For the first time she noticed the weakness of his mouth and that his lips were full and too prominent.

"By jove, that's better!" John Dale ejaculated. "When you wear those dark glasses I feel I'm talking to someone in blinkers—I never know what you're thinking."

"Perhaps it is a good thing," Doreen suggested.

"Now, don't be cruel to me, Miss Marston," he pleaded. "I want you to help me, I do really. You see, I know all about you, I know what a good girl you are, a heroine and all that sort of thing, and if you would only take an interest in a chap like me, you could do me any amount of good.

"It's this drinking. I know that you will say 'give it up', but it isn't as easy as kiss your hand. What I want is someone beside me, someone who will say to me 'John, you have had enough!' someone whom I will obey. You could help me if you tried. Will you?"

Doreen saw only too clearly the proposition that was being put to her. She saw herself from John Dale's point of view, as someone new, someone faintly interesting—firstly because she was a young woman, and secondly because he had now learnt that she was a kind of celebrity.

Had she been a peroxide blonde or a vivacious little red-head, he would have included her in his parties and taken the first opportunity of asking her to go to bed with him.

As it was, the instinct to conquer made him expect that in a girl of Anne Marston's type, he would find the maternal instinct, the desire to be confidant, guide and helper.

He was to be disappointed for Doreen's reaction was

one of disgust. Here was a man who had so much—money, health, a big position, at least in the country of his birth, who was chucking it all away because just like her stupid, unambitious father, he couldn't restrain his lust for drink.

She sat looking at John Dale, seeing him wasting, destroying, and deliberately besmirching a golden future.

He took her silence for encouragement.

"You see, I have never had a chance of knowing girls like you," he said. "My mother died when I was a child. My father is a fine old josser, but he's tough and so are most of his friends.

"I was brought up to grab what I wanted regardless of consequences. You will say I have been spoilt, perhaps I have—I admit that I generally give way to temptation, but at times I have tried to resist the old Satan in me and if you say the word, I'll try again.

"Give me a helping hand and I'll face the world and that extra drink with the courage of a lion and the abstinence of a monk. We are going to be pals, you and I. I knew that from the moment I spoke to you, standing against the rail over there.

"A girl like you could make a different man of me. You couldn't refuse a penitent sinner, could you? Tell me that you will help me—here and now."

Doreen took her feet off the rest in front of her chair and putting them firmly on the deck, stood up.

"Do you want to know what I really think about you, John Dale?" she said firmly.

He looked a little surprised at the tone of voice. Then he answered:

"Sure, shoot!"

"I think you are a fool," she said very distinctly, and walked away, leaving behind her a very surprised young man.

TEN

Doreen walked away from John Dale feeling angry and resentful.

She thought of his money, of his opportunities, of the kind of brute strength of which it was impossible not be be conscious when one was near him, and she felt as though his inner weakness made him into something unnatural, unclean.

She did not realise that deeper than her anger was a very personal reaction.

She had been envious of John Dale ever since she heard about the parties he gave on board—parties which she, but a week ago, would have been able to attend.

All her resentment at her personal appearance, at the clothes she was forced to wear, at the demure manner she must assume, surged to the surface in a sudden hatred against the man who, quite unconsciously, had called it into being.

She was overpowered by her feelings.

She could, at that moment, have hit him in the face, screamed abuse at him, and told him that he was unworthy in every way of the name he bore. But when she was alone, she felt these emotions ebbing away from her like a tide, and a sense of apprehension take their place.

It had been unwise of her to say what she had—it might indeed prove the false step that she had been so frightened of making.

What would John Dale think? It was neither the attitude nor the language he would expect from someone like Anne Marston.

Doreen pulled off her dark glasses and with an effort, prevented herself from flinging them on the floor and stamping on them. They were symbolic of her bondage to hypocrisy!

How mad she had been to think for one moment that she could go through with this ridiculous masquerade, which was foreign to everything in her nature.

She wanted to pull off her clothes, to get drunk, to paint her face and to run riot among the passengers, shocking and horrifying them in any way she could. She wanted to live, to be alive, to be a complete contrast to what, for the last thirty-six hours, she had been pretending to be.

She strode up and down the confined space of her cabin as though she were a wild animal behind bars. She started to laugh, then to cry, and only some small critical part of her mind, watching her with a deep cynicism, prevented her from having hysterics.

Then finally, when she had exhausted herself, she lay down on her bunk and closed her eyes.

She slept peacefully and unexpectedly. Running the gambit of so many emotions had been far more exhausting than she knew, taking toll of her weary body.

How long she slept for she had no idea, but when she awoke it was to the knowledge that in some extraordinary manner, she had found peace.

She lay in a drowsy contentment, experiencing a joy not of this world, but something which through divine mercy had pierced for a brief while the earthly barriers of the flesh.

A knock at the door startled her.

"Come in," she said.

It was nothing more alarming than her stewardess with a note.

"I have been asked to give you this, Miss Marston," she said and added, "having a rest? That's right. You will find the sea voyage does you a world of good."

"I hope so," Doreen replied.

"It will!" the stewardess assured her. "I have seen people come aboard on stretchers at Port Said and by the time we are at Gibraltar, they are running round the deck as lively as crickets. The sea is as good a doctor as any you will find in Harley Street. You can take my word for that."

"I will," Doreen answered with a smile.

She opened the note. As she had expected it was from John Dale.

"Dear Anne Marston. Don't be angry with me and hide yourself away. I have been looking for you for hours. You know I want to be your friend: won't you dine with me tonight in my state-room. If you will, I will give you my solemn promise that you wouldn't be ashamed of me. Yours penitently, John."

Doreen almost laughed. It was a schoolboy's attempt at reconciliation. At any rate he had not been shocked at what she had said.

Indeed she supposed from this invitation, that her attitude in some extraordinary way had stimulated his desire for her company.

Critically she began to think about him, striving to see him impersonally. Why, she wondered, should he bother about her—missionaries were hardly John Dale's line of country.

She decided that it must be because "she was different". How often she had heard that phrase used!

It carried her back to the days when she was very young, when she first went about with men. So many of them had said,

"You are different, Doreen, quite different to what I expected."

What they had meant was that she had an innocence and a freshness which had prevented them from expressing too freely their desires, or from seeking too ardently the intimacies they had hoped for.

"Has that old innocence returned to me?" Doreen asked now.

She thought bitterly of those who presumed to judge—men and women denouncing each other, passing sentence without mercy on their fellow creatures, always ready to convict the young and happy from sadism linked with jealousy.

It seemed to her that jealousy was only a deep-rooted envy of another person's capacity for pleasure.

That was what everyone was seeking, pleasure—their own particular, selfish pleasure. Even the missionaries, with their talk of a call from God, found in their dedication to a life of sacrifice and suffering, a pleasure peculiar to their temperaments and characters.

What was the difference, Doreen asked defiantly, between them and someone like herself, who demanded the love of a husband and the security of a home?

Those things would have given her pleasure, yet because she had failed to attain them, she must suffer both condemnation and contempt.

For the Anne Marstons of this world with their pinched lips, their ungenerous outlook on life, their fear of over-balancing from the perilous path of respectability, there was every possible reward that civilisation could offer insecurity.

For the Doreen Wallises the continual envy, hatred and malice of her own sex, the suspicious resentment of the older generation.

And the knowledge that should her foot slip on the precarious path she had chosen, a thousand hands would push her down, down into the quagmire of disgrace.

A week ago she and John Dale would have understood each other only too well. She would have encouraged him in his purpose, have taken what gifts he had offered her, and have done her best to marry him.

She would not have succeeded; of that Doreen was quite sure. He could meet thousands of girls of her type between London and Johannesburg, thousands only too willing to offer themselves and their easy virtue in return for a share of Joseph Dale's millions.

Many of them would undoubtedly find John genuinely lovable and in all probability never notice his now small weakness, but take it as a matter of course, while to them he would certainly not confess his frailty, or ask for their help.

Such women to John Dale meant amusement, and excitement and were an essential part of "good living".

But as a sex they would remain distinctly inferior—a decoration to life but never a fundamental necessity.

From an exceptional woman he might ask for inspiration, his respect for her emanating not from experience but from the idealism of mother-love which lingers in every man's heart, often buried but never entirely extinguished.

Doreen lying on her bunk with John Dale's letter in her hand, thought how in becoming Anne Marston she had stepped on to a pedestal.

Already she felt a little dizzy at her position, a precarious one from which she must be careful not to fall. Surely this letter was a warning?

In playing the part of Anne she had not run true to form; she had taken an individual line. The real Anne would have commiserated with John Dale; would have offered to help him; would have prayed for him.

Doreen had done none of these things. Letting her own feelings take the upper hand, she had said the first words that came to her mind. It had been dangerous, a risk she must have been crazy to incur.

But there was a light in the darkness of self-recrimination—her outspokenness had intrigued John Dale, that was why he wanted to know more.

Doreen re-acted that moment on deck.

She pictured the disdainful expression on her face, heard the contempt in her voice, and she knew that in walking away from John, leaving her sentiments of condemnation quivering in the air between them, she had seemed to him both attractive and desirable.

She must be careful: it would obviously be unwise for her to dine with him, much as she would like to. But she must answer this letter and the question was, dared she offer him any encouragement, however slight?

In spite of a warning voice telling her to go no farther, she was not prepared to ignore John Dale for the rest of the voyage. So much depended on her not losing her head under any circumstances. Yet supposing she allowed herself to become really friendly with him, was there any chance of his marrying her?

That, of course, would be the perfect solution to all

her troubles, but she was sensible enough to know that this was definitely an improbability.

John Dale was at least thirty-seven or thirty-eight; it was unlikely that he would be caught up in a board-ship romance.

Underneath that big open-handed play-boy attitude, there must be much of the tough, hard, astuteness of his father.

More than likely he was a snob at heart. She had seldom met the son of a self-made man who did not suffer from some kind of inferiority complex, and John's few words about working in a mine, confirmed her suspicion.

He had wished to assert himself, to prove himself not only the son of his father, but also a man.

The daughter of an obsure missionary, however much she might be in the public eye at the moment, was hardly a good match for the John Dale who would, in the years to come, step into his father's shoes.

No, marriage was an unlikely contingent.

What was far more probable was that she would get herself talked about, ruin the reputation with which she had come on board, and shatter the overtures of friendship already being made to her by respectable people.

No, she decided to herself, the risk was too great.

She wondered how Anne would have behaved at this moment. It seemed funny to think that she might have been lying here, on this very bunk.

"What would have been her thoughts?" Doreen wondered. "Did she ever think of men, save as souls to be brought nearer to that all powerful and jealous God, to whom she had devoted so many years of her life?"

Yet, Doreen questioned, had she really devoted herself? Had it not been just force of circumstances which had given her work in the Mission Settlement and which had caused her to behave with a heroism which had brought her the applause of the English-speaking world?

Surely it was environment more than anything else which counted, and the difference in her environment and Anne Marston's, might be responsible for everything which had made them as they were.

Such ideas were interesting but, Doreen told herself, they got her no further in answering John's letter. She changed her dress and smoothing her hair, went up to the writing-room. She sat for a long time, the pen in her hand.

Finally, after several attempts had found their way into the waste-paper basket, she wrote:

"Dear Mr. Dale. Thank you for your note. I am afraid that I cannot dine with you. I shall, however, hope to see you sometime on deck during the course of the evening. Yours sincerely, Anne Marston."

"Now, will he be snubbed or encouraged by that?" she questioned with a faint smile as she slipped it into an envelope.

After tea she had hardly been sitting for five minutes in her usual place on the windward side of the ship before John Dale was by her side.

"I thought I should find you here," he said. "Why won't you dine with me?"

Doreen put down the book she had been pretending to read.

"You must see that it is impossible," she said gently. "I am in deep mourning and, anyway, my absence at the Chief's table would cause a great deal of comment."

"Are you frightened of what people say?" he asked.

"I am not anxious for them to be unkind about me," Doreen replied.

"But I want to talk to you," he said insistently.

Doreen looked round. The deck was deserted. At this time of day most people were at the bridge tables, or listening to a concert in the lounge.

"Why not now?" she asked.

"I don't feel very brave at the moment," he answered with a grin. "You put the wind up me, you know!"

Doreen made no comment.

"I'm not laughing at you," he added quickly. "You

were absolutely right to say what you did and I think your words battered a bit of sense into my thick head for once. After you had gone I sat thinking 'if this is the way a really nice girl looks on you, John Dale, you had better do something about it.' "

"And so you are going to reform?" Doreen asked.

Despite every effort, she could not keep the sarcasm out of her voice. John Dale did not seem to hear it.

"I am," he said eagerly. "I am going to swear to you I will never . . ."

"But why to me?" Doreen asked.

"Why?" he echoed, "because I have got an enormous respect for you, Miss Marston. I think what you have done is fine, I do, really. You have got courage, and you don't boast about your achievements. There's pretty few men or women like that."

"Thank you," Doreen said. "But still, don't make your promises to me, make them to yourself."

"No," he answered. "I'm no guardian angel! I want to promise you. I swear that I will keep myself within bounds. I am not going to go on the water wagon—that would be rather ridiculous, wouldn't it—but I know when I have had enough and that's where I am going to stop. I promise, here and now, to be sober for the rest of the voyage."

In spite of her doubts, in spite of the knowledge that she had heard this often before, Doreen was impressed. For the moment, at any rate, John Dale was undoubtedly sincere.

"That's a promise then," she said quietly. "Given and witnessed."

"Give me your hand," John Dale commanded.

She did as she was told, and taking it in both of his, he said again:

"I swear it," then raised her fingers to his lips.

"He is going to be difficult," Doreen thought to herself.

Again she wondered whether this big seemingly childlike man was really so ingenuous as he seemed.

"Now," he said, releasing her hand, "we are friends, aren't we?"

"But of course," she replied. "As much as is possible between two people whose lives are so utterly different as yours and mine."

"They may be," he answered, "but I have a strong feeling that we have something in common. I can't explain what—perhaps you aren't as prim as you look, maybe I'm not as bad as they say."

"Do I look prim?" Doreen asked curiously.

"Well . . . it's those glasses of yours," he said apologetically, "and of course black clothes and not much lipstick make you different . . ." he faltered.

"To most of your girl friends!" Doreen added for him.

"Well, that's true enough," he admitted. "But do you know what I call you to myself?"

"No, what?" Doreen asked curiously.

"My little madonna," he said. "That is what you look like—one of those pictures in Italian art galleries. Heaven knows they have bored me enough when I have had to look at them yet, the other evening I had been thinking about you and wondering of what you reminded me, I suddenly remembered—'one of those madonnas', I said to myself."

"Don't," Doreen said in a stifled voice. "Please don't."

She got up from her chair, letting her book fall to the ground. She walked across the deck and stood staring out to sea. A moment later John was beside her.

"What is it?" he asked. "What have I said? Have I offended you?"

She couldn't answer him, couldn't possibly explain that she felt choked, suffocated and disgusted by her own hypocrisy.

ELEVEN

"I am supposed to be getting off at Marseilles tomorrow," John Dale said to Doreen. "But if you say the word, I will stay on the ship and come round by sea with you."

He had sought her out once again and was sitting by her side on deck.

More than one of the other passengers knitting or reading had watched his approach with curiosity, and Doreen was well aware that both she and John Dale had become the subject of much idle chatter.

"How can I help it?" she asked herself, but not with any great anxiety.

By cleverly confiding in Mrs. Waverton Watson, she knew that she had killed to a great extent any really unkind speculations.

She had drawn on her imagination a little where this good lady was concerned.

"I must admit," she had said to her, "that I had never heard of John Dale before you mentioned him in conversation the very first evening I had coffee with you. Naturally your words carried great weight with me and I was on my guard.

"At the same time I felt it would be wrong, and definitely against all the teaching in which I have been brought up, if I refused help where it was most needed."

"Help?" Mrs. Watson echoed curiously.

"I am afraid Mr. Dale is not happy," Doreen had answered in a discreet voice, as though she could say much more but would not betray a confidence.

"Some woman, I suppose, as usual," Mrs. Watson snorted. "Well, my dear, I don't wish to quench your ardour, but I assure you that is nothing original where young Mr. Dale is concerned. His love affairs are a byword in South Africa. Whenever he joins a ship he invariably leaves an episode behind him."

"I am sorry to hear that," Doreen said. "But if I can do nothing else, I can offer the best of my advice and pray for him."

She could not help a little smile of triumph at the success of her words. Mrs. Watson was undoubtedly impressed, and word went round the lounge that "that nice young Miss Marston" was doing her best to curb the wildness of John Dale.

It was not easy for Doreen, however, to keep up her pose of aloof adviser. John insisted on being at her side every available moment and it was almost impossible, aboard ship, to escape from anyone so persistent. It was almost ridiculous how impressed he was by her, and he was not unperceptive.

"You're human all right, under the marble veneer," he said. "I expect it is the way you have been brought up. If I could show you life as I know it, I wouldn't mind betting a thousand pounds to a penny you would enjoy yourself all right."

"I should feel like a fish out of water," Doreen assured him.

"I wonder," he said looking at her speculatively. "There's a glint in your eyes, sometimes, and something in your smile, which tells me you aren't half so prudish as you try to make me believe."

"I wasn't trying to make you believe anything of the sort," Doreen answered sharply. "You have made up your mind that I can reform you and there's nothing really very much for me to do, except to agree with all the good things you say and to frown disapproval on all the bad!"

"I believe you could be a marvellous inspiration to a man if you . . . tried," John said.

He hesitated before the last word and Doreen knew that he had been about to say "if you loved him", then changed his mind.

What was all this leading up to, she asked herself?

Could she love John Dale, and was she capable to making him love her enough to offer her marriage?

She had failed in the past to get what she wanted, but in this new guise and with this new aura round her, she felt that no man would ever dare to offer anything less binding.

Should she risk it? She asked herself that question again. She hesitated, then something in his eager weak mouth, in his eyes ringed around by lines of tired debauchery, made her feel disgusted, almost nauseated by him. It was so unpleasantly familiar.

She had met this type, without perhaps so much wealth or so much position, but with the same instincts, the same animal desires, not once but a thousand times!

Could she voluntarily, the first moment of her escape, go back—to drunkenness, to repentance and to an endless repetition of both? She knew her answer.

"No," she said clearly, "Of course you mustn't alter your plans and anyway, you would find the voyage very dull, because I feel sure all your friends are getting off tomorrow."

"Except you," he said.

"If you still want to see me again, once you have got back to England," Doreen suggested, "I will tell you where to find me. But honestly, it would be a great mistake for you to change your mind now at the last minute."

"Why would it be a great mistake?" he asked obstinately.

"For lots of reasons," she answered, "some which concern yourself and some which concern me."

"You are a funny girl, aren't you?" he said. "You have got me beaten. I must admit I don't know how to treat you."

"I shouldn't try," Doreen said. "I am not the right sort for you and you know it."

"Look here, Anne," he said irritably, "don't be so damned difficult. I want to be with you, honestly I do, and I can't see any reason why you shouldn't let me."

"I have told you that I will see you when we get back to England, if you haven't changed your mind," Doreen answered, "but I don't mind betting you will have forgotten all about me in a week."

"Very well, we'll see," he said. "Will you give me your address?"

He took out his notebook and wrote down what she told him.

"And the telephone number?" he asked.

"I haven't the slightest idea," Doreen said with a laugh. "But I should think my relations will be horrified if I am rung up on a long distance call by a young man! You will have to write or send me a picture postcard."

"I shall come down and see you," John Dale promised.

"Not without warning me, I hope?" Doreen said quickly.

"Are you ashamed of me or afraid of your relations?" he asked merrily.

"A little of both," she confessed. "You see, I haven't been home for a great many years and I am not quite certain what it will be like."

He nodded.

"I understand. You couldn't get up to London, I suppose? Make some excuse or other. I could get one of my friends to put you up. We would have a really good time—cabarets, night clubs and bottle parties, it would do you good."

Just for a moment Doreen was tempted. The life she knew so well, but in London—London which was the mecca of all pleasure-seekers at the moment.

How often she had heard people in Cairo complain that even the latest or gayest cabaret was not a patch on what was to be found just off Piccadilly.

Here was her chance; it was all too easy. John would pay for her, provide her with everything. He was not ungenerous, she knew that, and he was a very rich man. She thought of the clothes she could have, the things they would see, people they would meet, and the parties they would give. Just for a moment she wavered.

Then she remembered there was always the aftermath and she knew how quickly it came and how relentlessly it demanded the price of what had gone before.

She shook her head decisively.

"No," she said, "I think it is not only unlikely, but very impracticable."

"I will persuade you yet," he promised.

"You can always go on trying," she replied.

She looked at her watch; it was nearly one o'clock.

"I must go and get ready for lunch."

"I shall look for you here this afternoon."

He kept his promise and they had tea together. Later, when it came to dressing time, and the sun had already sunk in a blaze of glory over the sea, and the soft twilight was creeping heavenwards, veiling the coast of France, he asked:

"Meet me on deck after dinner tonight?"

"I have promised Mrs. Watson to have coffee with her."

"It is my last evening," he pleaded. "Come out afterwards for a little while."

Every night he had given her an invitation of the same sort, but somehow this was different.

"I will come for a moment," Doreen promised against her better judgment.

"I am being a fool and I am playing with fire," she told herself in her own cabin. Yet a spirit of adventure forced her to her feet as soon as Mrs. Watson had settled down at the bridge table and the coffee cups had been cleared away in the lounge.

"Where are you going, child?" Mrs. Watson asked.

"I thought I would go on deck for a moment," Doreen replied.

"It is getting chilly," Mrs. Watson said. "You are not in the East now. Take my wrap and put it round your shoulders."

"How nice of you! Are you quite sure you don't mind? I shan't be long."

"No, of course, take it," Mrs. Watson replied to her, then to the bridge table, "Is it my call? Two spades."

Feeling that she was no longer of interest, Doreen took the long white ermine stole from off the back of the chair.

It gave her a feeling of opulence and, somehow too,

of reckless excitement, as she stepped out on the deck. She removed her dark glasses and crossing the stole low over her breast, hugged the ends around her body.

It was certainly not in a mood becoming to a missionary's daughter that she went down to the dark end of the deck to meet John Dale. He was waiting for her. Long before she drew near to him she recognised the silhouette of his broad shoulders, saw the red glow of his cigar.

She came quietly up to him without speaking.

He stared at her for some moments.

"You look different," he said at length. "What is it?"

"My borrowed plumes, I expect," she replied, smoothing sensuously with one hand the soft fur.

"Where did you get it?" he asked.

"My good friend Mrs. Watson," Doreen replied, and she could not help the faint mocking note in her voice.

"I don't know how you can be bothered with that old tittle-tattle," John growled. "She is a menace on every ship that I have ever travelled on. I can't avoid her. I believe she does it on purpose to spite me."

Doreen laughed.

"Perhaps she is enamoured with your *beaux yeux*," she said.

He stared at her again, then put out his arm and slipped it through hers.

"You are different tonight."

"Must I always be the same?" she asked.

She knew she was being mad, crazy, that she was letting her real self come to the surface. It was penetrating through the mask that she wore. At the moment John was astonished; if she went on, he would be bewildered, then perhaps curious.

Yet there was a spirit of revolt within her—a spirit which drove her on in spite of her better judgment or instinct.

"I don't care what you are like," he answered, "as long as you are nice to me."

"And why shouldn't I be nice to you?" Doreen asked. "After all, you are a very eligible young man, Mr. John Dale, very eligible and, as far as I can see, very charming, especially to solitary young women travelling alone on the high seas."

She felt his hand tighten on her arm. There was something in the warmth of it, in the possessiveness of its clasp, which was a little intoxicating, which thrilled her.

"Anne, you are different tonight," John said again. "Different and rather marvellous."

"Perhaps you are very easily satisfied," Doreen said lightly.

She turned her head aside, knowing that the action was not unattractive, her neck framed by the soft whiteness of her furs.

"Which are you, Anne, saint or devil, because I am damned if I know?"

She turned her head to look at him, a half smile on her lips. They were parted and she stared up into his eyes. In that moment she knew again that old familiar breathless moment, which came invariably before she was kissed for the first time by someone new.

There was a vibration, an electricity between them. Doreen felt it running hotly through her veins. She knew that she was trembling and that John's hand on her bare arm had tightened until the pain of it was almost intolerable.

She gave a little gasp and swayed towards him.

A voice broke in upon them, a voice speaking quickly and anxiously.

"Oh, here you are, Miss Marston. I have been looking for you everywhere."

Just for a moment neither John nor Doreen moved. It seemed as though they could not, as though the world into which they had stepped together, would be immune against interruption.

Then hurriedly, with almost a convulsive gesture, Doreen freed herself from his hand and turned.

The parson from Rangoon was standing beside her.

"Is something wrong?" she asked and to her own ears her voice sounded strange and a little hoarse.

"I thought you might be able to help us," he said. "There's a native below in the steerage. He is desperately ill, in fact I think he is dying. But no one can understand what he says. I thought, perhaps, there was just a chance—with your knowledge of the different tribes—you might be able to talk with him. Poor fellow, he's in pain and he seems to be trying to tell us something."

Doreen stared at the parson as though she had been turned to stone.

"Will you come at once?" he repeated gently.

"Of course."

She heard her own words without realising she had uttered them. Then the whole situation seemed to clarify itself, so that with almost a sense of amusement she saw what had happened. She had been saved from John only to walk into another trap, a trap far more dangerous to her at this moment.

There was nothing to be done, she realised that. She turned to John Dale and slipping the ermine wrap from her shoulders, put it into his hands.

"Would you be kind enough," she asked, "to take this back to Mrs Watson, thank her and say I shall not require it again this evening?"

He did not know it, but at that moment John Dale held in his arms the superficiality of Doreen Wallis. Doreen discarded her old frivolous self and became Anne Marston.

Without another word or a backward look, she followed the parson down the deck. Her heart was beating suffocatingly. She put on her glasses again, she clenched her hands together as though in an effort to force a calm control upon herself.

"What can I do?" she wondered. "They will know, they will discover now that I am an impostor."

"Do you know anything about this man at all?" she asked. She tried to speak with concern, but her voice sounded brittle and shaken.

"Nothing," he replied. "Apparently he came on board at Port Said and he's supposed to be getting off tomorrow at Marseilles. The doctor tells me that he has obviously suffered many privations and sicknesses. He speaks a few words of French, but all day long he has been chattering away in some absolutely unknown dialect. He's a revolting looking creature too, but that won't worry you, will it?"

"No, of course not," Doreen said.

"He has been moved into a quarantine cabin."

As they went through the steerage, they heard bursts of laughter and the thin wailing cry of a baby mingled strangely with the twang of guitar strings which were being plucked by a pretty Eurasian girl sitting cross-legged at the foot of the companion way.

"Here we are," the parson said.

He knocked on the cabin door and it was opened by the ship's doctor.

"It is very kind of you to come, Miss Marston," he said, "but I doubt if you can do much good. The poor fellow seems to be sinking."

Doreen walked towards the bunk on which was the emaciated body of a native. There was a strong smell of dark flesh, almost overpowering in the small cabin.

The man was murmuring beneath his breath in a delirious manner. It was impossible to make any sense out of his words, most of which were completely incoherent. Doreen stood looking down at him.

What was she to do? What was she to say? She felt as though she were a prisoner in the dock. At any moment she might hear the cry of "guilty" and know that she stood convicted.

Two men were watching her, for the moment with confidence and without suspicion. She knew they were waiting and she turned to them, glad that her glasses hid what she felt must be the terror in her eyes.

"I can't recognise his words as belonging to any particular tribe," she said in a quavering voice.

"That is exactly what I remarked," the doctor agreed. "And he hasn't any tribe marks, except a cut on his left ear which might have been merely accidental."

The man on the bunk opened his eyes and spoke in a slightly louder, but no less rambling, tone.

"Speak to him, Miss Marston," the parson urged.

This was the crisis. Doreen stood staring at the native.

There was nothing she could do, she could only refuse and let them think what they liked. Then, as the seconds ticked away and she knew that both the doctor and parson were waiting, the native suddenly gave a convulsive cry.

It was almost like the scream of an animal. It echoed through the cabin and Doreen instinctively started away from him.

"It's no use. I am afraid I shall have to give him some more morphia. He won't understand you, Miss Marston, whatever you say to him."

For a moment Doreen could hardly believe that she had heard aright.

Then in her utter relief she felt a queer weakness grip her knees, so that it was with difficulty that she prevented herself from falling on to the floor.

"I am sorry," she said, in a voice broken with emotion.

The parson put out his hand and touched hers.

"You mustn't be too upset," he said. "It was tactless of me, perhaps, to ask you to come here after all you have been through these past weeks, but there was just a chance that you might help the poor fellow. I didn't want to miss it. Is there anything else we can do, Doctor?"

"Nothing," the doctor replied shortly. He had already given the man a hypodermic and was watching him.

"Then I will take Miss Marston away."

"Of course," the doctor answered, "and thank you for coming Miss Marston. If he's well enough to see you tomorrow I will let you know, but I think it is unlikely he will live through the night."

"I would like to hear in the morning," Doreen answered.

She felt as though she had aged considerably as she climbed from the steerage up to the second deck. Here she stopped and said good night.

"Are you going to bed?" the parson asked.

She nodded.

"I am tired," she confessed.

"Of course you are," he answered, "and I am sorry I have troubled you this evening, but you understand, don't you?"

"Of course," she replied.

She went along to her own cabin. On opening the door she saw there was a note lying on the floor. She picked it up and saw it was from John Dale. She opened it. There were only two lines.

"I am waiting for you on deck. I must see you again

John."

She looked at it for a moment. Then she tore it into several pieces and let them fall from her nerveless fingers. While they scattered on the floor, with a sudden rush of energy she slammed her cabin door and bolted it.

She pressed the bolt home firmly, putting all her strength against it, as though she worked in fear and in a kind of horror.

Then she leant back against the door itself, breathing with a quiet gasp of relief. She was safe.

By some miracle she had been rescued twice within the last hour.

TWELVE

Doreen had not expected anyone to meet her at Southampton. She had sent her grandmother a wire to tell her the approximate time at which the boat would dock, but otherwise she had felt it better to communicate as little as possible with her relations.

She had found amongst Anne's things a telegram from Mrs. Wickham, sent apparently soon after the story of Anne's bravery had appeared in the newspapers, and when she was still in hospital at Kartoum.

Piecing the story together, Doreen could only suppose that someone, perhaps the doctor in charge, had wired Anne's grandmother—as her next of kin—suggesting that it would be best for the girl to return to England as soon as she was well enough to travel.

The reply had been an invitation to come to Brookavon as soon as possible.

There had been no letters, although they could have reached her by air mail at either Port Said or Marseilles.

This deficiency did not surprise Doreen in any way, for she knew what bad correspondents all her mother's family were. Mary Wallis wrote home about once a year and Mrs. Wickham's letters were confined to a few lines at Christmas and on her daughter's birthday.

Very occasionally they would hear from Edith Wickham, but more often than not, she confined herself to a card of greeting on festive occasions.

During the last few days before the ship reached Southampton, Doreen had suffered agonies wondering if she would recognise her relations again, yet her very first sight of Edith Wickham walking through the crowds lining the landing-stage, recalled her vividly and unmistakably to Doreen's memory.

Aunt Edith had not altered in nineteen years, in fact she hardly seemed a day older than she had been when Doreen as a child, lonely and frightened, had landed at this very port.

Tall, thin, and wearing the same type of ill-fitting tweed suit as hundreds of other English country women do, Edith Wickham was, in her own way, outstanding.

She had once been a very pretty girl, pretty in the manner so admired by the Edwardians—which was statuesque, with sharp, almost classically perfect features, and the corn-coloured hair which must inevitably accompany pale and somewhat vacant blue eyes.

At eighteen Edith Wickham had been a beauty; she still had a faded, somewhat wistful echo of those good looks. She had not moved with the times.

She still did her hair in the same way as when she had "come out", wearing a rather frizzy fringe along the top of her high forehead and to keep her head tidy, a so-called "invisible net", kept in place by dozens of small hair pins which dropped around her like bronze rain whenever she became animated or unusually busy.

She had conceded one point to fashion: that was the discardence of the high-boned collars that she had worn with such elegance before the war.

Yet, because she could not tolerate a naked neck, she had assumed in their place a narrow band of black velvet tied in a neat bow behind.

She was never seen without this decoration; she wore it both in the day time with her tweeds and her knitted suits, and at night with the black velvet and lace tea gowns in which she presided at dinner.

As the unmarried member of the family it was, of course, her duty to look after her mother, and neither world wars, crises, nor the emancipation of women, had made any difference in Edith Wickham's life.

She had stayed on at the Manor, seldom leaving her mother even for a week-end.

In the village she made herself useful and, as was to be expected of her, she ran the Girl Guides, was a leading spirit at the Village Institute, and taught assiduously, if not with much originality, in the Sunday School.

In fact Edith Wickham was the backbone of all parochial entertaining in Brookavon, and while she expended so much of her energy and gave her wholehearted interest to everything that concerned the villagers, it was typical that they should speak of her always as "that poor Miss Wickham".

A sympathy which she would have failed to undersand had she known of it.

She was neither intelligent, talented, nor even particularly interesting. She had been a nice, clean, wholesome English girl, who would have made an excellent wife for a man of her own class who was not too imaginative.

The tragedy of Edith's life was that no man had ever asked her to marry him.

Once, very shortly after she came out, the son of a neighbouring landowner had taken a short-lived interest in her.

He had ridden over to the Manor on several occasions to pay his respects and had sat solemnly in the drawing-room while Mrs. Wickham made conversation and Edith, flustered and blushing, poured out the tea.

Then he had discovered—it was not difficult—that Edith had no money and was not likely to have any, with three brothers and twin sisters all having a rightful claim to a share of George Wickham's income.

He had been deceived by their mode of living, as many other better people than himself had been in the past, for Edith's father enjoyed living up to the hilt of his none too large income, and kept up a state at the Manor House, for which the family paid heavily after his accident in the hunting field.

Only then was it discovered and understood by his wife and children that a few thousands a year do not run to horses and carriages, to well-bred jumps, or the hundreds spent on the fashionable Continental resorts.

Mrs. Wickham never reproached his memory.

"I enjoyed it while it lasted," she said once.

She was quite unconscious that her family with difficulty refrained from saying that she, at least, had enjoyed the spending of their inheritance, while they were faced with nothing but the debts.

It was, of course, inevitable that the girls should suffer the most when the crash came.

The two eldest boys were at a university, and by scraping together every available penny, they were able to stay on and take their degrees.

The twins, Mary and Martha, were forced to make their début in the most meagre fashion, finding neither clothes nor parties provided for them, and having to make the best of tennis parties to which they could bicycle, or the local hunt balls to which, by hook or by crook, they could get a lift from some neighbour.

Edith, who was older, was pushed severely into the background, given an almost ridiculously small sum on which to dress, and told that the house-keeping was in her hands and that she must economise.

Conscientiously she did her best, while weeping many bitter tears at the beginning of each month when the accounts had to be paid, and any deficiency on the wrong side of the bank balance, was attributed to her fault.

Yet she was not soured or embittered in the slightest by what had happened in the past.

In her fifties she was the same good-natured, rather stupid girl, who had stepped so happily from the schoolroom to the drawing-room, believing with an unquenchable hope that a life of adventure lay before her.

Her very simplicity had brought her a certain happiness as the dreary, uneventful years passed by. Any occurrence out of the ordinary was of importance to Edith, anything unexpected, however small or insignificant, was a breath-taking event.

Now, looking for her niece on the quay at Southampton, her face was flushed with excitement as she watched the passengers from the ship disembark, one by one, down the steep gangway.

Almost simultaneously with Doreen's recognition of her aunt, the steward to whom Edith Wickham had been speaking, pointed her out.

"Here is Miss Marston," she heard the man say and Aunt Edith swooped forward with a shrill cry of pleasure.

"Anne! Welcome home," she exclaimed. "How thrilling it is to see you."

She kissed her and Doreen, with a sigh of relief, felt that a critical moment was past.

"How nice of you to come and meet me," she said.

"But of course! Didn't you expect me? You know I always come."

"Yes, yes," Doreen said hastily, feeling she had made a slip, "but at the same time I wasn't sure. You know how it is, one feels so forgotten after being away from England for years."

"You could never be forgotten. But since last time you have been through so much," Edith Wickham said in a low voice. "My dear, if you only knew how sorry we all are for you and, at the same time, so proud."

"Excuse me," a voice interrupted. "It is Miss Marston, isn't it? May I have a photograph?"

Doreen turned and saw a press photographer, his camera in his hand.

"Oh, I don't know," she murmured, glancing at her aunt.

"But of course you must let him take you," Edith Wickham said in a voice of flustered gratification. "And I hope it is better than some of the ones that have already appeared."

Doreen allowed herself to be led aside from the crowd moving towards the train and posed against a pile of luggage. When the photographer had finished, he asked her a few pertinent questions.

"Do you intend going back to Africa, Miss Marston?"

"It is impossible for me to decide that at the moment," Doreen answered. "I feel, at present, that I couldn't bear to look on the destruction of all that my parents have worked for. However, in the future, I may change my mind."

"And your immediate plans?" he asked.

"Are to stay with my grandmother at Brookavon," Doreen replied.

"Where we can get into touch with you should the occasion arise?" the reporter suggested. "Thank you very much, Miss Marston. I will send you a copy of the photograph."

"Thank you."

Doreen turned away and followed her aunt towards the small car in which she had come to meet her. Somehow or other her luggage was piled into it, although there was not much room.

Then they were off, driving out of Southampton —going home.

It took them nearly two hours and most of the way Edith Wickham talked vivaciously, much to the relief of Doreen, who was not only thankful that she herself had not got to make conversation, but was able, through her aunt's chatter, to recall to her mind many things which would be useful.

"Who shall I find at the Manor?" she asked, determined if she could not to be at a loss.

"There's only ourselves," her aunt replied. "Mother and I, and, of course, Richard."

"Richard?" Doreen queried.

"Yes, he's home for good now. He has given up any hope of getting results from those treatments in London. He will always be a cripple to a certain extent, I am afraid, and really we haven't got the money to go on paying doctor after doctor, to find that everything they suggest is a hopeless failure, after the first few weeks."

Richard? Doreen sat wondering how she could ask further questions. Now who was he? Had he been there nineteen years ago? If he had, she could not remember him.

There was an uncle whom she could not recall; it might be him, or it might be some other relative.

Luckily Edith Wickham enlightened her in the next sentence.

"It seems awful," she said in a hushed voice, "to think that Richard and I are the only members of the family left."

"Is he your eldest brother?" Doreen asked, drawing a bow at a venture. "I suppose I ought to remember, but I have forgotten."

"No, no, of course not," Edith said. "He's the youngest. I was the eldest of the family. Then Martha and Mary who, I believe, were a terrible disappointment to my father who wanted a boy. He needn't have worried because soon after they were born came Alfred and a year later, Matthew. They were both killed in the war.

"Then nearly five years after Matthew, when Mother really thought she had finished her family for good and all, Richard arrived—the baby of us all and that, I suppose, is why she is so fond of him. I don't think she has ever made any secret of the fact that he is her favourite."

"Why is he an invalid?" Doreen asked.

"He was always delicate, even as a boy," Edith said. "He had one leg shorter than the other, as well as curvature of the spine. He was always going to doctors.

"Then he got better and when war broke out, insisted

on joining up. He never got to France—after two months on Salisbury Plain he came back home crippled with arthritis.

"He had rheumatic fever, too, several years later and it has left him so weak and helpless that now he often spends half the day in bed. We have made the old schoolroom into his room—you remember how it opened out into the garden—so that he can go in and out of the house in his wheel chair without help."

"Now where was the schoolroom?" Doreen thought to herself. "I hope I shall remember the rest of the house when I get there. After only eight years away they won't expect me to lose my way, yet I can remember so little—only big rooms, too full of furniture, and a conservatory where there used to be a parrot. I wonder if it is still there?"

Her first impression of the Manor as they drove up the broad gravel sweep in front of the house, was that it had shrunk considerably since she last saw it.

As a child it had seemed to her a great mansion, but now she realised that it was a well-built, moderate-sized house, of weather-beaten grey stone, holding just that amount of dignity necessary to ensure its position in the small village through which they had just passed.

The Manor of Brookavon, with its surrounding orchards, fields with grazing cattle, old houses of black and white, was the personification of England at its most unchangeable.

An England where the cottages of the local people were clustered around the village green, and where the squire, to whom they looked to dispense protection and justice, was still treated as the final authority on every problem.

This was the England Doreen remembered, a pre-war world where the feudal system was still in existence, untouched by the fiery demands for equality and socialism.

More unchanged even than the village and the house itself, was the atmosphere which greeted her from the moment she entered the front door and came into the square oak-panelled hall.

It was the smell of age, of bees-wax, of pot pourri, good cigarettes and cigars, and over all, the scent of past generations, a strange atmospheric fragrance of people that had lived and died here in this very place.

It was all inexpressible, but it seemed to Doreen that she grasped at the mantle of eternity before it passed away into the pungent scent of mackintoshes, hanging in the lobby off the hall where Aunt Edith suggested she should hang her coat and wash her hands before going in to her grandmother.

Doreen gave herself a quick glance in the mirror as she turned to say she was ready. Here indeed was the acid test.

If her memories of her grandmother were not at fault, Mrs. Wickham was both frightening and austere, and she remembered, as a child, that nothing could escape the keenness of her eye.

She would be older now, much older, but perhaps she had altered as little as her eldest daughter, in which case, there was definite danger in the moment of meeting.

Once again the dark glasses were to prove themselves a protection which Doreen dared not discard.

During her last days aboard ship she had gone without them altogether, but that morning while dressing and packing, she made up her mind to use them, at any rate for a few days.

Now she was thankful for her decision.

"You will find your grandmother in the drawing-room," Aunt Edith said, putting away rugs and gloves in the great oak settle in the hall. "I will run the car round to the garage. I shan't be long."

"Oh do come in with me," Doreen said suddenly in a panic.

"Why?" Edith Wickham asked bluntly, then as if she read the answer in Doreen's pale face turned towards her, she added, "of course I will, if you want me to, but don't be nervous—mother's looking forward to seeing you. I expect you feel a bit strange coming back here alone, remembering that the last time you were with your parents. Poor Anne, but you must be brave, and we'll do everything possible to help you."

She slipped her arm through Doreen's and opened a door leading off the hall.

For a moment Doreen was blinded by the sunlight streaming through the long windows.

Then she had a confused impression of highly-glazed chintz, great cabinets filled with china, tables covered with ornaments, vases and bowls of flowers and in a flash, remembered the whole room—overcrowded, but with the certain charm of being continually lived in.

Sitting at a writing-table in the window was her grandmother.

"How little she is," was Doreen's first thought, for she too, seemed to have shrunk in the years that had passed.

But as Mrs. Wickham rose to her feet, holding out her hands in welcome, Doreen was conscious of a distinguished, almost beautiful face, of clear penetrating eyes that examined her closely, and of abundant white hair, dressed severely with incredible neatness.

"How are you, Anne?" her grandmother asked. "It is very nice to see you again."

She took Doreen's cold hand in hers and inclined her cheek towards her grand-daughter. Doreen kissed her, and experiencing an unexpected and uncontrollable shyness, murmured in a low voice which she hardly recognised as her own, that she was well.

"I met her at Southampton," Edith said, as though it were an achievement.

"So I gather," Mrs. Wickham remarked dryly. "Have you put the car away, Edith?"

"No, I am just going to," her daughter answered, almost guiltily.

"I should do so at once," Mrs. Wickham suggested. "Tea will be here at any moment now. I told Barton to bring it as soon as Anne arrived."

"I will go at once," Edith said and bustled from the room.

"Come and sit down," Mrs. Wickham said to Doreen, leading the way to a sofa.

Doreen did as she was told, unable to help a feeling of fear within her. It was extraordinary how awe-inspiring her grandmother was.

That first impression of her smallness had been only a momentary one. Now she seemed immense.

Her dignity surrounded her with an atmosphere which was almost of majesty.

"Tell me about yourself," she commanded. "Did you have a good journey?"

"Very good," Doreen answered.

"Was there anyone you knew on board ship and did you manage to make some friends?"

"I made a few," Doreen faltered.

She felt it was impossible to say more, to elaborate the voyage as she would have done to anyone else who was interested in her journey.

"You had enough money?" Mrs. Wickham asked sharply.

"Yes, thank you," Doreen replied. "Dr. Garston advanced me a little in Cairo for clothes and he also gave me my ticket. I understand that it came from some money that was already owing to . . . my father."

"I am glad that was all right," Mrs. Wickham said. "I was a little perturbed as to what to do. The doctor wired me from Khartoum but made no mention of money, but I felt that were you in need, you would have the good sense to cable me."

"Of course," Doreen answered, "I should have done that."

The door opened and she was thankful of the interruption. Tea was carried in by an old rather decrepit butler.

"I thought I heard Miss Anne arrive, madam," he said to Mrs. Wickham.

"That's right, Barton, she is here. Didn't Miss Edith ring the bell? Really, she gets more forgetful every day."

"No, I had no warning. I just had to use my ears and guess it was the car passing the pantry window," the old man grumbled with the privilege of an old retainer.

Then turning towards Doreen he said, "I am glad to see you, Miss Anne. It is a long time since you have been here."

"Thank you," Doreen replied. "I am very glad to be back."

THIRTEEN

Alice Wickham at seventy-five was known amongst her contemporaries, in fact to everyone with whom she came into contact, as "a character".

Actually she had possessed both character and personality from her early childhood, but what in childhood had been considered precociousness, in youth impertinence and in middle-age arrogance, was now, with silver hair and a life drawing rapidly to its close, considered a virtue and an asset.

Born in the days when a very large family was considered the natural and inevitable result of marriage, Alice had found that with several elder brothers and sisters, she must, if she wished to be noticed, assert herself.

She would have made a far better boy than a girl, for she had a masculine outlook on life and an obstinate determination where her own desires were concerned.

This in the days when to be truly feminine one must be timid and given to vapours, was naturally enough not looked on with favour.

Alice's parents paid very little individual attention to their children.

They were well off; they spent a great deal of their time travelling or entertaining large parties of their own friends, so the children had an adequate supply of governesses and nurses while they were young, and the boys were packed off to school as soon as they grew too old and obstreperous for schoolroom supervision.

Among those left behind at home, Alice easily became the leader, or indeed as the harassed governesses put it, the "ringleader of every escapade". Actually her supremacy went far deeper than mere leadership in games and daring.

By the time she was twelve, Alice ruled the schoolroom and when she extended her influence further, she found that by using her intelligence and by adopting diplomacy, she could also get her own way, to a large extent, with her parents.

It was not surprising that as a debutante Alice was a failure. She was extraordinarily pretty and very petite, but the men who referred to her as a "pocket Venus" and wished to protect such a fairy-like little creature from the cruel hard world, were quickly disillusioned.

Alice talked to them, not only as though they were her equals, but as though they were, in many ways, her inferiors.

This was naturally unwelcome, for Victorian manhood fancied himself as the supreme authority where the feminine sex was concerned.

However, in spite of a certain amount of unpopularity, Alice, like all strong characters, managed after a year or so to gather round her a *coterie* of her own.

Intelligent men who were bored by simpering, empty-headed women, found Alice both a relief and an inspiration, and the few celebrities that the family numbered amongst its acquaintances, were all Alice's friends.

They made no bones about the fact that they found the rest of the household dull and commonplace.

Among these kindred spirits there were several extremely eligible *parties* whom Alice might easily have married, had she been so inclined, but being already two generations ahead in thought, she claimed the right to choose her own husband because she should love him.

Alice's mother, after a few feeble and quite unsuccessful attempts to make her daughter behave conventionally, left the girl to her own devices, while her father, busy with his own interests, rebuked her when he got the opportunity, but as long as there was no open scandal, he was too indolent to trouble himself unduly.

Finally, to the surprise of everyone, Alice fell in love with George Wickham.

He was not particularly distinguished and he was certainly not the intellectual equal of many of the men who had courted her and been refused.

It was indeed difficult for most people to understand why Alice fell madly in love with him and was prepared, for the first time in her life, to acknowledge that she had met her superior.

Actually, George Wickham was an obstinate, slightly arrogant young man, but good-looking and extraordinarily charming, and he had been spoiled consistently since he was born because he was an only son.

He was not in the slightest bit impressed by Alice, but he admired her enormously, both for her looks and her quick wit which amused him.

Perhaps it was because he lacked that touch of awe and respect which had characterised everyone else's approach to her, that she was prepared to capitulate so completely the fortress of herself, having withstood every other onslaught.

All through her married life Alice was to love George with an adoration which never faltered.

She found him quite perfect in his own way, and while other people suffered from the strength of her personality, which grew more and more pronounced as the years went by, to George she was always a gentle yielding creature, ready to agree with whatsoever he suggested.

She brought up their children firmly and efficiently, making them completely subservient to her wishes. She made no secret of the fact that she found the girls boring and much preferred the boys.

When her two eldest sons were killed in the war, she knew that the larger part of her interest in life died with them, and although she appeared the same outwardly she was, in fact, a crippled woman.

She had planned so much for her sons, especially as George had been killed in the hunting field during the winter of 1913.

His death in the prime of life was a shock for everyone, but for his wife it was a tragedy beyond words.

Her family, her children and her friends expected Alice to be utterly crushed, to relax for the first time in her life and let the world see that beneath her dignified proud exterior there was the woman, passionate hearted, vulnerable and adoring, which George had known.

Yet the iron control which she had exercised all her life carried her through.

After a week during which she shut herself in her room, and firmly refused to see anyone, she came downstairs, pale but composed, to again take up the reins of the household, holding them tightly and firmly, as she had done through all the years of her married life.

George had gone, but the throne remained from whence she wielded her power.

The loss of her sons a few years later was a worse blow than even the death of her beloved husband, not because she loved them more, no one could ever approach the place that George held in her heart, but because she needed them more.

She wanted their youth, their strength and their affection, to carry her through the years which she saw looming ahead, when she would become an old woman, when her power would weaken and her kingdom become smaller.

She admired both her elder sons and she had an intense pride in them. Richard she loved with just a faint echo of that love she had given her husband.

For the girls she had a toleration, but often she found them insipid, immature and lacking in personality. In her innermost heart too, she despised the deep admiration they had for her herself.

She in her youth had admired nobody; she had gone her way regardless of authority, convention and prejudice.

Alice Wickham's originality had certainly not been quenched or diminished by marriage. Always she had managed to gather around her the interesting people, not always an easy task as they lived in the depths of the country.

Even there she did not escape criticism, because she would not tolerate people who were bores, or conform to the traditional behaviour expected from any chatelaine of the Manor of Brookavon.

Guests from London came and went and long before week-end parties were fashionable the Wickhams entertained from Friday to Tuesday all sorts and kinds of people.

Not content to behave in an unusual manner, Alice Wickham continued, all through her married life, to speak her mind both firmly and distinctly, regardless of the consequences.

She made enemies, but while they raged against her, she forgot their very existence.

She gained too many admirers, whom she often found a great nuisance, and whom she tried to disperse by a brusqueness that, strangely enough, seldom antagonised them, but only made them more firmly her slaves.

"Such people are insufferable!" she told her husband once, handing him two letters of fulsome gushing enthusiasm from women to whom she had been almost pointedly rude.

George had merely laughed.

"I have never known you suffer fools gladly."

"You aren't very helpful," Alice Wickham had retorted.

In all seriousness he had replied:

"You have never asked for my help!"

She had to admit it was true. Her own tongue was a weapon far more useful in her defence than any strong arm.

There was no need for George to constitute himself as her protector and as he had dryly remarked, with perhaps a touch of wistfulness, he had never been asked to do so.

Her passion to do what she wanted regardless of what others thought, was not unattended by incident and on more than one occasion she found herself involved in situations which were both delicate and compromising.

Even Alice was a little startled when, having gone alone to the rooms of a very eminent poet, she had literally to fight her way out.

But these foolish episodes were never confided to George. Alice believed that there was no sense in troubling him and it was indubitably true that she was quite capable of looking after herself.

It was perhaps fortunate that she was so self-sufficient, for besides the death of her husband and sons, the years had naturally taken their toll of a great many of her friends.

Most of them were older than she was, and as she said bitterly to her family on her seventieth birthday, the death column in *The Times* was the only social literature left to her.

But age could not force Alice Wickham to abdicate from a position of authority.

The old county people were still, to a certain extent, terrified of her. Her reputation for wit had certainly not diminished and if there is one thing the average British man or woman dislikes, it is to be made to look a fool by someone with a sharp tongue and a still sharper perceptiveness.

Alice Wickham at seventy-five was not an easy person to ignore, and there were few who dared to do so.

A few of the younger people tried from time to time to patronise the old lady, thinking that the Manor was a most convenient and comfortable meeting-place for their various activities, and being quite prepared to amuse themselves with listening to what its owner had to say, so long as eventually they would get something out of it.

They were speedily disillusioned.

They were either quickly dismissed and the place barred to them, in which case they were undoubtedly the losers, or having gone to criticise they stayed to applaud, coming away full of enthusiasm for Mrs. Wickham and not a little in awe of her.

Edith was, of course, a slave to her mother's wishes, a position which she accepted happily.

And Richard was content to live at home, knowing that there was no fuller life open to him, and grateful in many ways that the varied interests of his mother, modified to a certain extent the boredom he suffered because of his own incapability.

With Richard Mrs. Wickham was at her sweetest and most gentle. It was, indeed, surprising how tender she could be to him, while other people felt what the servants called "the rough side of her tongue".

Sentimentality of any sort was abhorrent to her nature. But of Richard she had an understanding which told her how he yearned for the virility which he could never have, and she tried with every means in her power to keep him from brooding.

Like all her children, Richard needed support and protection.

He could never be self-sufficient enough to enjoy life entirely intellectually, without the human touch and the bodily contact of other people.

Unlike most women, Alice had no desire to see her children married. For Edith's own sake she was sorry that she had no husband.

At the same time, Alice Wickham often thought how useful it was to have her eldest daughter with her, and to know that the most irksome duties could be placed upon her willing shoulders.

The twins had found themselves husbands without any help from their mother. She had disapproved of Mary's marriage, simply because she had known at the very first moment of their meeting, that Henry Wallis was a fool with a weak inferior character.

She had expected any daughter of hers to choose more sensibly and while her husband was against the marriage on financial grounds, she disliked it because she knew that eventually Mary would be both disillusioned and unhappy.

Martha's choice had been blessed from the very start, because her father had never been particularly fond of her and was delighted for her to be leaving home.

A full-blooded man, enjoying every moment of his life, it was annoying to have a child who quite obviously disapproved of everything he did.

George Wickham subscribed to the local church and attended morning service every Sunday of his life, accompanied by all those of his children who were at home. He thought of himself as a gentleman, a sportsman and a good fellow. Martha's attitude, if not a bombshell, was both disconcerting and irritating.

To her he was "a wine bibber, a flesh eater and a partaker of innocent blood", by which she meant that George enjoyed his glass of port after luncheon and dinner, that he ate heartily and well, that he was a hard rider to hounds and a good shot.

Martha announced that fox-hunting was cruel and that pheasant shooting was akin to wholesale murder.

As all the children had been brought up to consider such things the natural sport and relaxation of every gentleman, Martha's rebellion against the established order, caused almost a sensation in the household.

"She will grow out of it," Alice said soothingly to her husband as he recounted without much appreciation of the humorous aspect, how Martha had pleaded with him "to find God", after having asked if she might speak to him in the study.

But Martha did not grow out of it.

In fact, she became more ardent as she grew older, spending most of her spare time in church and making, as her father abruptly put it, "a damned fool of herself over the curate".

Donald Marston's proposal of marriage and his decision to become a missionary with Martha as his helpmate and companion, was greeted by George Wickham with an enthusiasm out of all proportion to the occasion.

He gave his daughter his blessing and an even more handsome wedding present than he would have offered under other circumstances.

Her absence from the household afforded him great relief, and he made no bones about saying so.

Alice often wondered to herself whether she would mind her sons getting married.

She doubted it, although a daughter-in-law might well have proved an irksome creature to whom she must be pleasant, whether she liked her or not.

But Alfred and Matthew were dead and poor Richard, however much he yearned for the companionship of some young and lovely creature, could never marry.

Alice would often watch the expression on his face when there were young people running about on the tennis court, or bathing in the swimming pool which had recently been built at the end of the garden.

She understood the urge within him for some fulfilment of those desires of which he was physically incapable; she could sense his desperate craving to know a virility which had always been denied him through his disability.

She could sympathise with the deep passionate hatred which he could not prevent because he was so jealous—searingly, miserably jealous of those healthy young bodies.

The two grandchildren which had been born to Martha and Mary had never interested Mrs. Wickham to any great degree.

She had herself taken maternity as it came to her, as a thing to be done conscientiously and well, but which was otherwise of little importance. She did not want to see a perpetration of the species and she could not understand the gushing enthusiasm of elderly women for their children's children.

Martha, as was to be expected of her, had always written home consistently and conscientiously.

Her weekly letter arrived on Monday mornings with Mrs. Wickham's morning tea, punctually and in the same well-regulated manner as everything else in that household.

She had put on paper every detail of the work that she and her husband were doing.

If the truth were known, Alice Wickham was often exceedingly bored by the long closely-written pages of thin notepaper. Martha had been verbose and she also managed to make everything with which she came in contact, appear dull and uninteresting in repetition.

Mrs. Wickham had seen Anne twice, once for three months when the child was only twelve years old and when another grandchild, Doreen Wallis, had also come home from abroad.

Looking back, Alice could remember very little about her eldest grand-daughter. She had seemed a quiet, self-possessed young woman, reminiscent in some ways of Martha in her youth, but with even less spirit and initiative.

She was not particularly pleased at the idea that she must make a home for the girl now she was orphaned, but that it was her duty to do so, of course, outweighed all other considerations.

"You should be able to find work for her among your varied activities, Edith," she suggested.

"Of course I will, Mother," Edith said enthusiastically. "She ought to be so helpful. After all, if she can look after natives, she ought to be able to do anything."

"Let's hope she isn't too much of a reformer," Alice Wickham said with a sigh. "Religion is never a comfortable thing to live with."

"I can't see any reason why she should try to convert us," Edith said seriously, her brow puckered at the thought.

"Are you quite certain you don't need it?" Mrs. Wickham asked.

Edith blushed.

"Really, Mother! What an idea," she said. "Surely you aren't suggesting . . . ?"

"I am not suggesting anything," Mrs. Wickham interrupted. "I only made the statement that religion is a difficult thing to live with and that I hope my granddaughter is not too enthusiastic a missionary."

"I should hope not, indeed," Edith said, but she remained anxious up to the very moment of Anne's arrival.

"You needn't have worried, Mother," she said that night after Doreen had gone to bed and she, as was her usual habit, had looked in at Mrs. Wickham's bedroom last thing. "She seems a very nice girl and quite ordinary. I am certain she won't try to save our souls or anything like that. I was a little worried after what you said."

Mrs. Wickham, sitting at her dressing-table, looked up at her daughter.

"Your great asset, Edith dear," she said, "is that you always take things at their face value. It makes life very easy for you, you ought to be grateful."

"I am sure I haven't the slightest idea what you are talking about, Mother," Edith said as she bent to kiss her good night.

FOURTEEN

"It is very peaceful here," Doreen said, looking at Edith across the table in the flower room, as they arranged roses and sweet peas in the big china vases which belonged to the drawing-room.

"Do you really think so?" Edith asked with surprise. "It always seems to me there is so much going on, arrangements of all sorts to be made, the telephone ringing and people dropping in when one least expects them! In fact I always say to Mother that I haven't a moment for the things I really want to do."

"What do you want to do?" Doreen asked, amused at Edith's idea that the Manor was a busy place.

"Well, I want to paint for one thing," Edith answered. "I love doing water colours—sketching, or even studies in still life. Mother doesn't think much of it, of course.

She never encouraged us even as children in what she calls 'drawing-room talents'. But you know, Anne, I really enjoy sitting with a paint box—not that I ever have time," she added with a sigh.

"I think all you do in the village is splendid," Doreen said.

"Well, that is a compliment from you," her aunt answered. "After all, look how much of your life you have given up to good works and to the heathen at that. For between ourselves, though you may think it awful of me to say so, I never feel that black people have as much claim on our charity as those of our own race and colour."

Doreen instead of feeling a hypocrite laughed out loud.

"You do put things amusingly," she exclaimed.

Edith flushed with pleasure.

"I thought you would be shocked," she said. "I'm sure you ought to be."

"I feel in the past I must have created the dreadful impression of being a prig," Doreen said.

It was not dangerous to talk to Edith Wickham like this. In spite of the fact that her aunt was fifty, Doreen always had the impression that she was speaking to a girl younger than herself.

She decided that it was not only because of Edith's sheltered existence that she seemed so childlike, but because of the genuine straight-forwardness of her character.

She was indeed a simple person, and there were no bumps, or twisted corners against which one might come unexpectedly and be surprised.

"Oh no," she answered now, "I never thought that. A prig is such a dreadful word, isn't it? But I must admit, if it won't hurt you to hear me say so, that your mother—fond as I was of her—used to make me feel guilty about so many things, and the last time you were here, of course it was for a very short while, you seemed so very different, not so understanding, or," Edith hesitated for words. . . .

"So human, perhaps!" Doreen suggested.

"That is just it," Edith said. "I always did feel that Martha and her husband were a teeny bit inhuman—you're not hurt with me for telling you?"

"No, of course not," Doreen answered. "You ought to know me well enough by this time, Aunt Edith, to realise that I couldn't be hurt by anything you said to me."

"I do like having you here," Edith Wickham said enthusiastically.

"Do you really?" Doreen asked. "If that is true, it is the nicest thing that has ever been said to me."

"You know it is true," Edith Wickham said earnestly. "And, what is more, I believe Mother enjoys it too."

"I shouldn't be too sure about that," Doreen answered wryly.

"Oh, but I know her so well," Edith went on, "and she likes you—she does really. I have never seen her so pleasant to anyone for ages, except, of course, Richard, and he's different."

"You make her sound a real dragon," Doreen said.

"Now you know I don't mean that," Edith expostulated, looking quite miserable at the accusation. "But I admit Mother can be difficult at times and she can make things most disagreeable for anyone with whom she does not see eye to eye."

"I don't believe it," Doreen said jokingly.

"Oh, but it is true," Edith said, taking her quite seriously. She lowered her voice and looked round. "If she wasn't my mother, Anne, I would say that at times she was really malicious to people. You can't really condemn it, because after all, she says the same to their faces as she does behind their backs. But she deliberately makes them squirm—I have watched them and felt so ashamed and sorry."

"I expect they deserve it," Doreen said cheerfully.

"It is easy for you to say that while you are in her good books," Edith said.

"In other words, wait and see," Doreen laughed.

"Oh, my dear, I hope she never alters as far as you are concerned," Edith replied. "You see, if anyone really gets on her nerves, we just keep them out of the way, not for Mother's sake, of course, but for theirs. She took a frightful dislike to the parson here once. I think it was partly his fault.

"He was a very stupid man and most bumptious, but really life was so unbearable, we were absolutely thankful when the Bishop decided to move him."

"How did you manage that?" Doreen asked.

"Well, we didn't exactly manage it," Edith confessed, "but of course, several people who were great friends of mother's knew the Bishop. I think they just dropped hints from time to time and so eventually the Bishop thought it was best to offer him another living—anything was better than having the whole parish go to rack and ruin."

"What a parochial upheaval!" Doreen teased. "And you in the thick of it. I don't wonder, Aunt Edith, you never have time for your sketching."

"There now," Edith said, putting down a large bunch of sweet peas with a gesture of dismay, "I am giving you quite the wrong impression, and I don't want to do that, Anne, you know I don't."

"You aren't doing anything of the sort," Doreen answered soothingly. "I only love to hear you telling me about these things, and after all, I have seen Grandmother in one of her . . . shall we say, worst moods."

"When the press reporters called the day after you arrived!" Edith said. "Yes, that was terrible, wasn't it? I forgot to warn you that Mother disapproves dreadfully of the newspapers. With the exception *The Times*, she thinks they are all common and sensational. Oh dear, those poor young men must have felt absolutely withered after she had finished speaking to them."

"Nevertheless, they got their photographs," Doreen said cheerfully, "and thanks to you, a very good tea, even if we had to give it to them in the servants' hall."

"One of them said it was quite an experience," Edith said cheerfully. "He said he thought people like Mother were an extinct pre-war race."

"Talking of wars, have you seen the papers today?" Doreen asked.

Edith shook her head.

"I haven't had a second even to glance at them," she confessed.

"Things look very bad," Doreen said. "It seems almost certain that we shall have to fight Germany sooner or later."

"Nonsense!" Edith Wickham said standing back from the table to admire her handiwork. "I don't believe all this crisis talk. We have had one war to end all wars. No one could be so stupid as to start another."

"I shouldn't be too sure," Doreen said.

"Well, I am certain God wouldn't allow it," Edith said, picking up a bowl of roses and preparing to leave the room. "I will take these into the drawing-room," she added. "We haven't done the Chinese vases in the hall yet."

Doreen walked to the window and looked out at the apple orchard.

The sunshine made the whole world green and gold, and it seemed impossible, in the midst of this pastoral setting, to imagine the devastation and horrors of war, or even the hustle and bustle of humanity.

"How peaceful!" Doreen whispered involuntarily to herself.

She had been at the Manor nearly a fortnight. Already it seemed to her as though the past was rapidly fading from her mind, as if it was being carried away from her on a swift tide.

Here she seemed to slip quietly into domestic tasks and into the general atmosphere of contentment, which radiated through the whole house.

Already she found it easy to talk to Edith about the local celebrities, village problems, or parochial differences. With her grandmother she had also a bond in common.

They were both intensely critical of people and at times vied with each other in exchanging opinions on the differences of character or personality they had noticed, or sensed, about the many various types of callers and visitors.

Doreen genuinely liked her grandmother, even while she was still a little afraid of her.

More than once she wondered if Mrs. Wickham was at all surprised at the pertinacity of her grand-daughter, yet after the first few days, it seemed to Doreen, that she was entirely safe.

It had been easy to make it very clear from the beginning, that she did not wish to talk very much about her father and mother, or of the tragedy which had made her an orphan.

It was fortunate too, that in a household so wrapped up in their own concerns, they appeared to have little interest, beyond a conventional politeness, in the life Doreen was supposed to have led before she came to them.

Richard, indeed, was the most difficult of her three relations. Doreen felt in some ways that he resented her presence and yet, she knew he strove to make her welcome.

She could not at first understand why, at times, he was frigid and disagreeable to a point of boorishness, while at others he went out of his way to be genial, seeking as a child might, to eradicate a bad impression he had made previously.

She longed to ask Edith about him, but felt shy at probing too deeply into the innermost lives of these people who were so kind to her.

Her grandmother was a person with whom it was quite impossible to be confidential, yet, could she have chosen, she would have liked that clever, witty old lady's honest opinion on Richard and his frequent strangeness.

Once when she had been walking down to the swimming pool, wearing only her bathing dress and a wrap of turkish towelling, she had met him as she passed through the rose garden.

"I am going down for a swim, Uncle Richard," she said. "Are you coming to watch me?"

"Can't you leave me alone!" he snarled at her suddenly. "I am busy."

Doreen had been too surprised to speak. He was sitting in the sunshine in his wheeled chair and although there was a book on his lap, it was closed.

Then she realised that his face was white and that his fingers were trembling.

"Are you ill?" she asked, starting forward.

"Go away!" he almost screamed at her. "For Christ's sake go away!"

She could only obey and leave him, feeling too astonished for any reciprocal anger. When she had finished swimming she made a wide detour to avoid the rose garden and went back to the house another way.

However, as she entered the hall she found Richard waiting there, a bunch of roses in his hand, which he thrust towards her.

"I picked these for you," he said gruffly, not looking at her, his eyes on the flowers. "I thought they would go with your room—the pink ones are almost the exact colour of the chintz, aren't they?"

"Yes they are," Doreen said. "Thank you so much. How nice of you."

"And by the way," he went on, speaking quickly in an unnatural affability, "I have got a book in my room which I think would interest you. It is a novel, but it is about Africa and I should think you would know a lot of the places it mentions. Shall I go and get it?"

"Oh, not now," Doreen said, "but I would love to borrow it if I may. I have just finished the book I was reading."

"I will go and get it then and put it on the table, so that you will find it when you come down."

Quietly, as though he was glad to escape from her, he wheeled himself away, over the oaken floor towards his own room.

"I don't understand," Doreen thought to herself, looking at the roses in her hand.

"Aren't you going to change, child?" came a voice from the top of the stairs.

Doreen wondered just how long her grandmother had been concealed in the dark shadows on the landing.

"Yes, I am just coming," she answered.

She went up the stairs, two steps at a time and on the top step stood face to face with her grandmother.

"Richard's roses," the old lady said gently, pointing to the blooms in Doreen's hand. "He is very proud of them. He looks after them himself, you know."

"They are lovely, aren't they?" Doreen replied. "He thought they would match the chintz in my bedroom."

Mrs. Wickham looked at her in a strange way and Doreen wondered what she was going to say.

Then, as though she changed her mind, she just touched the roses with her hand, and reaching for the banister, started to walk downstairs.

"Poor Richard!" she had murmured beneath her breath.

Looking through the flower room window, Doreen saw Richard coming up the curve of the drive, propelling himself and followed by a fat old spaniel, who occasionally condescended to leave the hearth-rug for a short walk.

The drive was slightly uphill and Doreen saw that Richard was exerting all his strength to keep his chair going.

"Poor Richard!"

She echoed the words of her grandmother.

He was so pale and emaciated that it was difficult to think of him as still a comparatively young man, years younger than Pepi, whom she had never considered old, and young enough, if he were not an invalid, to seek a young wife.

"What are you looking at?" Edith asked.

Doreen had not heard her come back into the room. She started.

"The orchard, the sunshine and Uncle Richard," she answered quite truthfully.

"Oh, has he come back?" Edith asked. "We shall have to hurry. It means that it must be nearly tea-time. Richard is always punctual."

"Haven't we nearly finished?" Doreen enquired, arranging delphiniums in a vase of Chinese blue which in reality was far too valuable to be used, but should have been placed in a glass cabinet.

"Yes, I think so," Edith replied vaguely. "I did the bedrooms this morning, when you were swimming."

"I am sorry!" Doreen said guiltily. "Why didn't you tell me? You know I would have liked to have helped you."

"My dear, you must enjoy the fine weather while you can," Edith said. "This has been a good summer, but last year it rained incessantly and the bath was absolutely wasted."

"You are so up-to-date here," Doreen said teasingly. "I never expected anything so luxurious as a swimming bath!"

"Don't say that to Mother," Edith replied warningly. "She would be furious; she likes to think that she assimilates all the best and most modern ideas, and nothing annoys her so much as when people infer that she is rather antiquated, or behind the times."

"She is a marvel," Doreen said with quite genuine enthusiasm. "Anyway, I am going to ask her advice this evening about myself. Do you think she will have a solution to my problem? She never seems at a loss where other people are concerned."

"What is your problem?" Edith asked.

"My future," Doreen said. "You have been very sweet about having me here, dear Aunt Edith, but I suppose that sooner or later, I shall have to think about getting a job, I must support myself in some way."

"Oh, must you?" Edith said in mock dismay. "I am sure Mother . . ." she hesitated.

"There you are, you see!" Doreen exclaimed. "You aren't certain what your mother will think, and that is just why I am going to ask her. After all, if she suddenly got tired of having me here, you know yourself, I should be in a very difficult position. It is much better for me to make the first move."

"Oh dear, I do hope Mother will think of something," Edith said, "but I am sure she will, she has never failed any of us yet."

Edith Wickham was right.

When tea was over and old Barton had carried away the great silver tray, which seemed almost too heavy for his bowed shoulders, had folded up the crochet-edged linen table-cloth, and put the gate-legged mahogany table in the corner of the room, Doreen found herself alone with her grandmother.

Richard had gone off into the garden immediately the meal was finished, whilst Edith had, with a tact that was obvious, made some excuse to leave the room.

Feeling rather like a schoolgirl about to approach her headmistress, Doreen after a moment's hesitation, took her courage in both hands.

"Grandmother," she said, "I want to ask you something. I love being here, you know that, and I am terribly grateful to you for having had me, but I must begin to think of the future. I wonder if I can get a job, or if you have any ideas as to what I could do. You see, I am not qualified for anything particularly."

"You must be good with children," Mrs. Wickham replied. "You have had a great deal of experience of them, even though they were black!"

"Yes, yes, of course," Doreen answered hurriedly.

She felt uncomfortably aware that her grandmother was looking at her with strangely penetrating eyes.

"Then you aren't entirely unqualified," Mrs. Wickham said.

"I shouldn't feel at all confident about looking after English children," Doreen answered quietly. "Mission work is a very specialised work, and after all, my position was a subservient one."

She could not face her grandmother while she spoke, but looked at the linen handkerchief she held in her hands.

"I remember Martha spoke very highly of your capabilities," Mrs. Wickham said.

Doreen felt she was battling against something she did not quite understand. She tried to answer lightly.

"I shouldn't pay too much heed to that," she said. "Parents all over the world are inclined to make out that their geese are swans."

"I personally should have thought you quite a capable young woman," Mrs. Wickham said dryly, "and you give me the impression of someone who, at least, has their wits about them."

"Thank you," Doreen said, half-curious, half-afraid, wondering what was in her grandmother's mind. "Won't you advise me," she went on, "you see, I don't know how to begin to look for anything."

"Well, as it happens," Mrs. Wickham said with a faint smile, "I had expected you to come to me about this very matter and so I have thought about you, dear child, these last few days and I think I have the very solution here in my pocket."

"What is it?" Doreen asked, somewhat apprehensively.

"It is a letter from a very old friend of mine, telling me that the German governess who had been looking after Michael Gillespie's daughter at Barnleigh Castle, has left at a moment's notice and in mysterious circumstances, in fact, it is assumed that she has been recalled to Germany."

"Yes?" Doreen said enquiringly.

"That leaves the child without a governess of any sort, and I believe that Michael Gillespie would only be too delighted to consider you for the situation."

"But why? He knows nothing about me. How does he know that I would be suitable?" Doreen asked quickly.

"He doesn't," Mrs. Wickham said, "and in my opinion, he cares less. He's a very busy man, or makes himself so, and he won't want to be worried with registry offices, references, and interviews. If he knows that my grand-daughter is willing to take the position of looking after his child, he will jump at the opportunity of saving himself trouble."

"He sounds a very casual father," Doreen remarked.

"He is a very strange man, my dear," Mrs. Wickham said. "He's a scientist and at the moment he is working on some experiment which keeps him shut up for eight to ten hours a day, so I am told. Few people see him, but few want to, for that matter."

"Why?" Doreen asked.

"What a lot of questions you ask, child," her

grandmother replied. "But still, you might as well know. He's a recluse and a woman hater. His wife, who was not a very desirable person, ran away soon after the child was born. That was soon after Michael Gillespie inherited the Castle.

"His uncle Colin Gillespie, was a great friend of mine. We were the same age and I had known him all my life; he was a frequent visitor here, especially during my husband's lifetime.

"He was a very popular man in the country, and I don't mind telling you, we were bitterly disappointed when his nephew, very shortly after settling in at the Castle, gave up every form of social connections or interests in the neighbourhood and made it quite clear that he wished to have little or no communication with the outside world.

"People tell me he was a very different man before he married. He was supposed to be a brilliant surgeon, but, apparently, he was also interested in research and during some experiments in a laboratory, there was an explosion, which blew off two fingers of his right hand and damaged one of his feet. After that his career was ended, of course.

"He may have had a great future—I never heard of him, but I do know that he has failed disgracefully as regards the inheritance left him by his uncle. The Castle grounds are going to rack and ruin.

"But that needn't trouble you. The point is that here is employment waiting for you at our very gates. Barnleigh Castle is about two and a half miles from here. Edith can easily run you over in her little car, or if she is too busy, I presume you could bicycle.

"I think that the best thing would be for me to write to Michael Gillespie tonight and say that you will call and see him tomorrow."

"Tomorrow!" Doreen echoed. "But are you certain, are you sure, Grandmother, that . . ."

"That it is a suitable career for you?" Mrs. Wickham said coldly. "Quite certain, my dear Anne. Had you any other ideas in your own mind?"

"No," Doreen faltered.

She realised that her grandmother disapproved of the somewhat unenthusiastic manner in which she had greeted her suggestion.

"You will still live here with us," Mrs. Wickham said, "and be under my chaperonage. I don't know whether you would prefer to be on your own, but personally I consider it would be a great mistake, and at least while I live, there is a home for you here."

"I am grateful, I am really," Doreen said. "It is only that I am surprised, in fact astonished, at your having a job ready for me, so to speak, up your sleeve. You can't expect us all to be as quick witted as you are, Grandmother."

She spoke with a hint of mischief in her voice and was pleased to see an answering gleam come into the old lady's eyes, but Mrs. Wickham did not relax her somewhat frigid austerity.

"It is settled then!" she said.

"As far as I am concerned," Doreen answered. "Of course, Mr. Gillespie may have other ideas."

"I think that is unlikely," Mrs. Wickham replied, rising from her chair and walking towards her writing desk.

Doreen with a little grimace, thought that if he had, he would in all probability have to change them.

FIFTEEN

"Are you feeling nervous?" Edith asked as she drove her small Austin along the narrow hedge-bordered lanes which led towards Barnleigh Castle.

"Terribly!" Doreen confessed. "I shouldn't have minded so much if I had a little more time to think it over, but it has all been such a rush, that I can't even begin to think of what I am to say to Mr. Gillespie."

"If you only knew how characteristic this is of Mother," Edith said, half-laughing, half-sympathetic. "Once she has made up her mind she never gives one time to consider anything. The whole thing is done, as it were, at a snap of her fingers."

"I think I am even more terrified of going back without the job than of being interviewed for it," Doreen said ruefully. "I would hate to admit to Grandmother that I have been a failure."

"I have often felt like that myself," Edith said with a sigh. "She has an extraordinary way of making one feel a fool. I remember that once when I was quite small there was an awful row because someone had drawn pictures on the bathroom wall.

"No one would confess to it and Mother stood there looking so severe that I suppose out of sheer hysteria I said I had done it, although I hadn't even been in the bathroom that morning.

"Of course, Alfred who was the real culprit, could not let me be punished and so he started to cry and owned up. I remember Mother was very angry with him, but she punished me too for being stupid.

"She spoke to me with a contempt which I have never forgotten. I suppose it was sheer nervousness which made me do such a thing, but Mother who has never suffered from nerves, can't understand other people having them."

"What is Mr. Gillespie like?" Doreen asked.

"I haven't seen him for years," Edith confessed. "When they first came here we called and I vaguely remember his wife. She was very pretty and very smart. Most people, including Mother, disapproved of her on sight. From what I remember of him, he was nice."

"And the child?" Doreen questioned.

"What did Mother say about her?"

"I don't think she mentioned her. Oh yes, I remember she did say last night that she was ten years old."

"I think you ought to know," Edith said hesitatingly, "that she is not a particularly nice child. I suppose she has been spoilt or brought up by inefficient servants.

Anyway, none of the families around here will have anything to do with her.

"They tried asking her to parties, but she behaved so badly that they gave it up and from all reports, she has a governess every two or three months."

"Well, that is a cheerful outlook!" Doreen exclaimed.

"I suppose really I oughtn't to have told you," Edith said anxiously, "but I can't help feeling that you should know. Perhaps you will be clever enough to handle her."

"What a hope!" Doreen murmured under her breath.

With horror she realised how very little she knew about children.

In Cairo some of her married friends had well brought up unobtrusive children, who came down to the drawing-room for ten minutes after luncheon and were whisked away by their nurses long before they could get troublesome.

But when she came to analyse it, she could hardly remember having a conversation with a child, or being alone with one for any definite period of time.

"Oh well," she thought defiantly to herself, "I have got to go through with this. I can't refuse, but I suppose, if the worst comes to the worst, I must just admit failure and face the consequences."

"There is the Castle," Edith said suddenly, and pointed to where a big grey turret rose above the trees.

"But it's enormous!" Doreen exclaimed.

"Oh, a great deal of it is in ruins," Edith answered, "but old Mr. Gillespie—who was Mother's friend—restored the Norman tower and rebuilt the south and west wings. He loved the place and was very proud of the fact that his family was mentioned in the Domesday Book."

They turned in at the lodge gates and drove up a broad avenue of oak trees with parkland stretching away on either side.

"Is he very well off?" Doreen asked.

"Who?" Edith questioned. "Michael Gillespie? Oh, I think so. He inherited a great deal of money from his uncle, but for all the help he is locally, he might as well be penniless. He occasionally sends a subscription to the hospital or the British Legion, but only if he has been written to at least a dozen times. Well, here we are. I will wait for you outside."

"Oh, come in with me," Doreen said hurriedly. "I shouldn't feel so frightened."

"Mother said you were to go in alone," Edith replied.

"And orders are orders!" Doreen said, trying to speak lightly, despite a sudden nervousness.

"Damn it all," she said to herself as she rang the bell, "what do I care?"

She thought of her appearance and realised that there was something, after all, in smart clothes and make-up. They gave one courage!

Now, in her plain black dress and cheap straw hat, she felt humble and a little crushed—a feeling she would never have experienced had she been calling on Mr. Gillespie as Doreen Wallis.

However, she held her head high as she followed a plump dignified butler through the huge oak-panelled hall and into a room which had big french windows facing the garden.

"I will tell Mr. Gillespie you are here," the man said. "It's Miss Marston, isn't it, miss?"

"Yes, that is right," Doreen said. "I think Mr. Gillespie is expecting me."

She looked round the room. It was beautifully furnished. There were walnut cabinets, needlework chairs and several attractive pictures, which even to her inexperienced eye, looked valuable.

At the same time the room had an unlived-in look and a strange musty smell as though the windows were seldom opened, or the fire lit.

There were no flowers—none of the little knick-knacks with which every woman ornaments a room and makes it essentially her own.

Doreen took off her gloves and sat down in an armchair. How strange it was, she thought, to be waiting to meet someone who might be her future employer.

She had played many parts in her life, but no one yet

had been interested in her efficacy as a teacher, or prepared to pay for them.

"Let's hope he doesn't delve too deeply into my capabilities," Doreen thought, realising that her ignorance was almost abysmal. "But I can get some books, I suppose!"

Should she get the job she imagined that she must spend at least part of her evenings reading up what she would have to teach on the morrow.

"I am mad," she thought to herself, "is this really a better life, fuller and more interesting than the one I have given up?"

Yet in Cairo she might at this moment have been facing complete penury. When she had discarded her old self, she had had exactly fifteen pounds in the bank and the ten pounds given her by Tony.

The small amount of money she should have inherited from her father was mortgaged for another five years. She had been unable to refuse him when he had asked her to sign her immediate participation away to moneylenders.

It had been a silly thing to do and she had known that once in the hands of usurers, it was difficult to get out again.

But Henry had been so insistent, so anxious, for the money "to tide him over a bad patch", and at the time she had consented, she had been as she thought, married to Pepi and secure in the belief that for the rest of her life he would provide for her.

But Cairo without money, and at a time when she was still weak from the effects of fever, would not have been very amusing. No, she was better off as she was.

With a start Doreen heard the door open. She had been waiting nearly twenty minutes. Now a man came hurrying into the room.

He was wearing a long white medical coat and she noticed that his right hand was gloved.

Her first thought as he crossed the room towards her, was that he was far older than she had expected.

Then she realised that she was mistaken; it was not

age, but an air of tiredness and fatigue which gave a false impression.

Michael Gillespie was tall, but he stooped a little and his dark hair was beginning to turn grey at the temples. There were deep lines running from nose to chin, a network of faint wrinkles round his eyes.

"I am sorry to have kept you waiting, Miss Marston," he said in a low voice, "but I am working and it is extremely inconvenient to be interrupted."

"I am sorry," Doreen replied. "My grandmother made the appointment thinking that the time would be a suitable one."

"Yes, yes, I understand," he said testily. "But I am in the middle of an experiment and these constant interruptions are most trying."

"I am sorry," Doreen repeated.

"Now let me see," he said, "what is it. . . ."

He looked as though he had forgotten on what mission she had come.

"I had your grandmother's letter somewhere," he added. "I wonder what I have done with it?" He felt in pockets.

"She only suggested," Doreen explained hesitatingly, "that if you were without a governess—she understood that yours had left—I might be a suitable person to undertake the education of your daughter."

"Oh yes, governess, yes, that was it," Michael Gillespie ejaculated. "I couldn't remember for the moment why it was I had to see you. Yes, I understand that the woman who was here with Sheila has gone—that is the fourth or fifth in the last six months, I can't keep count. Well, that will be quite all right. I hope everything will be quite satisfactory and that you will stay."

He held out his hand and Doreen realised in astonishment that it was a gesture of dismissal.

"But, but . . ." she stammered. "Surely we ought to arrange something—the times I come, or what I teach your child?"

"I leave all that to you, Miss Marston. Oh, and your salary will be paid by my agent, Mr. Johnstone. He sees to all that sort of thing for me. Please telephone him at the estate office and say I have engaged you."

"When would you like me to start?" Doreen asked.

"Whenever you like—tomorrow?"

"And your daughter," Doreen questioned, "shall I see her now?"

"Oh, Sheila. Yes, you will find her upstairs somewhere." He took out his watch. "I am sorry, I can't stay any longer. As I told you, I am working on an experiment and time is precious."

He went to the door and shouted "Walter!"

The butler was obviously not far away for Doreen heard his voice answer, "Yes, sir!"

"Take Miss Marston to the schoolroom," Mr. Gillespie ordered, then, without another word to Doreen, without even a look in her direction, he disappeared.

There was the sound of a door being slammed in the distance and the butler came into the room.

"Will you come this way, miss?" he said. "I think Miss Sheila is upstairs."

They walked up the broad carpeted staircase and Doreen was aware that the butler was glancing at her surreptitiously wondering, she supposed, if she was as incapable as her predecessors appeared to have been.

"What a wonderful staircase," she exclaimed almost involuntarily as they reached the minstrels' gallery running the whole length of the hall.

"The whole Castle is very fine, miss," the butler answered. "It is a pity so few people see it these days."

Doreen felt that his criticism was best left unanswered, but the man was apparently undeterred by her silence.

"Fine parties there used to be here in the old days," he went on. "Dancing down there in the hall and a string band—all in uniform—playing here in the gallery. There were hunt breakfasts, house parties for the races, people coming and going every week. Oh, we saw life, I can tell you, when the old gentleman was alive. Will you be staying, miss?"

Doreen shook her head.

"No," she said. "I am living with my grandmother, Mrs. Wickham, at the Manor."

The butler's face brightened into a beaming smile.

"There now," he said, "I wondered who you were and I might have guessed when I saw Miss Wickham in the car. I have known the Manor ever since I was a lad. My father was gamekeeper to your grandad. Eighty-nine he was when he died, and he wouldn't be pensioned off until he had passed his eighty-second birthday."

They passed through a green baize door which led to a long passage and to another flight of stairs. At the foot of it Doreen saw standing a middle-aged woman, wearing a starched white apron and the stiff white collar and cuffs beloved of all old-fashioned nurses.

"Well, what is it, Mr. Walter?" she asked in disagreeable tones.

"This is Miss Marston, nurse," he said, "a new governess for Miss Sheila."

"Another!" nurse ejaculated, looking Doreen up and down in a disdainful and antagonistic manner.

With difficulty Doreen managed to curb her feelings and hold out her hand.

"How do you do?" she said.

Nurse hesitated, then just touched her fingers in a chilly, off-hand way.

"If you ask my opinion," she said speaking in particular to neither Doreen nor the butler, "the child will be far better without a governess—they only upset her."

"I am afraid that is not Mr. Gillespie's opinion," Doreen said slowly and distinctly. "May I see Sheila, please?"

Nurse glared at her and said:

"She is upstairs."

She walked away down the passage, her starched apron rustling, her whole attitude one of intense disapproval.

"This way, miss," the butler said, pointing to the stairs.

When they were out of earshot, he lowered his voice and said confidentially, "Don't you take any notice of her, miss. She is a tartar as well we know. She has been with the child since she was a baby and hates interference. If the master knew half of her goings on he would have her out quick enough. But there, he takes no notice, one way or another."

Doreen felt she should not encourage this type of confidence. At the same time it was some consolation to know that in this extraordinary household, she had at least one friend. She knew that Walter's association with the Manor had already bound him to her with a bond of sympathy.

At the top of the stairs he opened a door into a big sunny nursery, at the far end of which, sitting in the window reading a book, was a child. She looked up as they entered and Doreen had a quick impression of big dark eyes and untidy lanky hair.

"What is it?" she questioned surlily.

Walter answered her.

"It's a new governess to see you, Miss Sheila—Miss Marston."

"Oh damn!"

The child threw the book down on the floor and got off the window ledge.

"Not another! I had thought now Fräulein was gone, I was going to have a holiday."

When she stood up, Doreen saw that Sheila was unexpectedly tall. Her face was small, heart-shaped, and appealing in spite of her present expression of animosity. She wore boy's shorts, into the pockets of which she had thrust her hands.

Doreen turned to Walter.

"Don't bother to wait for me," she said. "I will come down later. Thank you."

"Very good, miss."

He walked out of the room and shut the door behind him leaving Doreen alone with her new charge.

While she hesitated for words, the child spoke again.

"Nanny said that she thought it would be a long time before Daddy remembered to get me another governess."

"Well, it is bad luck for both you and nanny," Doreen

said, "but I happen to live only three miles away and so they didn't have to look very far."

"Aren't you going to stay here then?" the child asked.

"No. I am going to come daily," Doreen answered. "What time do you usually start lessons?"

"Never, if I can help it," Sheila replied, speaking in the rude aggressive voice she had used since the beginning of the conversation.

"Do you work in here?" Doreen asked.

"If you don't know, I'm not going to tell you," the child replied.

"All right then, don't," Doreen answered. "I will make my own arrangements. I shall come here at half-past nine tomorrow morning. Good-bye, Sheila."

She turned abruptly towards the door and sensed with some satisfaction that the child was both surprised and puzzled. With an effort of will she forced herself not to look back, but went out, closing the door behind her. At the bottom of the stairs she found Walter waiting.

"Is it all right, miss?" he asked.

"Quite," Doreen replied. "Why? Were you anxious?"

"Miss Sheila is a fair terror," he said. "You never know what she'd be up to. One of the governesses got a bucket of water on her head one morning and had hysterics. She left by the afternoon train too, said it wasn't what she was used to."

"I'm not surprised," Doreen answered. "Tell me, do I have luncheon in the nursery with nurse?"

"Oh no, miss!" Walter was obviously shocked at the idea of such a breech of etiquette. "You and Miss Sheila has luncheon in the dining-room, and the master joins you, if he isn't busy. It isn't often that he ain't, and so you don't see much of him. And nurse has hers taken up to her."

"I shall come at half-past nine," Doreen said. "Perhaps you will tell nurse to have Miss Sheila ready for me."

"I will tell her," Walter said cautiously, "not that she'll listen or make any effort to carry out your instructions."

They reached the bottom of the main staircase and walked towards the hall door.

"Will you tell Mr. Gillespie that I will write to him," Doreen asked.

"I shouldn't bother, miss," Walter said confidently. "Letters only annoy him. He will be expecting you, and if you will pardon me giving you the advice, you make your own arrangements, as suits you."

Doreen hid a smile. As she reached the door she held out her hand.

"Thank you," she said.

"It has been a pleasure, miss," Walter answered, as he let her out into the sunshine where Edith was waiting.

SIXTEEN

Mrs. Wickham listened with interest to Doreen's story of her reception at the Castle. She remembered Walter.

"He comes of a good family," she said. "His old father was a very superior type and most reliable. We had great trouble in pensioning him off. He just refused to retire although the work was quite beyond him towards the end. You will have to get rid of that nurse, I can see that."

"She is much more likely to get rid of me," Doreen replied.

Her grandmother looked at her with that strange expression, peculiar to herself, which her family knew well. It meant that she was contemptuous of some unexpected weakness.

"I shouldn't take up a defeatist attitude," she said severely. "As for the child, I feel confident that you will manage to make her see sense and instil some sort of discipline into her."

"I am glad you are so optimistic!" Doreen thought.

She herself felt extremely pessimistic about the future. She had been aware as she drove away with Edith from the Castle, of a distinct trembling in both her knees. It had not been an easy ordeal and one for which nothing in her past could possibly have prepared her.

"I wonder exactly how far my authority goes," she said now ruminatively to her grandmother.

"Just as far as you intend to make it," Mrs. Wickham answered. "My dear Anne, in a household like that, it should be very easy for you, gradually but determinedly to take command and get things arranged as you wish them to be."

Doreen laughed.

"You are marvellous, Grandmother! I know exactly what you mean and you would be able to do it perfectly, but though I am your grand-daughter, I just haven't got your gift of authority. I know my own limitations and face them quite honestly."

"Then I am disappointed in you," Mrs. Wickham said sharply.

"That's a compliment," Doreen exclaimed. "You sound as though you thought that I had possibilities, even though they do not materialise."

There was nothing Mrs. Wickham enjoyed more than when someone stood up to her in this sort of way.

Verbal warfare was a recreation that she often missed, when she was alone with Edith and Richard. Her keen eyes glinted with pleasure; her mouth curled in that faint smile which, in the past, had dismayed many people when some scintillating shaft of wit had pierced their most precious conceit.

Then before she could reply, as though Doreen's words recalled something to her mind, she said:

"By the way, I have some bad news for you all."

Richard who had finished tea and was just about to leave the room stopped, his fingers already on the rubber wheels of his chair.

"News?" he echoed. "About whom?"

"I had a letter from Lancelot Wallis today," Mrs. Wickham said soberly. "You remember, Henry's brother."

Doreen felt her heart leap with the shock, then a rapidly throbbing pulse brought the blood to her face. She lowered her head, pretending to be intent on petting Ned, the old spaniel who lay at her feet.

"What has he got to say?" Edith asked curiously.

"It is about Doreen—Mary's daughter. I am afraid that she is dead."

Doreen had a sudden, wild desire to burst out laughing. She knew it was hysteria; she knew it was only the sudden shock which made her long for some outlet to her feelings.

Yet she had to clench her hands together to prevent her shattering the rather hushed and sombre atmosphere with peal after peal of merriment. It was so ridiculous to sit there and listen to the news of her own death.

"Dead!" Richard said quietly. "Poor child."

"Hardly a child," Mrs. Wickham answered coldly. "Doreen must have been twenty-nine last birthday. Apparently she died in hospital in Cairo. A heart attack following a severe attack of fever.

"Lancelot says that he has only just received the particulars, as the authorities had some difficulty first of all in discovering Doreen's next of kin, and secondly in tracing him, because he has moved recently from the country into Leeds."

"He is a solicitor, isn't he?" Edith asked.

"Yes, he carried on his father's business," Mrs. Wickham replied. "I must say he seemed singularly undisturbed by my granddaughter's death, but at the same time, as he points out, it would be difficult now to do anything about it.

"Her death took place nearly a month ago and as she had enough money for the funeral, she was buried in the Cairo cemetery, next to Henry and Mary.

"What puzzles Lancelot, and not unnaturally, is that she apparently died under the name of 'Doreen Wallis' and yet, as far as we all know, she had been married for some years to a Greek. I'm afraid I have forgotten his name."

"Perhaps they were divorced," Richard suggested.

"That still would not account for her return to her

maiden name," Mrs. Wickham said. "However, as can be expected from Lancelot—you remember him, Edith, a dried-up stick of a man, he gives one few details and makes the whole letter read like a legal document."

"I wonder what she was like?" Edith said. "Do you remember when she first came here, Mother, all those years ago, what a funny little child she was—aggressive, rude, and a mass of nerves. She was terrified of us too. You remember her, Anne?"

Edith turned towards Doreen, who answered hastily:

"Yes, of course. We were here one summer together."

"I don't think you liked her very much, did you, Anne?" Mrs. Wickham asked.

Doreen looked up at her grandmother, then as quickly looked away again.

"I can hardly remember what I felt," she said. "It is a long time ago."

"Over nineteen years," Mrs. Wickham said. "I have often wondered what sort of life that child led in Cairo. I can't help feeling that neither Mary nor Henry were particularly good parents."

"Oh, I am sure Mary was," Edith expostulated. "She had a sweet nature, Mother . . . before she married."

"That makes you my only grandchild," Mrs. Wickham said to Doreen, ignoring Edith's last remark.

She said the words as though she meant them to strike some chord within Doreen herself.

"I hope I shan't be a disappointment," Doreen muttered.

Then feeling as though she could bear no more, she got to her feet.

"I'll get some sewing," she said and went towards the door. As she reached it she heard Richard say bitterly, in a low voice to his mother:

"Only one grandchild! Well, it looks as though it is the beginning of the end as far as the family is concerned!"

Doreen closed the drawing-room door behind her and ran upstairs. Now that she was alone and out of earshot, she somehow had no further desire to laugh, only to cry.

It was ridiculous, but she wanted to cry for what, as

far as the world was concerned, was the unimportance of Doreen Wallis. Was that all life meant, she asked herself?

That one was born to live, to suffer and to die, without leaving an impression behind, without being of any importance whatsoever?

It was absurd, but the casual remarks of her relations had wounded her. She knew, of course, that they had not seen Mary or Henry for many years and that the child who had spent one brief holiday at the Manor, could not be expected to hold a large place in their affections, or indeed in their interest.

Yet when Doreen thought of all she had endured and suffered in Cairo, of the unhappiness, heartburnings, and privations during her girlhood, of the shock of Pepi's death, of her own illness and desperate need of help, it seemed unfair that no one should mourn her passing.

Twenty-five pounds had ensured her a place in the cemetery, rather than a pauper's grave—the remains of Pepi's legacy and Tony's ten pounds with which he had asked her to buy a souvenir—

There ought to be some lesson, some ironical moral in that, she thought, but for the moment she could not see it. She only felt bitterly conscious of that lonely coffin with no mourners and no friendly salute or farewell.

Would Anne have minded, she wondered?

Now a new sense of what she had undertaken came to her. She was dead. It was a strange position to be in, this casting off of an old character and personality as though they were a suit of clothes, of being rehabilitated in thirty years of someone else's growing.

"I ought to feel light, gay and free," Doreen said to herself.

Instead she felt intolerably depressed and near to tears.

"It is no use sitting here moping," she thought. "I will go downstairs and get a book to read."

Richard told her to borrow any book she wanted from his own library. She knocked at his sitting-room door.

He answered "Come in" gruffly, as though he was annoyed at the interruption, but when she entered and he saw who it was, he smiled at her in a friendly fashion.

"Come in, Anne," he said. "Do you want me?"

"I have come to borrow a book. Can you recommend anything good?" Doreen replied.

"Yes, I can," he said. "I have got it here, somewhere. It is called *The Black Panther*. See if it is on the table over there."

Doreen looked where he pointed. Among a miscellaneous collection of books, papers and pipes, she found the volume.

Richard had discarded his wheel chair for a big leather one by the fireplace. He looked small and wizened in it and pathetically fragile.

"Don't go," he begged. "Stay and talk to me awhile."

There was a pleading in his voice which made Doreen look at him curiously.

"I would love to," she answered, "if you are quite sure I am not interrupting you."

"There is nothing to interrupt," he answered.

"I was feeling a bit depressed," Doreen confessed, sitting down opposite him in another chair, feeling the well-worn leather cool against her bare arms.

"Why?" her uncle asked.

"I don't know," Doreen answered untruthfully. "Unless, perhaps, it was hearing of my cousin's death. It struck me it was such a lonely way of dying and nobody here seemed to care."

"Isn't all dying lonely?" Richard asked almost savagely.

"But I don't see why it should be," Doreen replied. "Think of your mother, for instance, suppose she died. All her life she has been surrounded by admiring and adoring friends, when she has gone she will be missed, mourned and regretted. What is more, she will never be forgotten, not in our lifetime, anyway."

"And what consolation is that when you are dead?" Richard asked. "Will kind words or fulsome epitaphs warm you when you are under the soil?"

He spoke with such bitterness that Doreen realised

that quite inadvertently she had touched on a tender spot.

"Don't you believe in an after-life?" she asked.

"No, I don't!" Richard replied. "Does that shock you?"

"Not in the slightest," Doreen answered quickly. "I'm not certain that I do myself."

"And you a missionary's daughter?" Richard taunted. "I can't believe that that is a genuine sentiment."

"You forget that I did not choose my life," she said quietly. "If I was born into a certain position, that is hardly my fault—but my beliefs are my own."

Richard looked apologetic.

"I am sorry."

Doreen smiled at him.

"Why should you be?" she asked. "I'm the one to be sorry if I shock you. But I feel I can talk frankly to you and not have to be remembering the entire time what is expected of me."

"We all have to behave as others expect us to," Richard said.

"Why?" Doreen questioned.

"Because the whole structure of social life would fall to bits if we didn't. Can you imagine what would happen if everyone, whatever position they were in, were entirely natural or entirely honest?"

"Only by everyone donning a mask, in pretending to be what they aren't, and in living up to someone else's ideal, does the world continue in what it calls a state of civilisation."

Doreen stared at him.

"I wonder if you are right," she ruminated.

"Of course I am right," Richard replied. "If everyone relaxed even for a few hours, you would find parsons who were murderers, nuns who were prostitutes, bank managers who were thieves, and politicians who were cut-throat gangsters. No, they have to keep up a gigantic bluff for the sake of humanity itself."

"And you? Are you bluffing?" Doreen asked curiously.

"Of course I am," Richard said to her savagely. "Do you think that I want to lead the life of a pampered invalid, to be a man so broken and crippled that I only call forth tenderness and pity from all with whom I come in contact?

"I hate tenderness; I loathe pity. I want to be cruel, ruthless, virile, powerful and, if you like, sadistic. I want to have people in my power, just as I am in other people's power.

"I would like to make them grovel to me, to feel terrified of my authority—but dare I show those around me the truth? You know it would be impossible!"

He spoke vehemently and as his voice died away there was a hushed pregnant silence in the room, as though the air had been shattered by a scream.

Doreen understood; she saw how he was tortured by his own weakness; how he longed for escape, for a freedom which he would never find.

Quickly, instinctively, she sought within herself for words of comfort, knowing they must not be conventional ones, for she dared not show the pity she felt for him.

When she spoke it was in a cool logical voice.

"Aren't you confusing the mental and physical?" she asked.

"What do you mean?"

"Surely everything which you have just mentioned," Doreen replied, "can be supplied by your mental powers? The strength of cruelty, of domination and of power, is certainly not in the least dependent on the actual weight-lifting muscles in your arms, or in the strength of your body.

"All the tyrants in the past have been small men, most of them have suffered from some physical disability.

"You are lucky, Uncle Richard, many people in your circumstances want to win motor races, to be the first down the Cresta Run, or play Rugger for England. You can if you wish—drop the mask—and gratify all your ambitions."

"I never thought of it like that," Richard said. "I wonder if you are right."

"Of course I am!" Doreen exclaimed.

Then, so that he should not find too quickly the flaws in her argument, she added, "I am not in half such a fortunate position, because I don't know what I want."

"A husband, perhaps?" Richard suggested with a grimace.

"Oh, I suppose so," Doreen said lightly. "A house of my own, a husband, children, and a nice secure social position? That, I imagine, is the desire of ninety-nine women out of a hundred and the hundredth has got it already."

"Haven't you ever been in love?" Richard asked.

"I have thought I was," Doreen replied. "I have had a deep affection for somebody once and I was attracted physically, if one must put it that way."

"You will get everything you want in the future," Richard said reassuringly. "But for me there is no future."

"Why shouldn't there be a future for you?" Doreen asked. "In work, a career, or a successful mental effort! Now you are making yourself weak needlessly; you are sapping your strength in self-pity and, what is more, over the most unimportant part of yourself."

Richard sat forward in his chair and stared at her as though she were inspired.

"Anne! Anne! If I could only believe that what you say is true."

"It is true," Doreen answered. "It is just as true as you can make it. No one can make up your mind for you; no one can force you to live and to be alive—mentally. That world is an unexplored country for each one of us."

Richard covered his face with both his hands.

The dressing gong boomed through the house and Doreen got to her feet.

"Thank you for the book," she said gently, half afraid of disturbing him.

"Come here."

She obeyed, to stand at the arm of his chair, looking down at him.

"I think you have been sent to me from Heaven," Richard said slowly in a broken voice. "For the first time for many years you have brought a light into the depths of hell."

On an impulse, Doreen bent down and pressed her lips against his forehead.

"Your hell is a mirage," she said. "Get out of it! You can!"

Outside the room she realised that during the conversation she had poured out a part of her own vitality, so that she felt almost exhausted in a new and quite different way to anything she had experienced before.

"But perhaps I have been of some use to him," she thought as she went upstairs.

She saw how for years Richard had been swamped by his mother and because of his physical ailments, allowed to brood over himself and his empty life.

"It is absurd," Doreen said out loud. "He ought to have been given a proper job to carry out—estate work, management of some family business, anything which would take his mind off himself!"

Instead, for nearly twenty years he had pottered round the garden, seeing to the roses, doing just the few odd jobs that Mrs. Wickham allowed to slip from her own capable and dominating hands.

"She is too strong, too sturdy," Doreen thought. "She makes them cling to her, she supports them willy-nilly, whether it is for their own good or not and, if I am not careful, she will do the same to me. I shall become dependent on her, afraid, even as Edith is afraid, of her contempt, eager for her praise and goodwill."

Yet Doreen could not help admitting, in all fairness, that her grandmother was magnificent in her own way.

It was impossible to realise that in actual stature she was small, as she swept into dinner in front of her children and grandchild, wearing a dress of deep purple velvet with a collar of real Honiton lace.

At the head of the table in her high-backed chair, she looked like some painting by an old master.

She waited until they were all seated, then in some indefinable manner of her own, made them all realise that she had an announcement to make.

"I wonder what it is?" Doreen thought swiftly, both amused and intrigued at the slightly theatrical effect that her grandmother achieved with seemingly so little effort.

"Have any of you," Mrs. Wickham asked, "heard the latest news this evening?"

Doreen glanced at Edith, who had been down the village after tea.

"No, is there anything new?" she asked.

Mrs. Wickham paused and Doreen realised that she was relishing this moment, that she enjoyed being the centre of interest, of keeping all three of them waiting, hanging on her words, expectant of her pronouncement. At length she spoke.

"Germany marched into Poland this morning," she said. "England will declare war."

SEVENTEEN

Doreen arrived at the Castle a few minutes before half-past nine the following morning.

She carried with her one or two lesson books which she had managed to find in the well-stocked library shelves at the Manor.

They were old-fashioned, having been used by her mother when a child, but she felt they would do to start with and at least give her some guide as to what Sheila knew or did not know.

She had spent several hours the night before delving into them and was appalled at her own ignorance.

"Anyway," she thought cheerfully, "I shall at first have my hands full teaching the child manners. That seems to be a far more important necessity than any book learning."

Walter opened the door and welcomed her with a smile.

"All ready for work, miss?" he enquired.

"I suppose we do lessons in the room where I saw Miss Sheila yesterday afternoon?" Doreen asked.

"Well, miss," he answered doubtfully, "that was originally the old nursery. There had been continual trouble as to whether Miss Sheila shall work there or in another small room next door, which has always been considered the schoolroom, but which most of the governesses as have been here, used as their private sitting-room. You see, miss, nurse makes things very difficult."

Doreen did not doubt that and it was with a sinking heart she went upstairs and having opened the nursery door, found no one there but nurse herself.

"Good morning, nurse," she said brightly. "Where is Sheila? Is she ready for me?"

"I haven't the slightest idea," nurse answered insolently. "If you want her you had better find her."

Doreen felt furious and saw no reason why she should hide her feelings.

"I can hardly believe that your manners, nurse, are a good example for the child," she said. "Perhaps you would be good enough to show me where the schoolroom is. I understand from Walter it is on this landing."

Nurse seemed taken aback, and Doreen guessed that the other governesses who had come to the Castle, had been pathetic cowed creatures, who were anxious to keep their job and felt that as nurse was already firmly ensconced they had better keep in with her.

"It is the room on the left," nurse said abruptly, making no effort to rise.

"Thank you," Doreen replied. "If Sheila comes in here, perhaps you would tell her where I am."

The schoolroom was a small, rather charming room with windows overlooking the gardens at the back of the house. Doreen thoroughly inspected the premises and found to her delight a large and miscellaneous collection of school books.

Every governess, she felt, must have spent considerable sums on buying her own pet method of teaching and the result was several packed shelves and a cupboard where books, pencils, writing paper and maps were thrown in such confusion that Doreen suspected Sheila of having taken a delight in making a "pot pourri" of them.

After waiting for about half an hour, Doreen wondered what she should do.

She had been half expecting that Sheila might disappear and she felt that there were only two courses open to her, one to more or less ignore the child's defiance, the other to go in search of her.

The only guide she had at all to Sheila's mentality was her own childhood. Looking back she thought that at ten years old she might have done the very same thing.

With nothing to occupy her time, Doreen felt that this might be a good opportunity to explore the Castle itself. It would be wise for her to get to know her way about the house.

Resolutely, and at the same time slightly nervous of encountering nurse, she walked out of the schoolroom and opened the other doors on the landing.

One she discovered was Sheila's bedroom, a big light room, furnished with a child's bed and furniture of minute size.

The room opening out of it, she guessed, was nurse's, while another bedroom further along the passage was empty, but had doubtless in the past been occupied by the resident governess.

Otherwise there was only a bathroom and a housemaid's cupboard on the schoolroom landing, so walking downstairs, Doreen decided that she would send for Walter and ask him to show her the rest of the Castle.

Meeting a footman on the stairs, she asked him to find the butler, and a few minutes later he was at her side.

"Miss Sheila has disappeared, Walter," she said, "but if you could spare the time, I would like to see the Castle. It is rather bewildering not knowing one's way about in such a big place."

"She is a young demon, that child!" Walter exclaimed. "I guessed that was what had happened when James told me he had seen her snooping off across the fields soon after breakfast."

"In which case it is no use my trying to look for her," Doreen said.

"Oh none, miss," Walter replied. "If you will take my advice, you will go easy with her at first. Most of the governesses have tried being too strict too quickly, if you get my meaning. And, of course, nurse aids and abets her."

"I gathered that," Doreen said quietly. "And now for the house."

She enjoyed the morning immensely for Barnleigh Castle was magnificent. Colin Gillespie had spent a fortune on it before he died. Every piece of furniture was worthy of a museum, and most of the pictures were listed as National treasures.

The majority of the rooms were, of course, shut up, and Doreen could quite understand how disappointing it was for the servants to have to keep clean such acres of space, with never the reward of seeing their efforts admired.

It would have been satisfactory to know that the great drawing-room with its huge glittering chandeliers was sometimes filled with a gay, fashionable throng, to hear the click of the billiard balls in the oak panelled billiard room with its wide open fireplace, or to know that the state beds with their vast canopies of damask and coloured plumes, were being slept in by distinguished and important personages.

Doreen saw everything, save one wing of the house which was barred to her.

"That leads to the master's laboratory," Walter explained. "None of us ever goes through there. He has an assistant who lives in the village and who bicycles up every morning. He keeps it clean, I believe. But no one else in the house must pass this door."

"What a lot of footmen you have," Doreen remarked as for the third or fourth time during their tour of inspection, she found a different young man engaged in some form of work in the various rooms.

"They aren't footmen, miss," Walter said in scorn. "They are housemaids, or housemen, I suppose is the right term."

"Housemen!" Doreen exclaimed.

"Yes, the master won't have women here. I expected you'd have heard that! Everyone in the place with the exception of nurse, Miss Sheila and the governess, always has to be a man."

"Good gracious!" Doreen exclaimed. "What an extraordinary idea."

"We have a chef, a kitchen man and two scullery boys in the back, three in the pantry and four young fellows to keep the house clean. Quite a regiment we feel we are at times."

"And does it work well?" Doreen asked.

"Sometimes we has trouble," Walter admitted, "but usually I can manage them. I am in charge, you see, miss, although Mr. Johnstone, the agent, engages the staff. We has changes, of course, from time to time. I am about the only one who has been here a really long period, as one might say, but then I was with the master's uncle. Came to him as a pantry boy and worked my way up, until when the old butler died I took his place."

They had walked back to the hall by this time. As they entered, a big grandfather clock in the corner struck twelve.

"Twelve o'clock already!" Doreen exclaimed. "Time has flown, because I have been enjoying myself so much. Thank you, Walter. I think the Castle is wonderful."

"I must go and see about luncheon now, miss," he said. "It is at one o'clock."

"Do you think Miss Sheila will be back?" Doreen asked.

"There's no saying. She may or she may not. Just as the same as the master may or may not come in for his. But it's no use waiting for either of them, miss. When the gong sounds, will you come straight into the dining-room?"

"I will," Doreen replied and went upstairs.

There was nothing for her to do so she sat down in the schoolroom with a book and read until the great vibrating roar of the gong reached her ears.

A little apprehensively she went downstairs again and into the dining-room. To her relief, with the exception of Walter and two footmen, the room was empty.

She settled herself in the chair Walter indicated and helped herself to an egg dish from a huge silver plate. She had already started the second course when the door opened and Sheila came in.

The child was both dirty and untidy. Her cotton dress had a great jagged tear in it and she had obviously lost her hair ribbon.

She walked into the room with an air of defiance and self-satisfaction which was almost ludicrous. She took no notice of Doreen, but scrambled into a chair at the opposite side of the table.

"I hope you have kept something hot for me, Walter," she said. "I am ravenous."

Doreen looked at her charge.

"I have had a most amusing morning," she announced.

Sheila stared; she had obviously been expecting reproaches.

"What did you do?" she asked curiously.

"I went all round the Castle," Doreen answered. "What a splendid place for hide and seek and for all sorts of games. Don't you think we ought to get some children over sometime? It would be rather fun."

"All the children round here are smug pigs," Sheila answered.

"Are they?" Doreen said sympathetically. "What a nuisance. I remember, when I was a little girl, there was a child here who I simply hated. She was always telling me the things I ought not to do."

Sheila was obviously intrigued in spite of herself.

"And did you do them?" she asked, without much hope in her tone.

"Of course I did!" Doreen answered. "She was exactly what you would call a 'smug pig'. I used to pull her hair when no one was looking."

Sheila laughed with genuine merriment and Doreen knew that she had scored a point.

"I have often wanted to pull the girls' hair at the parties I have been to," Sheila said, "but most of them have got it cut too short."

"Yes, plaits were a great help," Doreen said. "But they were a nuisance too, one was always getting caught up in trees or bushes when one was climbing."

"I don't believe you climbed," Sheila said, making an effort to renew her antagonism.

"Well, we will have a competition and see," Doreen replied more confidently than she felt. "I'll give a prize for the one who gets the highest."

"What sort of prize?" Sheila asked suspiciously.

"A bar of chocolate, I think, don't you?" Doreen answered. "Do you like the plain sort or when it has got cream in the middle?"

Sheila put down her knife and fork and stared across the table.

"Do you know," she said, "I don't believe you are a governess at all. I think this must be some kind of a hoax."

Doreen was conscious that Walter turned away from the table, swiftly as though to hide a smile. She herself kept a straight face.

"I will tell you a secret if you like," she said, "but don't go telling people. I am an awfully bad one."

"Which means that you are a good one as far as I am concerned," Sheila said quickly and laughed at her own joke.

At that moment the door opened and Michael Gillespie came in. Doreen got to her feet.

"Good morning, Mr. Gillespie," she said.

He stared at her as though for a moment he could not remember who she was or why she was there.

"Good morning. Yes, yes, of course, Miss Marston," he answered. "Please don't move. Good morning, Sheila."

"Hullo, Daddy," the child answered without enthusiasm.

"Bring me something quickly, Walter," Mr. Gillespie commanded, sitting down in the chair at the end of the table. "I have got exactly ten minutes, then I must go back."

"What are you doing to the guinea pigs today?" Sheila asked.

"They aren't guinea pigs, they're rats," Mr. Gillespie corrected.

He looked exceedingly tired as though he had been without sleep for several nights. There was a grey tinge about his face and Doreen wondered why he was driving himself so hard and if these experiments were really worth the effort and the strain upon him.

"Can I come and see them?" Sheila asked.

"No, you can't," her father replied. "I have told you that before, Sheila. And, by the way, you are not to try and look through the windows. It is most disturbing and you frightened young Mackenzie so much the other day, that he dropped a test tube."

"Silly ass!" Sheila ejaculated.

Mr. Gillespie scowled at his daughter, but made no further effort to rebuke her. He was eating ravenously and Doreen wondered if he had missed his breakfast.

She broke the silence.

"I have been inspecting the Castle, Mr. Gillespie," she said. "I think it is one of the most beautiful places I have ever seen."

"Yes, nice, isn't it?" he answered absently, and she felt that he could not have thought out a more inadequate or inappropriate comment.

"Miss Marston wants to have a party," Sheila announced.

Mr. Gillespie stared across at Doreen with a sudden antagonism in his expression, which took her unawares so that she flushed painfully as she explained.

"Only children. It would be such a marvellous place for them to play in."

"We don't want a lot of children here," Michael Gillespie said roughly, "or at any rate, don't let me see them." He put down his knife and fork, pushed back his chair, and got to his feet.

"Are you going, Daddy?" Sheila asked. "You haven't had any pudding."

"I don't want any," he said. He walked towards the door and went out, without another word or a backward glance.

"Your father looks tired," Doreen said to Sheila.

"He is always tired and always disagreeable," the child answered. "I am sick of him."

Doreen felt that she had no appropriate reply ready and as they had now finished, she put down her napkin and looked at Sheila.

"Do you say grace," she said, "or don't you?"

"I don't," Sheila answered.

"All right," Doreen said.

She got to her feet.

"Before you rush off again," she went on, "you wouldn't like to show me the garden, would you? It doesn't matter if you are busy."

"All right, if you want to see it. I have got to take my pony some sugar, anyway."

Sheila had spoken without enthusiasm, but once again Doreen felt she had scored a point.

They went out through the front door towards the stables.

"Do you ride alone?" Doreen asked.

"Billy comes with me," Sheila replied. "He's the stable boy, but William is lazy."

"Who is William?" Doreen enquired.

"He is the groom and he is always pretending to Daddy, if anything is said, that he is looking after the horses. But he doesn't do anything of the sort, he just sits about smoking a pipe and drinking beer, which Daddy pays for. I know he does because I heard William tell them to put it on the grain account over the telephone. He didn't know I was listening; I was hidden in the loft."

It was only to be expected, Doreen thought, that in a household where there was no authority, it was certain there were to be bad servants, who would take advantage of it.

She hesitated before she made her next suggestion, then asked:

"I suppose you wouldn't like me to ride with you? But perhaps there isn't a horse."

"Can you ride?" Sheila asked.

"Of course I can," Doreen answered, thinking of those years as Pepi's wife, when she had ridden early before breakfast.

"I bet I can ride better than you," Sheila challenged.

"I wonder," Doreen said coolly. "You see I have had the advantage of having really good horses and of looking smart on them. I hate to see people who look like a bundle of rags, hunched up on a horse's back, don't you?"

"I think people who fuss about clothes are a bore," Sheila said antagonistically.

"Oh, if they are really fussy, like silly little girls who can't do anything because they are frightened of spoiling their best dresses or of getting their hands dirty!" Doreen replied. "At the same time, I like to look nice, and if possible, nicer than other people. Pretty clothes make one feel important."

She spoke with genuine feeling in her voice and Sheila was obviously interested.

"Do they really?" she questioned.

"Really," Doreen replied.

"Nanny says any old thing does to wear in this benighted place," Sheila said.

"Don't you believe it," Doreen said lightly. "Clothes are important wherever you are. If you learn how to look nice now, you'll look nice when you grow up. That's when you'll want to be pretty and have a lovely time."

Sheila walked for some way kicking loose stones in front of her. Doreen felt she was thinking and made no effort to interrupt. At last the child spoke again.

"My mother was very pretty," she said, "and she was very bad too. That is why I am bad."

Doreen felt that here was a danger spot. She had already decided that Sheila must be approached by unconventional methods if she were to obtain the child's confidence and trust. But she knew that she must proceed warily.

"Who said your mother was bad?" she asked.

"Nanny told me," Sheila answered. "She said she was a weak, bad woman, who treated my father shamefully. I don't blame her, I'd treat him shamefully too, if I got the chance."

"But she was very pretty, you say?" Doreen asked.

"Very, very pretty," Sheila said with conviction. "Daddy has done away with all the photographs of her. Nanny said he burnt them in one big fire in the library, but nevertheless, I know she was pretty—the prettiest person in the world."

"I expect you will be like her," Doreen said clearly.

"Me!" Sheila ejaculated.

She stared at Doreen as though she had gone mad, then moving across the path so as to get nearer to her, she lowered her voice.

"Do you mean you think I am going to be pretty?" she asked.

"I think you could be if you tried," Doreen answered coolly.

"Tell me how, tell me how," Sheila said in an excess of excitement and slipped her arm into Doreen's.

EIGHTEEN

"Are you going to the Castle this morning?" Edith asked Doreen on Sunday. "I could drop you there as I have got to go almost past the gates to see the A.R.P. Warden in Barnleigh village. You had better take advantage of my offer—I suppose now that war is certain our petrol will be rationed and we shall all have to go about on bicycles."

"I shall go today," Doreen answered, "although I

have quite made up my mind that in future I shall ask for my Sundays off."

"That sounds as if you were a housemaid," Richard said from the other side of the breakfast table.

"Don't mention such a thing in connection with the Castle," Doreen replied laughing. "Nurse and I are the only females allowed to pass the portals."

"I don't suppose that will continue for very long," Edith said. "Most of the men servants are certain to be called up and I believe the agent, George Johnstone is in the Yeomanry."

"I had never thought of that," Doreen confessed. "What will Mr. Gillespie do?"

She was soon to find out. An hour later Edith dropped her at the gates and she walked up the drive, finding it longer on foot than she had thought. She rang the front door bell and it was opened by Walter.

"Good morning, miss," he said. "I thought it would be you. I am glad as how you have come. Things are very difficult here."

"What is the matter?" Doreen asked.

"Well, miss, we are very much depreciated since yesterday, as you might say. Both my footmen went this morning by the early train, and chef is packing now. Three of the housemen have got their papers ordering them to report tomorrow morning, which leaves three of us in the house, and none of us knowing which way to turn. Mr. Johnstone is with the master now."

"Good gracious!" Doreen said. "Whatever are you going to do?"

"And that's not all, miss," Walter went on, obviously relishing his task as news-teller. "Mr. Johnstone has just informed us that about forty evacuated children are arriving today from Melchester."

"Forty children!" Doreen ejaculated. "But whoever is going to look after them?"

"I believe as how they are part of a school," Walter said, "and that some of the teachers are coming with them."

"Thank heaven for that," Doreen said, "but where are you going to put them?"

"I am waiting to ask the master," Walter said.

At that moment the library door opened and Michael Gillespie came into the hall accompanied by George Johnstone. The agent, who was in uniform, had not met Doreen before, but before they could be introduced he walked across to her with outstretched hand.

"You are Anne Marston, aren't you?" he said. "I have heard a great deal about you and I was looking forward to meeting you. I am only sorry that this is hail and farewell."

"Are you leaving at once?" Doreen asked.

"I am afraid so," he said ruefully. "I have just been handing over my keys of office."

"A lot of good they will do me," Michael Gillespie said angrily.

They were the first words he had spoken, for he had not even vouchsafed a good morning to Doreen.

"I don't know what the devil we are going to do. Did you hear what Mr. Johnstone said," he went on turning to Walter, "we have got forty children coming today from the convent in Melchester."

"A convent!" Doreen exclaimed. "Then I shouldn't worry—the nuns will look after the children and you won't be bothered by them."

"And where do you think we are going to put them?" Michael Gillespie asked almost angrily. "And anyway, who is to arrange the household here? I am up to my eyes in work, with two men arriving from the Ministry today. They have got to be housed somewhere, too."

"Well, why not let Miss Marston see to it?" Mr. Johnstone broke in heartily. "If all I have heard about her is correct, forty children and a couple of scientists are child's play compared to what she has had to manage in Africa, and as Mrs. Wickham's granddaughter, she certainly has a second claim to efficiency."

"Oh, but I couldn't," Doreen said hastily.

But not before she had seen a light of relief come into Michael Gillespie's face.

"But of course!" he said. "I never thought of that. That would be a solution."

"But it is impossible . . ." Doreen began, only to be interrupted by George Johnstone.

"Nonsense, nonsense!" he said. "You mustn't be modest with us, Miss Marston. After all, this is wartime, and we have all got to put our hands to the plough. Walter will help you in the house, won't you, Walter?"

"Come into the library both of you," Michael Gillespie said abruptly, and turning led the way.

Doreen had no choice but to follow him, the agent at her heels. Michael Gillespie sat down at a large desk on which there were a pile of account books, and a big bunch of keys of all shapes and sizes, each one bearing a label.

"Won't you sit down?" he said, and Doreen meekly obeyed.

While George Johnstone walked across to the fireplace and lit a cigarette.

"The position is this, Miss Marston," Michael Gillespie started.

As he spoke she noticed how tired he looked, as though he had been up all night.

"I don't know if you are aware of it, but I am engaged on a series of scientific experiments which may, in the event of the present circumstances, prove of immense value to the Government.

"I have, as it happens, been working for a great number of years on various antidotes to poison gas. I have had a certain amount of success, but only a faint interest has been taken in my work, owing to the fact that everyone in this country was filled with an incurable optimism that war would never come again.

"However, quite recently the Ministry of Health and the War Office accepted certain serums I had prepared. Last night they telephoned me to the effect that they were sending down two of their chief research men to work with me in speeding up the production, and in continuing the experiments that I already have under way."

He paused and looked down at his gloved hand with its two missing fingers.

"I suppose, after all, in my own way, I shall be on National Service."

"Good heavens, Michael!" George Johnstone interrupted. "But of course you will be. Do you imagine that you would be doing more good by sitting in a trench? If you do, you're a damned fool and you know it."

"I would willingly change places," Michael Gillespie said.

Doreen knew from the expression on his face that the injury he had sustained years ago to his hand and his foot must be continually irksome to him, giving him a feeling of frustration, and perhaps, being partially responsible for the hermit-like life he had chosen for himself.

"I suppose all men mind a physical disability more than anything else," she thought, remembering Richard. Then an idea came to her.

Michael Gillespie went on talking.

"I, therefore," he said, "have no time to see to the household, or to make any arrangements for these children, which, I understand, are to be billeted here. Someone has got to do it and until you arrived, Miss Marston, George and I were at our wits' end, wondering who we could ask to take over the job."

"Honestly, it wouldn't be difficult," George Johnstone broke in. "Walter knows all the families on the estate. Most of them have got strapping young women who would only be too pleased to come up and work at the Castle."

"Women?" Michael Gillespie questioned.

"Yes, women, Michael," George answered. "You have got to face this now, whether you like it or not. I suppose you know that ninety per cent of your staff have already gone."

"Walter told me," Michael Gillespie answered.

"Well, you are lucky that he is too old to serve," George said. "Because what you would do without Walter, I can't think. He's a tower of strength, Miss Marston, as you will find out. He has kept order and peace in this house for ten years, in spite of Michael's ridiculous ideas of only employing masculine labour.

"At first I expected to be fetched out of bed every night to settle a drunken brawl, or a free fight in the pantry. There were two or three incidents, I believe, but Walter made peace by his own methods, and very able methods they have proved to be."

"Incidents? What sort of incidents?" Michael Gillespie questioned.

"Oh, you weren't told, old chap," George answered. "You wouldn't have listened anyway. You were too busy. But now let's face it, the women are coming into their own again at the Castle, and you have got to put up with them."

"If I must, I must," Michael Gillespie answered irritably. "Well, Miss Marston, that is all, I think. Here are the books."

"Those are the household accounts with red covers," George Johnstone explained. "The black ones are all the estate books. They needn't trouble you—you can't tackle them as well."

Here was the opportunity Doreen needed to broach her own idea.

She was amused to notice that Michael Gillespie had not asked her whether she had made up her mind to accept the responsibility which he had offered her, but had assumed with a brusqueness which was characteristic of him, that she would acquiesce without comment.

"May I make a suggestion?" she said. "My Uncle Richard—I think you both know him—would be quite capable of taking over the accounts and running the estate, at any rate until you can find someone better."

"Richard would be invaluable!" George Johnstone said before Michael Gillespie could speak. "I never thought of him. Do you think he would?"

"I will make him," Doreen answered with a smile.

"Well, that is splendid. It solves yet another of our problems. If you could speak to him on the telephone, I would drop in at the Manor now, on my way to the station and give him the books and make a few of the explanations necessary."

"I will speak to him at once," Doreen answered.

She got to her feet then hesitated.

"There is only one thing, Mr. Gillespie," she said. "I

would like to do this job for you, and I will do my best to be efficient, but will you give me complete power to engage or to dismiss whosoever I please?"

"Of course, of course!" Michael Gillespie said testily, as though such a question was unnecessary and rather annoying. "All I ask is that I am not bothered and that my department is allowed to carry on without interruption from the household."

"The feminine side of it, at any rate," George Johnstone said facetiously.

Michael Gillespie appeared not to hear him. Instead he walked towards the door.

"I must go back to the laboratory," he said. "Tell Walter to see that the car meets the 12.10 train from London."

He left the room without another word and Doreen faced George Johnstone with a faint smile on her lips.

"You don't know," she said, "what you have let him in for. I haven't the slightest idea how to begin such a task."

"Don't worry, you will be splendid," he replied heartily. He looked at his wrist-watch and gave an exclamation. "By jove! I must be off though. Look here, ring up your uncle and tell him I am on the way. Say I can't stay for more than three minutes. I have got the devil of a journey across country."

He held out his hand.

"Good-bye," he said, "I feel I couldn't leave the old place in more capable hands."

Doreen laughed.

"You are an optimist. Good-bye and good luck."

"Telephone at once," he instructed her.

"I am going to," she said. "I might as well do it from here."

She picked up the receiver on the desk and in a few moments was through to the Manor.

"Ask Mr. Richard to come to the telephone," she said to Barton. After a long wait she heard Richard's voice at the other end.

"Who is it?" he asked.

"It is Anne," she replied.

"Anne!" he said in surprise. "I wondered who it could be. I was in the rose garden."

"Listen, Uncle Richard," Doreen said. "We need your help and we need it badly. Edith was right, George Johnstone has been called up and he and I have decided that the only person who could possibly carry on his work, and look after the estate, at any rate for the moment, is yourself."

"What are you talking about?" Richard said. "I don't understand."

Very patiently Doreen explained. Her uncle was at first incredulous, then gradually she heard a new note in his voice, half apprehension, half excitement.

It took time but she managed to convince him that he was really wanted; that here was work, the work that he had been denied for so long.

"At any rate," she said finally, "you must take it on for the present, even if you find it too much for you later. George Johnstone is on his way to see you; he told me to tell you he could only stay three minutes."

"I will go down to the gates to meet him," Richard said.

"I should," Doreen replied. "He has got the estate books with him."

"I will go and meet him now," Richard repeated.

There was a little pause, then he said in a low voice:

"You are quite sure I can do it?"

"Sure?" Doreen questioned. "I am absolutely certain that you are the very person for the job."

With that she rang off and crossing the room, opened the library door. Walter was waiting in the hall. Before she could speak, he came forward with a beaming smile.

"Mr. Johnstone has told me, miss, that you are to take over here. I am very pleased indeed and, if you will not think it impertinent of me to say so, what we have always wanted here has been a lady like yourself at the head of things."

"Thank you, Walter," Doreen said. "Mr. Johnstone told me that you were a tower of strength! You will need to be, for I am very inexperienced in these matters."

She was to learn in the half-hour that followed how inexperienced she was while she and Walter planned out the new household.

Her acquaintance with the management of half a dozen native servants in Cairo was not much help when it came to the question of staffing a place the size of Barnleigh Castle, and of trying to understand, in a few moments, the intricacies of English life below stairs.

Doreen tried to grasp the different departments, the etiquette of the housekeeper's room and the hall, the apparently impregnable barriers which debarred a servant, however willing, from doing any work that was not his, and the courtsey titles of Mr., Mrs. and Miss given to the upper few.

It was all a bewildering maze of detail which she realised had to be mastered if she were to undertake her duties efficiently.

The staffing of the place was, fortunately, not very difficult.

"There's Perkins' girl," Walter said. "She's willing to come into the house, he's the under-gardener. And there's Mrs. Robinson at the Lodge, she was in service before she married and she will come back as head housemaid, at any rate to tide us over.

"We could get Mrs. Plowman in as cook—she has been here before in a crisis, but don't say a word to the master, miss. He didn't know, and what was the point of my telling him?"

"What men have we got left?" Doreen asked.

"There's one of the housemen," Walter said, "he is deaf in his left ear and they wouldn't take him when he tried to join the Territorials with the others; and there's Jacobs, the odd man, he's fifty-five and gets bronchitis real bad in winter. I doubt if they will want him for any war service."

"Well, you had better have both of them in the dining-room," Doreen said. "It will save Mr. Gillespie being annoyed by women waiting on him and we must try to keep the rest of the staff out of sight while he is about. Now what about the children? Where are they to go?"

"Well, miss, I was thinking like this," Walter said. "It seemes a pity to put school children, of whose habits we know nothing, in the best rooms. Supposing we used the nursery flat and the floor below it?

"Miss Sheila and nurse aren't likely to spoil the best rooms to the same degree as a lot of young children. The rooms on the floor below the nursery were, in the old days, all kept for bachelors.

"There's one or two valuable pictures which we could remove, but if you will look at the inventory, miss, you will see that most of the things are good, but not listed in the antique section."

"I think it would be a brilliant idea, Walter," Doreen approved. "And Mr. Gillespie's guests, the two scientists who are arriving today, they also can be put in the best rooms."

"I hope as how they will be careful," Walter said gloomily. "I don't trust them scientists."

"We will impress on them that they must not damage anything!" Doreen said with a smile. "But I really feel relieved about the children."

"What is more, miss," Walter went on, "there's a back staircase leading down to the games room where Mr. Collin Gillespie used to hold the tenants' ball once a year."

"Where they could feed and play!" Doreen exclaimed. "Oh, Walter! It gets better and better. I had better go and see Miss Sheila and nurse and tell them they must move their things."

She went upstairs to the schoolroom. As she reached the top landing, she was greeted by a whoop of joy.

"I thought you were never coming!"

She stared at Sheila in surprise.

"What do you think of me?" the child asked. "I look pretty now, don't I?"

It was with the greatest difficulty that Doreen controlled her laughter, but she realised that this was an important moment, more important perhaps, than the reorganisation of the household and the billeting of evacuated children, or even, as far as Sheila was concerned, the inevitability of war.

The child had dressed herself up in what must have been her very best party dress two or three years ago. It was a very short, faded organdie, creased and crumpled from being put away.

Round her waist she had tied a sash of bright magenta ribbon and on her head she wore a wreath of roses and daisies which might, at one time, have decorated a hat. She had back-combed her hair until it stuck out round her head in an untidy fuzz.

And from some hidden source, of which Doreen could not guess, she had found lipstick and powder and applied them plentifully to her face.

As Doreen had not spoken for a moment, the child came nearer and took her hand.

"I do look pretty, don't I?" she reiterated, but this time there was a note of anxiety in her voice.

"I think you look lovely," Doreen replied. "Now I am going to have a try and see if I can make you look even better!"

"That will be fun," Sheila said, leading the way with dancing steps through the open door of the schoolroom.

NINETEEN

It was extraordinary the amount of work that managed, somehow or other, to be got done by Sunday evening, and Sheila enjoyed the upheaval more than anyone else.

Doreen explained to her that her help was wanted and that she was relying on her to do as much as she could to get the place ready for the children who were arriving.

It was perhaps the first time in the whole of her life that anyone had ever appealed to Sheila in the right way, or let her prove herself a sensible human being, rather than a naughty little girl invariably in need of correction.

She helped Doreen to move the pictures and all the

unnecessary ornaments and furniture from the guests' rooms, which were to be allotted to the children and the nuns.

She even volunteered to leave a large number of her toys upstairs in the nursery for them, and was delighted when Doreen told her that she could have her choice of the State rooms on the main landing.

"And where are you going to sleep?" she asked, and her face fell when Doreen replied:

"I am not staying here, Sheila. I go back to my grandmother at night."

Circumstances were soon to make her reverse her decision.

The only person who gave no assistance of any sort and whose contribution to the efforts made by everyone else was to be more disagreeable than usual, was nurse.

She grumbled, she was openly defiant of orders given by Doreen and expressed her opinion frequently and within everyone's hearing, that the Castle itself was far too large and too prominent on the landscape, to be overlooked by enemy aircraft and would doubtless be the first place in England to receive a bomb.

Doreen ignored her at first, but later in the day, when her insolence became unbearable, she spoke sharply.

"I don't think you quite understand the position here, nurse," she said. "Mr. Gillespie has given me complete charge of the house. You must either obey my orders and accommodate yourself to the new conditions which exist here, or I am afraid you will have to make other arrangements for your future."

Nurse stared at her as though she had taken leave of her senses. But she had a trump card to play.

About half an hour after tea—a meal snatched while they were still working—nurse came into a bedroom where Doreen, with the help of one of the newly recruited housemaids, was making up a bed and said:

"Can I speak to you, Miss Marston?"

"Of course, nurse," Doreen replied. "Is it anything very important?"

"If you could spare me a few moments of your

valuable time alone," nurse said with a dark look at the new housemaid, "I shall not keep you long."

"All right," Doreen answered wearily.

She was heartily sick of nurse and her grumbling by this time. She finished off the bed and said to the girl, "Start in the next room, will you, Marion? I will come and help you as soon as I can."

As the door closed Doreen straightened her back and said:

"Well, nurse, what is it? As you see I am rather busy."

"I am afraid that I have got to leave at once," nurse said with an air of triumph. "I have just been speaking to my old mother at Melchester. She is very frightened of air raids and I have decided that she must be evacuated to a safe place.

"Of course, I am deeply grieved at leaving Miss Sheila at this moment, but I am sure some arrangements can be made for the care of the poor child. I will return as soon as is conveniently possible."

Doreen was well aware that nurse thought she was disrupting the household by her proposed absence. On the face of things, it did seem rather difficult to know what to do with Sheila, who would not care to be left alone the very first night that she was to sleep in a strange bedroom.

"If you have made up your mind to go, nurse," Doreen answered, "there is nothing more to be said. Perhaps you would be good enough to give me your address."

"I am only doing my duty, Miss Marston," nurse said with a sigh. "I am sure you will agree with me that one's kith and kin must come first. As for little Sheila, I have been father and mother to her and I am afraid she will break her heart tonight at the thought of my leaving her for the first time since she was born."

"A lot you care, you disagreeable old woman," Doreen thought. In fact she guessed that nurse was hoping Sheila would make a really tempestuous scene. She hurried in search of the child.

She found her downstairs with Walter, arranging chairs, tables and toys in the big games room.

"Sheila," she called, "I have got something to tell you. Can Walter spare you for a moment?"

Sheila came running towards her, a really happy smile on her face.

"Walter says I am as good as any footman," she told Doreen proudly. "I have arranged all these chairs myself—do you see?"

"I don't know what we should have done without you," Doreen assured her solemnly. "But listen, darling, I have got something to tell you. Your nanny has got to go away tonight to look after her old mother who is in a town. They want to take her into the country, so that she will be quite safe in case of an air raid."

"Am I going to be left all alone?" Sheila asked with the instinctive selfishness of a child.

Her mouth drooped, her brow puckered, and she looked as though she might burst into tears.

"Of course you aren't to be left alone," Doreen answered. "In fact, I have already thought of a plan. You have chosen the big blue room to sleep in, haven't you, the one with the lovely four-poster bed? Well, there's a little dressing-room next to it, you know the one with the funny picture which we laughed at of the lady on a swing. Would you like me to sleep there? Then, if you are frightened, which, of course you wouldn't be because you are much too big, I could pop in and join you."

"Would you really stay?" Sheila asked. "That would be fun, wouldn't it?"

"It would!" Doreen echoed. "And I could tell you a story before you went to sleep."

"Oh, I would love that!" Sheila said. "Will it be a story about a really bad child? Nannie's stories are so stupid—they are always about terribly good children who never do anything. I want a story about a child who is bad and who does really bad things."

"I will try and think of one," Doreen promised, "but bad children always turn out frightfully clever and brave in the end, you know, so that everyone admires them and thinks how splendid they are, but of course that is after they have given up their badness."

"How long are they bad for?" Sheila asked curiously.

"Oh, only until they are about ten," Doreen answered cautiously.

She left the child secure in the knowledge that things would turn out all right.

She went to the telephone to let her grandmother know she wouldn't be home and ask if it would be possible for anyone to pack a small suitcase of her things and bring it up to the Castle. To her surprise as she entered the library, she found her uncle there.

"Hullo, Uncle Richard!" she exclaimed. "Nobody told me you had come."

"I'm not paying a social call," he said. "Johnstone told me that I would find various papers and deeds in this desk and I am looking for them. You don't think Gillespie will mind, do you? Johnstone said I was just to come in and get them."

"Don't you disturb Mr. Gillespie on any account," Doreen said hastily. "Anyway, I don't believe he knows anything about the place."

"I rather gathered that," Richard answered, "and I must say, Johnstone has left everything in perfect order. It won't be difficult to keep things going."

He spoke in a businesslike manner which made Doreen smile. She saw that he was already taking his new responsibilities seriously.

"I am just going to ring up the Manor," she said, "and tell Grandmother I can't get home tonight. Nurse has elected to go away and evacuate her mother, so I can't leave the child."

"You aren't going to stay here," Richard said.

"Why not?" Doreen enquired.

"But, my dear girl, that is impossible," he said. "Think of your position—you must have a chaperone!"

Doreen laughed.

"Really, Uncle Richard! I don't think that is very important at the moment! But we are expecting at least six nuns within the next hour and although they may not have had husbands, they would certainly be considered enough chaperonage for one unimportant governess and a very busy scientist."

"I am quite sure Mother wouldn't like it," Richard expostulated.

"Well, she will just have to put up with it," Doreen replied. "I can't leave the child alone here, with no one in charge."

"Surely one of the servants could keep her company?"

"All of them are new, with the exception of the men servants and I don't know if you consider it right to leave a butler or footman in charge of a child of ten, but I certainly don't."

"Well, please yourself," Richard said, "but I warn you, Mother will disapprove most strongly."

"I wonder?" Doreen said. "I have a feeling that at a time like this, your mother would be far more broad-minded about that sort of thing than anyone else."

She was right. When she telephoned the Manor, she was lucky enough to get through to Edith. When she explained what had happened, Edith volunteered to go and tell Mrs. Wickham and also to bring along a suitcase.

"Well, was Grandmother horrified?" were the first words with which Doreen greeted her when she arrived half an hour later.

"I told her exactly what you told me."

"What did she say?"

"She sent a message to say mind you were very careful that the beds were aired."

Doreen burst into a peal of laughter.

"I was right!" she said. "Good for Grandmother! She can take anything in her stride. Poor Uncle Richard has been most Victorian about it. He really believes that I shall be damned socially for the rest of my days."

While they were talking Walter came hurrying in to say that the children and nuns had arrived in two charabancs. Doreen went out to greet them and escorted them immediately to their own quarters.

The children were wide-eyed with excitement.

"I have ordered a light supper," Doreen said to the

sister in charge, "then I thought you would like to get them off to bed."

"We are very grateful," she answered. "We wish to put you to as little trouble as possible. Tomorrow, perhaps, we could work out some schedule by which we can relieve your staff of every possible labour."

In spite of the preparations that had been made there was still a lot to be seen to, and afterwards Sheila had to be put to bed. The evacuees had arrived very late and the dinner gong boomed through the house before Doreen had finished settling the child for the night.

"Aren't you going to change your dress?" Sheila asked. "I thought ladies always put on evening gowns with low backs and low fronts. Nanny says they are designed by the devil, and that's the way my mother used to dress, but when I asked Daddy, he said all decent people dressed for dinner and that was why he wasn't decent."

Doreen laughed.

"I haven't got time to change tonight," she said. "We have been working too hard, but one evening you shall see my only evening dress, and you will be very disappointed, I promise you!"

"But then you are only a governess, aren't you?" Sheila said. "That makes it different."

Doreen tried to laugh but she was conscious of a chill as she kissed Sheila and went downstairs.

"Only a governess!" So that was what she had come to now. It was ridiculous to mind the chance words of a child of ten, who had been brought up by a prejudiced and snobbish nurse.

At the same time, it defined her position and took away the inner glow of satisfaction which had been radiating from her ever since she had taken charge of the Castle first thing that morning.

She was tired and her muscles were aching from moving furniture and making beds, but she had enjoyed what had been an unusual experience.

She had been interested in interviewing the good-natured, willing country girls whom Walter in some mysterious manner of his own, had managed to get up to the Castle within a few hours.

She had liked planning the simple but nourishing menus, both for the dining-room and for the children and the nuns. It had given her a sense of power that she had not experienced for many years.

Now, like a bubble, her whole elation had been burst by Sheila's words, "you are only a governess!"

Walter was waiting in the hall.

"The master has just sent a message to say that dinner must be kept back for twenty minutes, miss," he said. "I was just coming up to tell you."

Doreen turned and hurried up the stairs again. Twenty minutes would give her time to have a bath and to change.

Her suitcase contained the simple black evening dress which she had worn aboard ship and the new head housemaid, who was apparently well up in her duties, had laid it out on the bed ready for her and drawn a bath in the adjoining bathroom.

It took Doreen fifteen minutes to bath, put on the dress and rearrange her hair.

She powdered her nose, then with a feeling of annoyance because of the words which still echoed in her mind, she opened her handbag and took out the pale lipstick that she had bought in Cairo.

She touched up her mouth and thought how even a little more colour made an extraordinary difference.

"Not that anyone will notice it," she told herself, "but it gives me confidence."

She peered at herself in the big carved mirror which hung over the dressing-table. There was no getting away from the fact that she was looking better; her hair which had been so limp and brittle after fever, had now regained its life and elasticity.

Her skin, too, was better than it had been for years and in spite of the lack of cosmetics, there was a faint flush in either cheek and her eyes were bright and clear.

She slipped downstairs just as she heard the sound of men's voices coming from the closed off wing of the

Castle. None of them had changed, but for the first time she saw Michael Gillespie without the white coat which always reminded her irresistibly of a chemist.

In grey flannel trousers and a well-cut tweed coat, she realised for the first time that he was good-looking. He was talking animatedly too, which dispersed, for the moment, his air of exhaustion and fatigue.

It was, however, only temporary and the moment he was silent or relaxed, she knew that he was desperately tired. He looked up in surprise at her approach.

"I hope you don't mind, Mr. Gillespie," she said hurriedly in explanation, "but I am staying here tonight. Nurse has been called away on family matters and I didn't like to leave Sheila alone."

"Of course, quite all right," he said and turning, introduced her to the two new-comers.

They went into dinner and although Michael Gillespie was silent and quiet, eating little and refusing any form of alcohol, the other two men were both amusing and interesting.

Unlike their host, they were obviously quite prepared to forget shop, out of working hours, and to enjoy feminine companionship, however limited.

More than once when they were all laughing heartily at some witticism, Doreen glanced anxiously at Michael Gillespie to see how he was liking this new departure.

She knew from Walter that his dinner usually consisted of cold meat and a salad, carried on a tray to the library or, more often than not, into the laboratory itself.

When dinner was over they all went to the library for coffee. When she had finished hers, Doreen felt that it would be correct for her to withdraw.

It was only half-past nine and she supposed that as she had no schoolroom in which to sit, she would have to go to bed. But as she rose in her seat, one of the newcomers spoke.

"You aren't leaving us, Miss Marston?"

"I thought perhaps you might want to talk business,"

Doreen answered. "I know Mr. Gillespie usually works until all hours of night."

"Oh no, that is too much!" the other man answered. "All work and no play was never a good motto. Besides, one gets stale—don't you find that, Gillespie?"

"I have never thought about it," Michael Gillespie answered awkwardly. "But perhaps you are right. I don't remember when I last had more than four hours' sleep."

"You must be crazy!" one of the new-comers said. "That is the way to crock up and be of no use to anybody. We shall have to bully him, Miss Marston, and make the laboratory out of bounds, except at certain hours."

"I certainly think he has been doing too much," Doreen said gently, afraid that her employer might resent her expressing her opinion.

"Well, if we aren't going to work," Michael Gillespie said, "I shall change my mind and have a cigar."

He got up and took one from the big silver box which Walter had left beside the coffee tray.

"I'll tell you what we must do though," one of the guests said, "we must put that call through to London before it is too late and insist on those new supplies being sent down by the morning train. We shall be stuck if they aren't here by tomorrow evening."

"There's a telephone here," Michael Gillespie answered, "or would you rather speak in the morning-room, which is next door."

"I will go next door," he answered. "I have got one or two things to say to old Freddie, who I believe is on duty tonight. You had better come and speak to him too, Donald," he added to the other man. "We have got to give him a fairly coherent description of what we require, and that extremely good claret I drank at dinner is liable to make me forgetful."

The two men left the room and Doreen sitting quietly in a big armchair, wondered what Michael Gillespie was thinking.

He was lighting his cigar, using two or three matches

in the process, warming it, watching the glowing end with the intentness of a connoisseur.

His face was grave, but at the same time, she thought that the expression of irritation and tension was not so obvious as it had been on their previous encounters.

He looked up suddenly and saw her watching him.

"Are you wondering if I am upset at this violation of my sanctuary?" he asked.

It was the first time he had spoken to her as though she was a human being and not a mere cypher to whom he was giving instructions. She was surprised, too, at his perception.

"Yes," she answered, "that is exactly what I was wondering. Do you mind very much?"

"I think nothing is worse than anticipation," he replied. "I have been afraid of disturbance for so long that now it has come, it is immeasureably less horrifying than I had expected."

"I am glad," Doreen said simply.

"I suppose only a fool would dream that he could isolate himself completely from life and from humanity?" Michael Gillespie said.

"Most people are afraid of loneliness," Doreen answered.

"Well, we certainly aren't going to be lonely here," Michael Gillespie said sarcastically.

"I will tell you who is going to enjoy the change enormously," Doreen said with a smile, "and who, I believe, will ultimately benefit by it—that is Sheila."

"Good. I am glad to hear that."

Michael Gillespie's voice seemed to be more frigid again, or was it imagination. There was an awkward silence and Doreen got to her feet.

"It's been a long day," she said, "I think I will go to bed. Good night, Mr. Gillespie."

"Good night," he said curtly.

He walked across the room and opened the door for her. She didn't look at him as she passed, but she sensed that something had upset him.

Could it be her reference to Sheila? Could he have

read some inner meaning in her casual words—a desire for frivolity, perhaps?

It was ridiculous and it was difficult to understand. Those irritating words of Sheila's recurred in her mind:

"You are only a governess!"

TWENTY

When nurse wired to say that she could not return immediately as her mother was ill, Doreen found that she must stay on at the Castle for an indefinite period.

The fact of her being there simplified matters considerably, for there were innumerable things to see to and it was soon obvious that she could have no routine hours, but must be on duty from the moment she awoke in the morning until she went to bed at night.

The evacuated children settled down happily, but were responsible for innumerable breakages and for miscellaneous collection of requirements which Doreen found almost impossible to procure.

Sheila was easier to manage than she had anticipated. The child was so excited and so interested in the developments going on around her, that she had no time to think about herself, or to plan misdemeanours.

Doreen rapidly came to the conclusion that the whole reason for her naughtiness lay in the fact that she had been bored.

It was easy to understand as she grew more familiar with the child's character, how nurse had continually harped on the fact of her mother's frivolity and evildoings.

It was, indeed, difficult to find any trace of Michael Gillespie in his daughter. His desire for solitude, his affection for work and his extraordinary concentration, were all lacking in Sheila's make-up.

She was like quick-silver and, when it suited her, wilful to a degree, unless her attention was being continually absorbed by superficial entertainment.

Gradually Doreen began to build up a very clear idea of what Mrs. Gillespie had been like. She could imagine her as frivolous, pleasure-seeking and, above all, anxious for attention.

Sheila craved to be admired, to be continually the centre of interest. Nothing more unsuited to her nature could have been chosen than her upbringing for the past ten years.

Everyone at the Castle congratulated Doreen on her handling of her new charge, with the exception of Michael Gillespie himself.

Actually the credit was due, not so much to her tact and diplomacy, as to the circumstances in which, for the moment, they all found themselves.

Although she never professed to be a child lover, it would have been difficult for Doreen not to have liked Sheila, for the child took a tremendous fancy to her, following her about like a small dog, attentive and trusting, ready to do whatever she suggested.

Her very first effort at inciting her towards tidiness and cleanliness had been amazingly successful. But the pendulum had, of course, swung in the opposite direction and Sheila insisted on decking herself out, even in spite of Doreen's restraining influence, in hair ribbons, necklaces and any form of unsuitable ornamentation which was available.

But this, Doreen thought, was a fault on the right side, and although it might be unconventional teaching, it certainly succeeded in making Sheila wash her hands before meals, take care of her nails and brush both her hair and her teeth.

However, Doreen was yet to meet with unexpected opposition.

There had been an unusual amount to see to one morning and although she had managed to get in nearly an hour's reading and writing in the schoolroom, she had been forced before luncheon to leave Sheila to her own devices, while she interviewed the head housemaid, who had been having trouble with the laundry.

When the gong went for luncheon, Doreen ran down stairs, hoping that Sheila wouldn't have disappeared.

She met Michael Gillespie and the two other scientists in the hall, for since the new-comers had arrived at the Castle, there was no unpunctuality for meals—they insisted on leaving the laboratory as soon as the gong sounded.

They all walked in chatting to find Sheila already in the room. She was seated in her usual place, but she had chosen to decorate herself with a mass of flowers from the garden.

A wreath of carnations was perched on top of her dark head and round her neck was a garland of sweet peas. Bracelets of other flowers were tied round her wrists and bunches of pinks and violas were pinned on her cotton dress.

"What have you been doing, Sheila?" Doreen asked, beginning to laugh.

Sheila preened herself like a small peacock and replied:

"I am the flower fairy. I do look pretty, don't I?"

The two scientists assured her that she was the Queen of the Fairies herself and Doreen was passing the whole thing off as a joke, when suddenly she saw Michael Gillespie's face.

He was scowling, staring at the child with what was quite unmistakably real anger. Sheila was too excited, too pleased with herself to notice him, but as they sat down at the table he said to Doreen in a furious undertone:

"You have no right to allow this sort of thing. The child should be ashamed of herself."

Doreen was piqued. She felt he was unreasonable.

"I should have thought it was very harmless," she answered, speaking quickly, without choosing her words.

"That is for me to judge," he replied.

Their eyes met and in that moment Doreen was conscious that she was dealing with someone whose will power was strong and by no means dormant. But she felt defiant rather than afraid and answered back.

"I thought you had left her in my charge?"

Michael Gillespie looked at her steadily, then coolly, with what was obviously meant to be a direct rebuke to her personally, he turned to the child at the other side of the table.

"Go upstairs, Sheila," he said, "and take that rubbish off. You look ridiculous."

Sheila's smile and laughter faded. She stared at her father, at first with surprise, then with a flush of anger.

"I won't!" she said. "My flowers look beautiful—everyone thinks so but you, and you are an old kill-joy—we all know that."

"Do as you are told," Michael Gillespie said quietly.

"I won't," Sheila answered again, gripping the table. "I want my lunch and I am going to stay here."

Michael Gillespie got to his feet. To her horror Doreen realised that he was going to forcibly remove the child from the room.

She could imagine what a disturbance and scene it would cause, and she was also afraid for Sheila.

In spite of everything, the child was sensitive and Doreen knew, even without experience, that such a humiliation must leave a scar which it would take years to efface.

Hurriedly she got to her feet.

"Please leave this to me," she said with an air of command.

She walked round the table and put her arms round the child.

"Listen, Sheila," she whispered. "You and I will go and have our luncheon somewhere else. Your father doesn't like your flowers, but I do, so we will go away together and leave the men to themselves."

Sheilt was not to be smoothed so easily.

"I won't go, I won't," she said. "I don't care what he says. He's beastly and unkind."

She pushed Doreen's arms away.

"Leave me alone!" she screamed in sudden fury. "I want my lunch and I am going to have it here."

Doreen stood back, not knowing what to do, conscious that she had failed and conscious, also, that

Michael Gillespie was approaching the child, obviously determined to put her out of the room.

"Please don't," she said pleadingly to him.

He hesitated, but not before Sheila had also realised his intention. Clinging on to the table with both hands, she roared her defiance.

"I won't go," she said. "My mother ran away from you and I wish I could too. I wish I could go to her and never see you again. You are a beast and I hate you!"

There was a moment's utter silence when Sheila's voice ceased.

The effect on Michael Gillespie was frightening. His eyes blazed and for one horrified second, Doreen thought that he was going to strike the child.

Then abruptly, he turned on his heel and walked from the room, slamming the door behind him. An astounded and rather stupified company was left behind.

Sheila was still clinging to the arms of her chair; she started to cry. Her tears came slowly, at first the whimper of a frightened child, then gradually they became a passionate storm which there was no stemming.

Doreen put her arms about her.

"Hush, darling," she said. "It is all right. It is all over now."

Her words had no effect; it was doubtful if Sheila even heard them. She was sobbing as though her heart would break.

At last desperately, Doreen picked her up in her arms and carried her out of the room.

"Can you manage, miss?" Walter asked as he opened the door and she knew from the tone of his voice that he was deeply sympathetic.

"It is quite all right," Doreen replied. "See that the gentlemen have their luncheon."

She laid Sheila on her bed and fetched eau-de-Cologne for her forehead, but it was nearly half an hour before the child stopped crying.

Then she was utterly exhausted, her face swollen, her whole body trembling from the force of her emotion. Doreen covered her up with an eiderdown and lowered the blinds.

"Try and get some sleep, darling," she suggested. "I will go and get you a hot water-bottle. Your feet are cold and when you wake up we will have a lovely tea together."

She opened the door of the room and found on a table outside, a tray with some cold meat and fruit, obviously brought up by the thoughtful Walter.

"I don't feel like eating," Doreen thought.

But she realised that when Sheila was asleep she would have to eat a little, so as not to disappoint Walter's kindness.

She got her hot water-bottle and went down the passage towards the housekeeper's cupboard, where she could fill it. At the top of the stairs she walked straight into Michael Gillespie.

"I was just coming," he said, "to find out how Sheila is. I hear that neither of you have had any luncheon."

Doreen felt a sudden burning resentment that this should have happened. She had been working hard all the week; she was tired and, at the same time, not unnaturally elated both at her success in managing the Castle and in looking after the child.

She tried to control the hasty words of reply which rose to her lips. Then on the floor at their feet, she saw a carnation. It had obviously fallen from Sheila's wreath as she had carried her upstairs.

It was bruised and beginning to fade. Somehow the mere fact of it lying there made her angry, as she had never been angry before, with the man who had caused all this trouble and unnecessary suffering.

She drew herself up and looked him straight in the face.

"Sheila is quieter now," she said, "but I can imagine nothing more calculated to damage and injure a child than the scene we have just experienced in the dining-room."

"For which you blame me!" Michael Gillespie remarked with a twist of his lips, which was not a smile but something bitter and sneering.

"If you want the truth," Doreen replied, flinging all caution to the winds and forgetting she was speaking to her employer, "I think you were both unreasonable and cruel."

"That is your personal opinion," Michael Gillespie said. "But it does not mean you are correct in your supposition."

He spoke coolly, but Doreen was aware that he was as angry as she was.

"Any woman," she replied hotly, "seeing a child neglected, spoilt, then treated in a manner most calculated to make her feel a nervous wreck, would be entitled to speak her mind.

"You have left Sheila all these years to the mercy of that abominable old nurse, who neglects her in the most disgraceful manner and fills her mind with all sorts of rubbish, both about her mother and about you.

"Now because the child is a little exuberant, a little over-excited at being treated as a reasonable human being, you interfere unreasonably. To my mind you could not be more cruel to Sheila than if you had deprived her of food and nourishment. I think you must be crazy!"

"If that is your last word, Miss Marston," Michael Gillespie said icily, "I think this conversation had better end."

"I quite agree with you," Doreen retorted.

She walked away from him without another word, passing through the swing door which led to the housekeeper's cupboard and heard it shut behind her with a decisive sound which, in some ridiculous manner, relieved her feelings.

"I hate him," she said out loud.

Only when she had taken the hot bottle back to the child and picked up the tray of food to take it into her room, did she realise what she had done. That was obviously the end of her first job.

She could hardly expect to speak to her employer in such terms, then continue in his service.

"Well, I'm not sorry," she told herself defiantly. "He deserved it—every word that I have said is the truth. I don't care. I am glad to leave here."

That was untrue and she knew it. She pulled her suitcase from under the bed and started to pack, and while she did so her anger and defiance gradually vanished.

A wave of despondency swept over her.

"I am a fool," she told herself, "a stupid fool."

She knew now that she had been really happy this past week.

She had no time to think about herself, to worry about her own feelings, or about the danger she had incurred in passing herself off as Anne.

She knew that she was doing a good job of work and there was a definite satisfaction in the knowledge that she had to a great extent gained Sheila's confidence and that the child was happier, as well as better behaved.

She enjoyed too, and she admitted it, the company of the three men at dinner every night and the evenings when they sat round in the library talking and laughing.

She had found that she could be both an amusing and entertaining companion without relying in any way on sex.

It was like exploring some new country, for her to spend a considerable amount of time with men without continually being aware of her physical attractions. The scientists and Michael Gillespie treated her with courtesy and a respect which was precious because it was novel.

Now this brief interlude was ended. Her temper had betrayed her—a temper which she was certain Anne would never have displayed and which, she knew, she would have difficulty in explaining to her grandmother.

She was not far from tears when finally her suitcase was ready.

"I will go downstairs and telephone to the Manor," she thought. "If Edith can't come and fetch me, I had better order a taxi."

She peeped through the communicating door between her room and Sheila's. From the bed came the sound of gentle breathing and she knew the child was asleep.

"I had better get the second housemaid to sleep in my room tonight," she thought. "She is a nice girl and Sheila likes her. There is no reason why the child should suffer more than is necessary."

She walked down the stairs and into the library to the telephone. She was just dialing the number of the Manor when Michael Gillespie came into the room.

He was wearing his white coat, so that she knew he had come straight from the laboratory. He stopped on seeing her.

Quickly she replaced the receiver.

"I am sorry if you require this room," she said. "I will go to the morning-room. I was telephoning home to ask them to come and fetch me."

"Come and fetch you?" he repeated. "What do you mean by that?"

"That I am leaving," Doreen answered. "Actually I was going to leave a note for you."

"But why are you going?" he asked.

She stared at him and saw that there was genuine surprise in his face. For a moment she felt bewildered.

"I hardly expected that you would want me to stay after our conversation just now," she said.

Then with a flash of humour which came from nervousness, rather than a desire to be facetious, she added,

"I thought I had better resign before I was kicked out."

He shut the door behind him and came into the room.

"But you can't do that!" he said. "You can't leave me here alone to cope with everything."

Doreen felt the blood rush to her face in relief and in incredulous astonishment.

"I expect you could manage," she stammered.

"You know I couldn't," Michael Gillespie said. "Miss Marston, I apologise, I apologise in all sincerity for what occurred today. It was—well, I can't explain, some things are too difficult to speak of to anybody, but will you let me, in justification, tell you that I had a reason for my actions. But you mustn't go—that would make things impossible.

"If you will stay, I will give you my promise that nothing of this sort shall ever occur again."

It was all rather bewildering, this humility, this sudden complete change of front from a man, who a moment ago, she had been hating as an antagonist.

"If you are quite certain you want me . . ." Doreen answered.

She too spoke humbly, a little awed, and conscious quite unreasonably of a sudden sympathy for Michael Gillespie.

"I am quite, quite sure," he said solemnly, "that we could not manage without you."

A sudden gladness lightened Doreen's face.

"I am glad," she said childishly. "I will go and unpack."

She turned towards the door, but his next words arrested her.

"Do you like being here, then?" he asked.

In response her smile was radiant.

"I have only just discovered how much," she replied and left him alone.

TWENTY-ONE

To Doreen's surprise, she and Michael Gillespie were alone for dinner that night.

She had decided the menu with cook in the morning and had ordered for four as usual, but when she came downstairs a few moments before the dinner gong was rung, Walter informed her that the two scientists had been invited by a neighbour—General Morton—to meet a Ministry of Health official, who had arrived unexpectedly in the neighbourhood.

"The master was asked too," he added confidentially. "But, of course, he refused. I haven't known him to dine out for years."

Doreen felt a little apprehensive about a *tête-à-tête* dinner after the difficulties earlier in the day. She waited in the library where, because it was a cold evening, a fire had been lit.

She had brought downstairs with her some mending of Sheila's, which, as nurse was away, she felt was a part of her duty.

She was sewing when the door opened and Michael Gillespie came in.

He had changed into a dinner jacket for the first time since she had been at the Castle.

"I am sorry if I am late, Miss Marston," he said. "It is so long since I wore evening clothes, that I have almost forgotten how to dress."

"I am very flattered if you have troubled on my account," Doreen answered, making her tone as light as his, realising that he was trying to ease the situation.

"Perhaps I feared another lecture from you," he said.

There was a twinkle in his eyes which told her that under his grave exterior there still lurked in Michael Gillespie a sense of humour and perhaps a sense of the ridiculous.

She was saved from making a reply by Walter announcing that dinner was served and they walked in silence into the dining-room.

The meal was excellent and Michael Gillespie insisted on Doreen having some claret.

"It will do you good," he said. "You must be tired, and I am still feeling rather guilty about your luncheon."

"Walter saw that I didn't go hungry," she said with a smile.

"I am glad about that," he said solemnly.

She had the feeling—though she could not account for it—that something momentous was happening that evening.

Instinctively she guessed that this was the first time Michael Gillespie had entertained a woman alone for many years.

She felt that he was trying to be at his best, perhaps to make amends for the scene earlier in the day, or perhaps because he genuinely wished to prove himself not so bad as she had inferred.

Dinner over, they went back to the library for their coffee and as Walter took away the silver tray and closed the door behind them, Doreen wondered whether

her grandmother's broad-minded approval of her taking up her new position at the Castle, would include dining alone with the owner of it.

She picked up her sewing, bent her head over the work and even as she did so, was silently amused at herself. She was well aware how demure she must look in her black dress with its white collar, her neat hair and lowered eyes.

"Really womanly!" she thought.

Then as if in telepathy, Michael Gillespie's next words told her that he was thinking the same thing.

"I thought none of your sex sewed these days," he said. "I have always been told that manufactured goods are far better and far more efficient than anything made at home."

"I'm not making, I'm mending," Doreen corrected.

"At any rate you are sewing," he answered. "I don't believe I have seen a woman do that since my mother died. She used to embroider exquisitely, and one seldom saw her without some kind of needlework in her hands."

"I am afraid my knowledge of sewing comes more from necessity than from inclination," Doreen said.

Michael Gillespie got up, took a cigar and stood with his back to the fire as he lit it.

"You are a surprising person, Anne Marston," he said, using her Christian name for the first time.

"Am I? Why?" Doreen answered.

"I have always had a hatred of the capable, efficient type of woman who runs missions and who is prepared to brave darkest Africa to convert the happy heathen into miserable Christians.

"The ones I have met were, perhaps, not representative for they were narrow-minded and unspeakably unattractive."

Doreen thought of the mission colony in Cairo and laughed.

"I know exactly the type you mean," she said.

"Then you mustn't blame my assumption that you would be of the same calibre," he said.

"Did you think that?" she asked.

"That first morning you came to interview me here,"

he answered, "I was very agreeably surprised. Since then my astonishment has increased daily."

"In spite of my plain speaking?" Doreen said gently.

"Perhaps because of it," he said. "You were right and I was wrong. I am not such a fool as to deny that."

She looked up at him.

"No one could make a more handsome apology," she said. "Thank you."

"And your opinion of me still stands, I suppose?" he questioned.

Doreen looked away from him into the fire, faintly embarrassed.

"Does it matter very much what I think?" she asked.

"Yes, it does," he replied. "After all, you are in control of my household and you are living here."

"Only temporarily," Doreen corrected.

"But why?" he asked. "Why should you ever go?"

"For one thing," Doreen replied, "nurse will be returning and as long as you employ her, Sheila must be in her charge, except at lesson times. Secondly . . ." she hesitated, she had been going to say "my grandmother needs me," but she knew it was quite untrue.

"Well, secondly?" Michael Gillespie prompted.

Then as she did not go on, he added,

"I don't believe there is a secondly. As for nurse, do you consider her indispensable?"

"On the contrary," Doreen answered. "I think she is a bad influence on Sheila, and although I hate to be the means of anyone losing a job, I definitely think the child is too old to need a nurse."

"I have thought that for a long time," Michael Gillespie said. "I have kept her because the governesses would not stay and because when Sheila was a baby, nurse was both good with the child and loyal to me."

"It would be difficult to get rid of her then," Doreen said.

"I don't think so," Michael Gillespie replied. "I will get Johnstone . . ." he corrected himself ". . . your uncle, to write her a nice letter offering a pension of two pounds a week and send her fifty pounds as a parting present."

"That is certainly generous," Doreen said.

"I can afford to be," he answered shortly.

Doreen laughed.

"That is an admission people seldom make. It has been my experience that even the richest are always complaining of their poverty, no one ever has enough."

"Do you want money?" Michael Gillespie asked sharply.

"Of course," Doreen answered. "Who doesn't?"

"I for one," he answered. "I believe it to be an insidious poison which ruins not only every unlucky individual that possesses it, but also the reason why civilisation does not progress further.

"There are wars, crimes, unemployment, or general lack of decency, and the incentive to all of them is the desire for money—the greed for gold."

"It is a nice theory," Doreen said, "but perhaps you have never been poor; perhaps you have never wondered where your next meal is coming from; never been prepared to sink to almost any level to ensure that one is not left destitute and hungry."

"No, I have never known that," he said, "but I have known worse. I have known a misery which has crippled my whole outlook on life. I have endured what has been a hell on earth, simply because I have been blessed by too many of this world's goods."

Doreen answered him frivolously.

"Well, I wouldn't mind trying it for a change—the life of 'a poor little rich girl' would be very welcome, I assure you."

"That is what Sheila will be," Michael Gillespie said. "At the moment she has lived through ten years of it. Do you think she is happy?"

"That is hardly her fault!"

"Meaning that it is mine?" he asked.

Doreen bent her head and took several stitches before she answered.

"Must we start this again?"

"I think we must," Michael Gillespie answered grimly. "You are a disturbing element in this house.

Never before have I been challenged; never before have I had to account for my actions."

"And never before," Doreen added, "has one of your servants been so rude to you."

"Yet I asked you to stay!" Michael Gillespie said.

"I am still wondering why you did," Doreen answered. "My box was packed, I fully expected to go."

He walked away from the fire and sat down in the arm-chair opposite her.

"I am going to do a thing," he said, "which I never in my wildest moments expected to do. I am going to confide in you. I don't know quite why I should, except perhaps in the few days you have been here, you have proved yourself so valuable, both to the house and to Sheila, that I daren't risk losing you. And if you are essential to my well-being, I would like you to understand my point of view."

Doreen put down her sewing and let her hands lie idly in her lap. She looked at Michael Gillespie and realised that she had been right: something tremendous was happening this evening.

There was an expression of resolve and determination on his face, and his chin was set as though he faced tremendous odds. She knew she was waiting for the barriers of his reserve to fall, barriers which had been built up for many years.

Swiftly the thought came to her—Michael Gillespie had not always been like this!

He had not always been serious, solemn and grave, but had been as other men, ready to enjoy life, to accept light-heartedly all the good things it could offer him. What had happened, she wondered?

What tragedy had left him crippled in spirit, a man who seemed always to be experiencing pain.

She waited in silence, until with a sudden movement, Michael threw his half smoked cigar into the fire.

"I was angry at luncheon today," he began, "because when I came into the room I saw, not Sheila the child of ten, but her mother, the woman who was my wife, sitting there.

"I am not being disloyal only truthful when I say that

Sheila's mother was not a wicked woman, but a very stupid one, who was easily influenced by bad company.

"Actually she had only one failing, one weakness, but it smashed our marriage completely and ruined my life.

"That weakness was vanity! It sounds almost farcical, doesn't it, to make so much of what is, I suppose, an indivisible part of every woman, but my wife's vanity drove her to such lengths that it is almost impossible now to describe to you what a horror I have of over-ornamentation, and the shock of seeing in Sheila an echo of her mother, after I had begun to realise fully the type of person I had married.

"I was twenty-nine at the time of my marriage. I was very ambitious and doing exceedingly well as a surgeon. I had already begun to build up a certain reputation for people talked about me as a 'coming man'.

"I had been so busy getting into that position that I had little time for sociabilities, and when I fell in love with Elsie, I suppose it hit me harder than it would most men of my age.

"She was very lovely and when I first met her, she had quite recently gone on the stage. But she had none of the usual background of an actress's life.

"Her father was a conventional country J.P., her mother was an exceedingly attractive woman, who was connected with several well-known families and who, I gathered, disapproved most strongly of her daughter's desire to be in the limelight.

"However, after several years of argument, Elsie got her own way and through friends, was tried out in a very small part in a West End production.

"I was called in to operate on her for an acute appendicitis and immediately she was convalescent I spent every available moment that I could, taking her about and continually beseeching her to marry me.

"I suppose I must have been very young in some ways, or perhaps merely foolishly innocent. It honestly never crossed my mind that there were other men in Elsie's life.

"The man who had got her the job on the stage seemed to me an effeminate sort of chap, and I couldn't imagine any woman as lovely as Elsie, bothering about him for one second.

"Most of her other male acquaintances appeared to be the usual nondescript idle crowd of wasters that one meets at cocktail parties or finds propping up the latest and most fashionable bar of the moment.

"I admit I never gave them a serious thought. I believed with supreme egotism that I would make Elsie love me and I was prepared to spend my whole life doing what I could to make her happy.

"It was shortly after we met that my uncle, Colin Gillespie, who owned this Castle, became dangerously ill. He was informed by his doctors that he had only a few months to live and he sent for me.

"He told me that I was his heir, that the Castle and everything he possessed would be mine at his death.

"I was glad, of course, in some ways, but I was too anxious to make a success of my career, to think of giving up my work at the hospital, or my rooms in Harley Street, and retiring to the country.

"Looking back, I suppose from that moment Elsie's attitude towards me was less elusive and more possessive, but still she could not make up her mind to marry me.

"I wanted her so badly that I was quite prepared to be patient, to let her come to me in her own way, believing optimistically that sooner or later, such a love as mine must get its reward.

"I couldn't see as much of her as I wished because of my work, and I think, once or twice, it did cross my mind that when we did go out together, it was a nuisance to have to be continually sitting in restaurants, and to go from night club to night club, where we were as often as not joined by a crowd of Elsie's innumerable friends.

"I had been brought up in far too hard a school to realise that I had any personal importance apart from my capabilities.

"I did not realise that Elsie continually boasted about the brilliant young surgeon who was so much in love with her, or that behind my back she referred to me as 'my millionaire doctor'.

"If I had known, I doubt whether it would have made any difference.

"At that time I should have thought it amusing or quaint and wouldn't, for a moment, have understood that everything and everyone with whom Elsie came in contact, must, in some way, flatter herself.

"She was lovely—I have already told you that. She certainly lavished every attention on her looks.

"I believe that occasionally my patience was strained to its utmost when we were dining out and she would disappear to the cloak-room for nearly half an hour, merely to titivate her hair, or improve her make-up.

"I was to learn, when we were married, what an important business such a proceeding was and to discover too, that it took my wife nearly two hours to dress, either in the morning, or before going out to dinner.

"Finally I married her. I shall never forget the happiness and elation that I experienced when she told me she had definitely made up her mind and that she wished the ceremony to take place as quietly as possible at a registry office.

"I thought that here, at last, was genuine proof of Elsie's love for me. I had quite expected that I must suffer the ordeal of a huge wedding at St. Margaret's, Westminster, or St. George's, Hanover Square, that there would be bridesmaids, ushers, speeches and a big reception.

"But Elsie apparently wanted none of these things; she only wanted to be united to me, quickly and quietly, with no other witnesses save her father and mother.

"I was too happy even to speak when she first told me.

"I planned the wedding as she had suggested, but at the last moment the registry office was packed with her friends.

"They hurried us off afterwards to an impromptu, but very noisy, reception in a private room at the Savoy. The Press, too, turned up in force.

"There was a battery of cameras and every newspaper next morning carried photographs captioned

"BEAUTIFUL SOCIETY ACTRESS WEDS WEALTHY SURGEON".

"When I asked Elsie how the secret had leaked out, she laughed.

" 'I didn't see why I should miss all the fun,' she said and her words even then struck me as strange.

"I had imagined that the quiet little wedding we had planned together was her ideal, as well as mine.

"All the reverence, all the sacredness, that I had expected from our wedding day was drowned in cocktails, in the chatter and laughter of people I hardly knew, but who treated me with a familiarity which, somehow, I greatly resented.

"We went to Paris for our honeymoon, but here again we were not alone.

"There were parties in which we were always surrounded by friends; we drove to the races in different cars; we lunched at opposite ends of tables; we went to bed so tired that Elsie barely had the energy to wish me good night.

"It was then, very gradually, I began to see that such an existence was the breath of life to my wife.

"Without it she could bear neither herself nor me. She had to have the unceasing admiration, an adulation of other people. It was, as I have said, vanity, but vanity distorted until it was almost madness.

"It was during our honeymoon that I learnt for the first time that she wished, on her return, to take up residence at the Castle and to have a smart service flat in London.

"I explained to her very patiently that it was quite impossible. She would not listen. We had scene after scene; finally I knew that I either had to lose my wife or my career.

"I was fool enough to love a woman more than what, to every doctor should be not a job of work, but a calling as sacred as that undertaken by a priest. I gave in.

"I threw up my practice and we came home to the Castle in state.

"Only one thing I reserved for myself—the right to continue in a research which had already been interesting me for several years, but over which until then I had been unable to spend much time. Elsie agreed to that.

" 'It will give you a nice hobby, dear,' she said. I winced, but I did not contradict her.

"The next month was spent in getting things straight in the Castle, rearranging the rooms and furniture and also in choosing a flat in London and decorating it.

"I proceeded to build the laboratory, determined that somehow or other I should be able to convince Elsie that I must eventually work continuously and seriously.

"After the first flurry of getting in was over, I began to find that I had more time on my hands than I had anticipated.

"My wife was busy with her old crowd of friends, surrounded by men who flattered and toadied to her, by women who all seemed to me so alike with their painted faces, high-pitched voices, that I never knew them apart.

"After three months Elsie told me that we were going to have a child. I was delighted, so delighted that it took me some time to realise that Elsie did not echo either my pleasure, or my excitement.

"I put it down to her condition, and I tried as the months went on, to account for her constant irritability and impatience with the same excuse.

"It seemed to me that she had taken a dislike to me personally. She hated me to touch her, and while she was gay, amusing and the life and soul of any party, the moment we were alone she became sullen and morose.

"Only one thing seemed to matter: that I should tell her on every possible occasion how lovely she was and how her looks were quite unimpaired by the process of child-bearing.

" 'You are a doctor,' she kept saying to me, 'surely you can do something to stop me losing my figure?'

"I thought, at first, her fears were natural, then I began to realise in a kind of horror, that she herself loathed with a bitter loathing, the idea of being a mother.

"I suppose I was old-fashioned. My own family life had been a particularly happy one.

"My mother had meant a lot to me and I had never

believed that a woman could actively dislike children and everything to do with them.

"Even in my medical career I had never come up against anyone quite so self-centred as my own wife.

"In some ways it seemed to be understandable that she should mind more than some women, because at four months it was definitely obvious that she was pregnant and several of the doctors with whom I discussed the matter, thought she might prove to be abnormal.

"At six months Sheila was born, a normal healthy child, weighing over eight pounds. Then for the first time I understood.

"My eyes were opened and I realised what perhaps a more astute man would have gathered long before—that Sheila was not my child."

TWENTY-TWO

Michael Gillespie had never, even in his wildest dreams, intended to confide in anyone what his life with Elsie had meant to him.

The final revelation of how unimportant he had been to her and how she had tricked him into being the father of her child, and had shattered every ideal and illusion that he had ever had, was his secret burden.

But he had felt compelled by some instinct stronger than his own reserve, to make some sort of explanation to the girl who was so ably managing his household and for whom he had a grudging respect.

However, when he had seen her sitting in the firelight with her sewing in her hand, looking with her Madonna-like head and demure clothes, so unlike his distorted imagination of all women, he found the first break in a silence of nearly ten years.

It released his tongue so that he could not stop, but must go on, pouring out all that had been cooped up within himself since the very night of Sheila's birth.

It all came back to him so vividly as he spoke.

He had rushed away from the expensive nursing home where, after seeing the baby, he had had one brief glimpse of his wife, pale and exhausted lying against lace pillows and surrounded by flowers.

And he had gone out into the night on foot to continue walking until dawn.

He had no idea where he went; afterwards he had only vague memories of crowded busy thoroughfares, of streets in which he was the only passer-by, of dark sinister alleyways when his footsteps seemed startlingly loud.

More than once during his roamings women spoke to him. He gave them money, feeling a sympathy and understanding for their needs which forced prostitution upon them.

But of his wife—what could he think? He was bewildered and stricken by something which was deeper than anger and beyond misery.

As a doctor he knew from his brief first glance at the child that he could not be mistaken or deceived.

Then as he walked he realised a hundred small incidents, a thousand clues which might have given him some inkling of what was happening.

But he had been blind, blind in his love for Elsie, obsessed by her beauty, enchained by the attraction that she had for him, even in her most indifferent moments.

When dawn came he walked slowly back to the luxurious flat which was redolent of her personality, and in which he had never felt at home or at ease.

When he got there, he realised he could not face the white and gold drawing-room, the dining-room with its panelled walls and damask hangings, or the bedroom done up in peach-pink with shaded lights and fragrant with exotic sensuous perfume which was characteristic of Elsie herself.

It was so early that none of the servants were awake.

He went to his dressing-room quietly. He packed a

suitcase and left London. He sent no word to the nursing home, or to his wife.

He went back to the Castle and for a week stayed there alone, among the shattered ruins of what he had once believed was to be the fine edifice of his life.

He saw how utterly foolish he had been to give up his career, to sacrifice for any woman, however beautiful, those long years of apprenticeship and those first exhausting efforts, which had gradually given him standing in the medical profession.

Could he go back?

Already he sensed some overwhelming change within himself, which must exclude such a possibility.

He went into his laboratory and he worked as he had never worked before. It was then that the accident happened.

Perhaps it was carelessness; perhaps he took a greater risk than he might have done had he been clear-minded and level-headed.

He was never quite certain what did happen, for the first thing he knew about it was when he found himself in bed with nurses and doctors in attendance and learnt that the fingers of his right hand were damaged for ever.

It was less of a shock to know that he would always limp slightly and that all active exercise must be debarred from him.

He could have borne that more easily than the knowledge that, whether he wished it or not, he could never practice again as a surgeon, that he must find even his work in the laboratory restricted.

Gradually he was nursed back to health and strength, but some vital part of himself seemed missing.

He grew old in a few weeks; he grew bitter and resentful.

It was impossible, of course, for him to see Elsie, for she was still in the nursing home, still unaware of what her husband had discovered, or of the change that his feelings had undergone.

She wrote him brief, frivolous little letters, harmless in themselves, save that for the first time Michael reading them in criticism, rather than in love and affection.

He saw at last how selfish, how egotistical and how incurably vain she was. There was hardly one line of reference to her baby.

Every word was about herself and her fear of not regaining her figure.

She told him how she was exercising, how masseurs, beauty specialists and health experts were continually in attendance, and where before he would have laughed and thought it slightly childish, this now increased in him to what was paramount to a deep hatred.

At last after six weeks in London she came back to the Castle.

She travelled down with two nurses in attendance and she came into the house looking more incredibly lovely than he had ever seen her.

She was pale and slightly exhausted by the journey, but when she entered Michael's bedroom, where he lay with his bandaged hand and his feet in an iron cage, her first words were characteristic:

"How do you think I look, darling?" she asked.

He answered her in monosyllables, but it is doubtful if she even noticed that his manner was in any way strange towards her. She was so preoccupied by all that she was going to do now she was well again.

The child was handed over to a nurse and bundled away into the nurseries at the top of the house.

The servants may have noticed that Michael never asked to see it, but as far as Elsie was concerned, she seldom saw the baby herself and it would have surprised her had anyone taken a genuine interest in it.

After two or three weeks at the Castle during which time the place was filled with friends and with the more youthful and gay neighbours from the countryside, Elsie went back to London.

Michael's convalescence was slow, but when at last the doctors pronounced him as well as they could make him and his nurses packed their boxes preparatory to leaving, he too went to London in search of his wife.

He had not announced his arrival, but went straight to the flat, arriving one evening about cocktail time.

He let himself in with his key and he found her alone

in the drawing-room with a man he had never seen before, but who was quite obviously on familiar terms with his wife.

They were sitting very close together on the sofa and his arm was round her shoulders. Elsie was neither startled nor embarrassed by her husband's sudden entrance.

"What a surprise, Michael!" she said brightly.

Then slowly, very slowly and deliberately, as though she had no intention of disturbing herself unduly, she rose to her feet.

She was looking particularly beautiful in a soft transparent rest gown of pale pink chiffon, but to Michael at that moment, she appeared as something so obscene and so horrible, that he could hardly control himself as he looked at her.

It relieved his feelings to turn to the young man on the sofa and say to him curtly two words:

"Get out!"

"Michael! What do you mean?" Elsie exclaimed.

He ignored her and staring down at the apprehensive frightened expression on the man's face, he added:

"Do you hear me? Get out and quickly!"

"You can't behave like this," Elsie cried. "You must be mad, or drunk! What is the matter with you, Michael? This is Jack Tilney—*the* Jack Tilney."

"I have never heard of him and I don't want to," Michael said. "Well, sir? are you going, or do I have to throw you out?"

The man murmured something incoherent and getting hastily to his feet, edged towards the door.

"But you can't! This is impossible—I don't understand," Elsie cried. "Jack, stay, I'll explain, I'll make him apologize."

She ran after the man, putting beseeching hands on his arm.

Michael stood watching the scene, his hands deep in his pockets. Something cruel, sardonic and very foreign to his nature, made him almost enjoy his wife's discomfiture and the young man's fear.

Mr. Tilney left and left quickly. Then Michael was

face to face with the infuriated virago who was his wife.

"How dare you behave like this! What does it mean? Have you taken leave of your senses?"

"If you will be quiet," Michael said in icy tones, "there shall be an explanation, but it will be for you to make it."

"What do you mean?"

"There are many things for us to discuss together, my dear Elsie," Michael said, "and as it will take some time, I suggest that you sit down and take things calmly."

Something in his tone frightened her. Instinctively she sensed danger, her anger disappeared, she went very close to him, and looked up into his face with an appealing gesture.

"What is the matter, Michael?" she asked. "Why are you so cruel to me?"

Two months previously he would have taken her instantly into his arms.

One pleading look from her large eyes would have made him hesitate, the touch of her hand on his arm would have undoubtedly altered his resolution.

Now it was too late.

Her body meant no more to him than if she had been hunch-backed and hideous, and because of the immunity he felt, it amused him to look down at her for a long minute, to let her gradually and incredulously understand his indifference.

"Michael!" she said again.

Her voice was low and her warm red mouth was not far from his.

"I am afraid it is too late for that sort of thing, Elsie," he answered.

His tone was abrupt and crudely it jerked her to reality like the lash of a whip.

"What is the matter?" she again asked.

This time there was a tremulous anxiety in her voice.

"Whose child is it?"

She must have felt completely safe; she could never for a moment have anticipated that he might guess the truth, for at his question she went very white and there was no doubting that the shock of his words were almost overwhelming.

She could only stare at him in silence.

"Well, I am waiting," he said.

He saw then that she was struggling in a kind of paralysed agony to force her brain to concoct some explanation, some story which would convince him. Reading her thoughts, he laughed brutally.

"Lies won't help you," he added. "I want to know the truth."

She told him then, told him brokenly and at the same time with those terrible little touches of egotism which showed up so vividly the shallowness of her nature.

It had been some young man she had met for a very short space of time—a penniless young lord whose one claim to fame was that he had won some motor-racing trophies, and managed to have his name incessantly in the society papers.

Elsie had liked being seen about with him, had encouraged his attentions, while she had, at the same time, been encouraging Michael.

Both men had flattered her; their position had been a sop to her vanity, one had merely demanded more than the other.

When she had finished telling him exactly what had happened, Elsie looked up at her husband.

"I am sorry, Michael," she said.

"You will be," he answered.

"Why? What are you going to do?" she whispered.

"I am going to divorce you," he said. "You and your child will leave my house as soon as possible."

It took her some moments to understand him but when the full realisation of what it would mean dawned upon her, she was like a creature demented.

She saw that at one blow Michael could destroy all that she felt was worth having; her social career, reputation and money would be gone and she would be hampered also by a child she did not want and did not care for.

"You can't do this to me, you can't!" she screamed.

Then when she saw he meant it, her pleading turned to fury. Losing all control of herself, she tried to hurt him in every way possible.

He had believed that he had already savoured the very depths of unhappiness and disillusionment, but there was more to come.

He was to learn of Elsie's many lovers; the fact that she had never cared for him in the slightest, but had married him because he had money and because there was no one better available at that particular moment, to save her from the predicament she was in.

He was told of infidelities which had occurred the moment they returned from their honeymoon.

She screamed at him and laughed at him for a gullible fool, while in the next breath she begged him to take no action against her, but to let her continue as his wife.

Finally, when they were both exhausted, he left the house and went to sleep at his Club.

In the morning before he went round to see his solicitors, he rang up the flat, intending to relent his severity far enough to allow Elsie to stay on until the end of their lease and to make arrangements for her to have the child there.

He was told by her maid that she could not speak to him then, but it was of vital importance that he should call for a letter which would be waiting for him, any time after twelve o'clock.

Wondering a little at this, he nevertheless went round as he was asked. He found that Elsie had already gone and that the place was stripped of all her personal possessions.

The letter explained everything.

"I am going to America with Jack Tilney," she wrote. *"Although you may not have heard of him, most civilised people who attend the cinema have. He is in the middle of getting a divorce and as soon as he is free, I shall marry him. In the meantime, he has promised me a brilliant career on the films. If you want to divorce me you can do so, citing who you please, it won't matter in America, they think nothing of such things over there.*

"As for the child, I leave her in your care unconditionally. I understand that legally she bears your name and if you don't like that, you must just put up with it. It will be no use sending her after me because I shall merely send her back again. Good-bye, Michael, you were always far too serious to be a really amusing companion. Yours, Elsie."

There was nothing to be done. Michael knew that as usual Elsie, thinking only of herself, had managed to make the best of a bad bargain.

He discovered that Jack Tilney was, in fact, a well known film actor, whose salary in dollars ran into fabulous figures.

He was also quite prepared to believe that if Elsie had made up her mind for a career on the screen, she would doubtless get it, one way or another.

He decided, therefore, to start divorce proceedings, citing Jack Tilney. His position as regards the child was put to him very plainly by the solicitors.

"I am afraid, Mr. Gillespie, that legally she is your daughter and must be accepted as such. No question of her illegitimacy can be raised in the Courts. She was born in wedlock. If you divorce your wife you will be given full custody of the child and I should think, in a case like this, your wife would only get discretionary access."

Grimly Michael realised that there was nothing to be done.

He had got to accept the child and bring her up as his own. He thought bitterly that she would be his heir, would inherit all the vast fortune that Colin Gillespie had left him.

In a frustrated bitterness he vowed there and then that women should play no further part in his life, not even in his household.

When he got back to the Castle he dismissed every servant in the place who was of the female sex, with the exception of Sheila's nurse. He cut himself off from every Club, Association or social community to which he belonged.

He infuriated the county by refusing to give a subscription towards the hunt and by announcing that he was wiring his estate, so that it could not be ridden over.

He could have thought out no better way to antagonise his neighbours.

Thus began his life of a hermit and gradually he became absorbed in his work of research to the exclusion of all else. It was lucky, perhaps, that he had this tremendous interest, for otherwise his mind might easily have become deranged.

He was not really immune to people's feelings; he had not the temperament for living entirely on his own, without companionship, but having chosen his course, he would not turn aside from it.

He forced himself to go on, to forget his money, his position and his pseudo-paternity, while he worked for seventeen or eighteen hours a day in his laboratory.

As Sheila grew older he began to see the child occasionally. When she got to the stage of coming down to meals with the governess, she was forced to his notice.

He could not look at her without seeing again many characteristics of her mother.

She was not to know, poor child, that the disagreeableness and what was often paramount to unkindness from the man she called "Father", came because her eyes reminded him of his youth, which he believed had gone for ever, and of the day when he had known happiness before he had been disillusioned.

Of Elsie he heard nothing for many years. Then when Sheila was about seven, he was informed by his solicitors that she had been killed in an aeroplane crash whilst flying from New York to Palm Beach.

Several other passengers from the same plane had been saved, but Elsie had died from burns.

Michael had expected the news to mean nothing to him. But as he finished reading the letter, he realised that he had a sense of loss, and also a sense of pain.

Whatever Elsie had done, however she had behaved, she had meant something so tremendous in his life, that even after seven years it was impossible for the wound to have completely healed.

He had been maimed by his association with her, as surely as he had been maimed by the explosion which had caused the loss of his fingers.

Love such as he had felt for Elsie could not be rooted up and thrown away because logically it was the right thing to do.

He mourned his wife in death, but it neither softened his heart, nor made him feel more kindly towards the outside world. If anything, it hardened his resolution to carry on in solitude, to isolate himself still more completely from his fellow creatures.

He had succeeded admirably until some weakness which he had not hitherto suspected made him talk to the new governess—to a girl whose puritanical appearance was in utter contrast to the woman of whom he spoke.

He heard his voice running on and he hated himself for his lack of control and her for prompting it.

There came an agonised silence between them after he had told her that Sheila was not his child. He heard Doreen's exclamation of surprise.

Then abruptly he got to his feet.

"There is no point in my telling you this," he said angrily.

Doreen looked up at him and instinctly felt the change in his mood, knew the sudden reaction he was experiencing. She was about to speak, about to try and find adequate words with which to convey her sympathy and to disperse, if she could, his resentment.

Then she saw the look on his face and recoiled from it.

"He hates me," she thought. "He hates me because I have gained his confidence."

At that moment the telephone rang.

TWENTY-THREE

Michael picked up the receiver.

"Hullo—yes, yes, hold on." He turned to Doreen. "It is for you," he said.

"For me?" Doreen echoed in surprise. "At this time of night—what can have happened at the Manor?"

Michael did not answer her. He handed her the receiver with a strange look in his eyes which for the moment she could not interpret.

"Good night, Miss Marston," he said abruptly.

"Are you going?" she asked.

There was a note of dismay in her voice. This seemed an unexpected ending to the evening they had spent together.

"Yes," he replied. "I think I have talked quite enough for one evening. Good night."

She watched him walk towards the door at the far end of the room, then half afraid he would turn and see her, she spoke into the telephone.

"Hullo—Anne Marston speaking. Who is it?"

"I will give you three guesses," a cheery voice said.

Before she could remember to be formal, she had recognised the voice.

"John!"

"Exactly, John! Are you surprised to hear a voice from the past?"

"How did you know I was here?"

"You may well ask. I ought to have been a member of the C.I.D.! I have rung you up at the address you gave me for the last three evenings and each time the same doddering old servant informed me that you were out.

"It was only tonight when I got on to a more or less intelligent human being, who I gather was your uncle, that I found out that you were staying away. What has happened? Have they turned you out, or have you made influential friends in the neighbourhood?"

Doreen laughed.

"Oh, influential friends. I am glad you were impressed by my new address. Did my uncle tell you why I was here?"

"No, he merely said that you were staying at Barnleigh Castle and that doubtless you would be available if I telephoned you. Well, spill the beans, or is the information to be censored?"

"No, you can hear the whole truth. I have become a governess."

"Good Lord!"

There was surprise and consternation in John's voice.

She laughed.

"I thought you would be surprised. I am myself."

"Well, look here," he said seriously. "Governess or no governess, I have got to see you. I am coming down tomorrow and you must take your afternoon off."

"But I can't," Doreen expostulated. "I am far too busy. I am looking after the house and forty evacuated children as well."

"Aren't you important!" he mocked. "Nevertheless, I insist on seeing you, so you might as well make up your mind to it right away. I shall motor down, leaving London first thing in the morning, so I ought to be with you about lunch time. Be waiting for me on the doorstep and we will go and eat at the local inn, if there is one."

"But of course I can't do that," Doreen protested. "Honestly, John, it is very nice of you, but I must refuse with thanks. I have got far too much to do, so much in fact, that it would be just a waste of your time coming all that way, especially to see me."

"Now listen," he said, "and get this into your head right away. I am going to see you, if I have to fight my way into the Castle. So it will save a lot of trouble if you give me a time that suits you and I will be there."

"What do you want to see me about?" she asked.

"That's better!" he said. "You are taking a bit of interest in me."

Doreen had an uncomfortable feeling that in spite of Michael Gillespie's firm good night, he might have waited for yet another word with her. It was impossible for her to go on talking to John Dale in this way.

"Listen," she said desperately, "if you really mean that it is important, I will come out with you for an hour or so tomorrow afternoon, I cannot promise more."

"All right," he said. "I will be content with the crumbs which fall from the Castle table. But you promise not to fail me."

"Of course I won't."

"Well, what time shall I get to you?"

"About half-past two. I will be ready then, but I really must be back in time for tea."

"Well, I warn you," he said, "that I shall try and persuade you otherwise, but we will wait and see."

"You are quite certain it is really worth coming?" Doreen questioned.

"Quite!" he replied. "Sleep well, my dear, and be a little curious as to why I want to see you."

"I am."

"Good-bye then, until tomorrow."

"Good-bye."

Doreen put down the receiver and stood staring at it reflectively. She felt half excited, half apprehensive. What did this mean, she asked herself?

Why should John want to see her so urgently? Why should he take the trouble to motor all the way from London, just for an hour's conversation?

She was well aware that he meant what he had said. He would, if needs be, have forced himself into the Castle, rather than accept her refusal to see him.

She had always known there was an obstinacy and determination about him, in spite of other weaknesses.

In a way, it was rather attractive to be bullied when for the past weeks she had been giving orders and had been the driving force for so many people.

Swiftly she began making plans for tomorrow. She would arrange for Sheila to ride and if she could get the child off soon after luncheon, that would leave her free until tea-time.

She picked up her sewing from the chair and walked towards the door. Outside the hall was empty.

She supposed that Michael Gillespie had gone to his laboratory. From his point of view it was still early and he would doubtless work far into the night.

She turned out the light in the library and shut the door.

As she did so, she became conscious of a cold wind blowing through the hall and realised that it came from the front door. Someone had left it open.

Her supposition was not correct: Michael Gillespie had not gone to the laboratory; he had gone for a walk.

She hesitated for a moment, as though she would go to the door and look for him.

Then feeling that after his last words he might consider it an impertinence, she went slowly upstairs feeling, in spite of her employer's confidence, he was still a stranger to her, still someone she did not understand and of whom she was not a little afraid.

It was fortunate that the next day was fine and sunny, Doreen had wondered what she would do if it were wet so that Sheila could not ride. She sent a message down to the stables first thing in the morning:

"Miss Sheila's pony with William in attendance were to be at the front door at a quarter past two."

When she came down with the child ready dressed, it was to find no William, but young Billy, the stable boy, in his place.

"Where is William?" Doreen asked. "I sent a message that he was to take Miss Sheila for a ride this afternoon."

"I know that, miss," Billy answered. "I told him myself."

"Well, why isn't he here?" Doreen demanded.

Billy went very pink in the face. He opened his mouth as though he were about to speak, then closed it on an embarrassed silence.

"Well?" Doreen asked. "There must be some explanation."

"He said as 'ow he wouldn't take his orders that

way," Billy blurted out, crimson as any young turkey cock.

Doreen was silent for a moment.

"Very well," she said at length. "You will have to take Miss Sheila, Billy. But be very careful of her, won't you? She needn't be back until about a quarter past four, but keep near the house and don't go on the main road."

"I understand, miss," Billy said.

"Oh, you can trust me all right with Billy," Sheila interrupted. "He has taken me before lots of times and he won't let me do anything in the least dangerous. William doesn't care. He said once that if I broke my neck it would be a damned good thing."

"Well, please don't do it this afternoon," Doreen said.

"I won't," Sheila promised.

Doreen watched them ride off, then going into the house, went to the telephone. She rang up Richard Wickham where she knew she would find him—in the Agent's office—and told him what had occurred.

"The outside servants," she said, "are nothing to do with me, but I have heard stories about William before and I would be glad if you would find out if he's really essential to the place. The child has got to ride and I have got to give the orders—you do see that this is an impossible position?"

"Of course I do," he said soothingly. "Don't get angry, my dear. I will see to it. It sounds to me as though he is a bad lot altogether. The stable accounts are in such a mess that I haven't really been able to get down to them."

He lowered his voice.

"Between ourselves, Anne, George Johnstone let a lot of things slide. I am surprised."

"Well, I am sure you will manage all right," Doreen said.

"Oh, I'm not doing so badly," Richard boasted. "Things straighten themselves out as you go along, you know. By the way, did a young man get on to you last night?"

"Yes. Thank you for giving him the telephone number."

"Apparently old Barton had been very off hand with him," Richard said with a chuckle. "He obviously doesn't approve of followers in the family."

"What are you inferring?" Doreen asked.

"Oh, nothing!" Richard said hastily. "But, by the way, is he Joseph Dale's son? He told me that he had travelled over with you on the boat and I just wondered."

"Yes, he is as a matter of fact," Doreen admitted.

Then hastily before she could be questioned further, she added:

"I must go now. Good-bye, Uncle Richard, and thank you for saying you will see about William."

"Just leave that to me."

There was a note of confidence in Richard's voice which had never been there before. Doreen knew that her plan of getting him interested and at work, had succeeded beyond the bounds of her highest expectations.

He was not only busier than he had been in the whole of his life, but he was also, if one could judge in such a short space of time, better and healthier.

For the first time for twenty years he had something else to think about besides his own body and his inability to do the athletic things which other men of his own age could do.

Had he been forced to show immediately an efficiency he did not possess, the whole plan might have failed, but as things were, Michael Gillespie's indifference to everything that happened on the estate was a blessing.

Richard Wickham could take his own time, could gradually assimilate the difficulties, the negotiations and the many transactions which had taken place in the past, or been half planned for the future.

Things were made easier for him too by the fact that he was well known in the neighbourhood.

The farmers, labourers and the cottagers, were as familiar with the Manor as they were with the Castle itself. In fact, in most cases, they knew Richard far better than Michael Gillespie.

The work itself was not exacting, once he could bring

his unaccustomed mind to assimilate figures, and it gave Richard a sense of importance to start off, soon after breakfast, every morning for the Estate Office.

He had two ways of getting about, one was by an electrically-propelled chair and the other was in a small two-seater car, driven by the man who did odd jobs at the Manor, and which had been specially built to carry the invalid chair he used in the house.

It was surprising how he could manage to visit all sorts of people and places by one method or the other.

When he returned home at night, he was tired but not exhausted, comfortably weary, but not as he had often been in the past, despondent and irritably miserable.

As Doreen finished speaking to her uncle, she looked at the clock and found that it wanted only a few minutes to the half-past.

Hurriedly she ran upstairs and fetched her hat and coat and was waiting on the steps for John Dale by the time she heard the sound of his horn as he turned in at the Lodge and saw his car coming up the drive.

She was anxious, for reasons which she did not express even to herself, to get him away from the Castle as soon as possible.

She did not even wish the servants to see him and the moment he drove up to the door, she ran down the steps.

He was driving himself and was alone.

"Here I am," he said, holding out his hand.

She had forgotten how big and broad-shouldered he was, or that his voice had that dominant, noisy quality, which seemed somehow tremendously vibrant, after the quiet English voices that she had heard lately.

"You are very punctual," she said.

"I have had a couple of hours to kill in the immediate neighbourhood," he answered. "What a one-eyed place! In this part of the world no one would guess there was a war going on."

Doreen glanced over her shoulder towards the house.

"Shall I get into the car?" she suggested.

"In a hurry?" John asked with raised eyebrows. "You aren't going to ask me in, then?"

Doreen shook her head.

"It is my afternoon out!" she laughed.

She got into the front seat beside him and they drove slowly away down the drive.

"Do you know," he said as they went, "I had forgotten how pretty you are."

"Thank you," Doreen replied. "That is the first compliment I have had since I got here."

"What's the matter with the place?" he asked. "Are the men all mobilised or are they blind?"

"We don't waste words in this part of the country!" Doreen answered.

"And you keep your feelings on ice," John said. "I love England, but after a time it gets me down, I have a yearning for the wide open spaces."

"Where men are men!" Doreen finished for him.

"Well, it is true," he answered. "Half the people in this country are wrapped up in cotton wool. A breath of fresh air or a strong word or two, knocks them sideways."

"Is this an advertisement talk for South Africa?" Doreen asked.

She was laughing and enjoying the slightly frivolous conversation, simply because for the first time for weeks, she was speaking easily and naturally to a young man.

After the gentle conventional atmosphere of the Manor and the many responsibilities she had undertaken at the Castle, this was a perfect reaction, and she knew that she was enjoying John Dale's cheery companionship.

She expected him to make some amusing answer to her question. Instead he spoke gravely.

"In some ways that hits the nail on the head."

"What nail and whose head?" she asked.

The narrow lane through which they had been driving opened out on to a wide common.

Without comment John turned the car off the roadway and on to the grass. Here he stopped and switching off the engine, turned in his seat to face Doreen.

"Yours," he said.

His answer came so long after her original question, that for the moment she looked bewildered, having lost the thread of their discussion.

"Start again," she said, "and at the beginning. I don't know what we were talking about. There's a lot I want you to tell me. Why are you here? Why did you telephone me and what have you been doing since we last met on the boat?"

As she spoke she pulled off the small hat she was wearing and threw it on the floor of the car. She ran her fingers through her hair, then looked up at her companion.

He was staring at her, but he was not smiling.

"Well," she said a little impatiently, "begin."

"I was just trying to choose the right words," he explained. "You see, Anne, I have come down here for a very special reason."

There was a grave tone in his voice which arrested her.

"Which is?" she asked, keeping very still, her fingers linked together in her lap.

"To ask you to marry me," John Dale said.

For one wild moment Doreen thought he was joking. She turned swiftly, her eyes searching his face, the instinct for self-protection bringing to her lips a frivolous, joking answer, which would show him that she knew he had spoken in jest.

But it was obvious that he was serious. In spite of herself her eyes dropped before his. She felt her heart begin to beat quicker with an almost frightening impetuosity.

"I don't understand," she faltered.

"I know you don't," he said. "But it is like this. I have been thinking about you ever since we met. You may not believe me, but it happens to be true. When we were parted it seemed to me as though all the other women with whom I came in contact, lacked something, perhaps it was a seriousness, perhaps it was the fact that you had made me see how ridiculous my own life was.

"From that moment when you called me 'A fool' I

knew I was one. I was chucking away so much, missing so many interesting and vital things, wasting the years of my life when I might make something of myself.

"Don't think I gave in without a struggle. I tried to forget you, I tried to cut you out of my thoughts, to even laugh at all you stood for.

" 'A missionary's daughter and John Dale don't mix,' I said to myself, but it didn't work.

"I went to parties, I drank as much, if not more, than usual. All the time everything was ruined for me by hearing your voice say 'you are a fool.' "

"It is not a pretty expression," Doreen said in a weak voice.

"But it is true. That was what got me between the eyes. It is true and you were the first person who had the guts to tell me. Finally I began to see that somehow you had got hold of me.

"I didn't enjoy things because you weren't there; I didn't want to go about with the usual crowd who, up to the time I had met you, seemed to me to be the top.

"Then there comes the war. Anne, I am going back home. I would have been down here before, only I was waiting to wind up my business and to make arrangements to sail for South Africa.

"I am going to join up with our own boys and I will be in France with the first batch to be trained. I have talked to the old man two or three times on the telephone, and he is fixing the whole thing for me."

"That is splendid," Doreen said enthusiastically.

"But wait," John went on, "I haven't finished yet. I am leaving on Monday and I want you to come with me."

"To come with you?"

"Yes, as my wife. We will have to be married before we go, because it is going to be mighty hard on passport facilities if we don't.

"Once you are Mrs. Dale I can pull a mass of strings in the old man's name, and we will have our honeymoon at sea. You will be an old married woman by the time we arrive in Capetown."

"But I can't," Doreen said quickly. "I couldn't."

"Why not?" he asked. "Is it the speed that is worrying you?"

Instantly she asked herself the same question: "Why not?"

Some cool, calculating part of her was astounded at her own hesitation, at her own reluctance, not only to grasp the situation, but to understand all it implied.

Marriage! The word should have meant something thrilling and overwhelming to her. It was what she had hoped for for so long.

It was like coming unexpectedly to one's journey's end, but the elation that should have been there was lacking. Doreen found herself striving to make commonsense pierce its way through her chaotic thoughts.

This was John Dale, son of Joseph Dale, a rich, very rich man, young, strong and in love with her. What more did she want? Why was she hesitating?

Why didn't she turn and give him the answer he was waiting for?

The silence between them seemed endless, yet she could not force herself to break it, could not even turn her eyes to the man who sat beside her.

Then with something akin to panic she felt his arms go round her, felt him draw her into his embrace.

His lips were on hers, fiercely, passionately, possessively, and she felt herself drowning in his strength, against which she had no resistance.

"You have got to be my wife," he murmured. "I want you. God, how I want you—and I can't do without you."

He kissed her again and again. She felt that his kisses in their intensity bruised and seared her mouth. She struggled a little, but it was like fighting against superhuman odds. He was blinded by his desire for her.

She saw the fire in his eyes and felt powerless, impotent and, somehow, utterly unprotected.

"Please," she pleaded, "please let me go."

"I want you," he said again hoarsely.

"I must think, I must," she answered, pressing against him with her hands.

This time her words seemed to penetrate, so that

reluctantly he eased the pressure of his arms and she could move a little away from him.

She was still encircled and was conscious that she was breathless and dishevelled by the violence of his kisses.

"Well," he said, his voice deep and emotional. "What are you going to say to me?"

Then she knew the answer, knew it as truly and as irrevocably as if someone else had said it for her.

The very certainty of what she was about to say made her strength come flooding back to her, so that she could resist him and turn away from this great bear-like man who physically held her so easily in his power, but whom, she knew in reality, was a weakling.

"I can't marry you, John," she said coolly. "I am sorry, but my answer is definitely no."

TWENTY-FOUR

Afterwards Doreen was to wonder at her resolution, at her firmness, and at the strength of will which made all John Dale's pleadings, persuasions, and even ultimate bullyings, of no avail.

Yet because of this new strength, a new understanding seemed to come to her too, and they had parted in a friendly way.

"I shall write to you, Anne," he said, holding both her hands as she stood at the Castle door to say good-bye to him.

"Yes, do," she answered.

"And I shall go on hoping."

She knew at that moment that she had really moved him, for there was something in the way he said those simple words which meant more than all the passion and the blustering to which she had been subjected during the afternoon.

It had been difficult at first to make John believe that she meant what she said.

It was not so much conceit, as the inability to understand, that caused John Dale, who had been spoilt and run after by women all his life, to fail to grasp that the one woman on whom he had set his mind, was refusing to marry him.

If Doreen had hesitated, if she had weakened for a moment, she believed that she would have found herself being carried towards London with the certainty that as quickly as the law would allow it, she would have become a married woman.

But the finality of her tones and the strength of purpose which underlay them had a sincerity which even John Dale could not ignore.

Yet her attitude to him was the more incomprehensible because she could give him no reasonable excuse.

He was not to know that from the first second his lips touched hers, it brought to her a revelation of the truth, not of himself, but of someone else.

The violence of his passion neither shocked nor disgusted her, or indeed had it meant anything more than the passing of an emotional storm in which, unfortunately, she was the victim.

When he had offered her everything that his wealth could buy if only she would reconsider her decision, his voice meant little more than the distant thunder over the hills, or the darkening clouds of a storm.

Something new, something radiant had arisen within her heart which displaced everything else and minimised all that was occurring into unimportance, for in John's arms, with his lips against hers, Doreen had learnt that she was in love.

Love, as she had never known it, vibrated in all its radiant wonder through her whole being.

She was in love—her heart sang with the words; her eyes were opened to a glory she had never believed existed in the world she had found so difficult and often so dismal.

She knew now why the past weeks had gone by in a

happiness and contentment out of all proportion to the actual circumstances.

Why she had awoken, morning after morning, to a world so lovely and so beautiful that she must catch her breath and close her eyes, lest it was but a dream which would vanish again as swiftly as it had come.

She had gone about her duties at the Castle as though they clothed her like a regal mantle and had decked her as if with jewels.

Everything was fresh and easy, every difficulty was surmountable. Yet she knew now she had been waiting always for something more; for a footfall in the doorway, for the sound of one voice, the sight of one particular person.

Now she understood why she had been so anxious to please, why her heart had beaten fitfully, first in interest, then in anger, afterwards in sympathy.

She was not certain when these feelings had deepened into the love which she found pulsating through her now. It seemed as though it had always been there, from that first moment when Michael Gillespie had come into the drawing-room to interview her for the post of governess.

She knew now why the sight of his wounded hand and his slight limp had hurt her. She had believed it to be pity that she had felt for him, but pity was not a knife between one's breasts—an agony which pierced into one's innermost consciousness.

That was love—love for one person whom one would enfold and protect against every injury of body and soul.

Strangely enough, this overwhelming emotion was in itself no surprise.

She had always known love would be like this, when at last it came to her, and the glory of it made her tremble and be still in John Dale's arms, unconsciously surrendering herself because he was so utterly unimportant.

Only as she watched him drive away in his big grey car and heard the sound of its engine gradually fade into the distance, did she remember that she had thrown away the most advantageous offer of security that she had ever received in the whole of her life!

However much John might go on hoping, it would not be easy for her to change her mind in the future.

In a few days he would sail for South Africa and when he returned as a soldier to fight in France, there would not be any likelihood of seeing him.

He had gone, gone from her life because of the answer she had given him and she must go back to her work, an employee dependent on giving satisfaction to a difficult and often incomprehensible employer.

How different her position would have been as John Dale's wife. She knew that the extravagant pleasures he had offered her were not exaggerated.

He was rich—rich beyond all her dreams. She knew also that he was right when he said she could do so much for him. If she loved him, there was little a clever woman could not do with a man who loved her in return.

But Doreen knew now that even if she never saw Michael again, she could never love John Dale.

As yet the revelation of her own love was too sudden for her to make plans, to formulate her own desires.

She only knew that she loved Michael and that she would give up hope of heaven, if needs be, for his sake.

As she walked up the stairs, the memory of the expression on his face the evening before, when the telephone rang, came back to her. She shivered.

There had been dislike in his eyes, a kind of repugnance because, against his will, as it were, he had broken through his reserve to speak to her of the past.

"Michael, Michael!" she whispered and his name on her lips was like a precious gift.

Alone in her own bedroom she stared at the glass. Her cheeks were flushed; her eyes shining.

"I look like a woman who has been kissed by her lover," she thought to herself.

Then laughed at how very opposite that was to the truth.

"I shall see Michael tonight," she thought.

All that was feminine in her made her regard her reflection in the mirror with anxiety. Why wasn't she prettier? Why should her attractions draw to her side someone like John Dale, but not the man she wanted?

She wondered about Sheila's mother. What had Elsie been like? Michael had said she was lovely. Doreen knew that she could not compete with the memory that Michael must have of his first wife's beauty.

And because Elsie was dead time could never take its toll of her youth and radiance. Always and for ever Elsie's memory would remain in Michael's mind, undimmed and unfaded.

How could someone like herself hope to supplant a creature, who for all her sinning, had managed by her physical perfections to keep a hold upon him?

For it was Elsie who still held him back from being a normal man and it was his recollection of her which forced him, in the prime of life, to deny himself the society of all women and the natural comforts of home.

Doreen had a wild desire to run away, to leave the Castle, to leave Michael. She felt that she was up against such overwhelming odds that her defeat was but the matter of time.

Slowly tears gathered in her eyes. But before they could fall, she lifted her chin high and faced herself defiantly in the mirror.

"I won't give in," she said out loud. "Michael, Michael, I love you."

The sound of her own words gave her new strength. She knew that her way was already predestined. She must go forward; there was no retreat.

She could not, she dared not, face a future without Michael and somehow, in some mysterious way, she knew that things would right themselves.

She turned away from her dressing-table and went in search of Sheila.

It wanted only a few minutes to tea-time and she guessed that the child would have come in and be waiting for her downstairs in the library.

She was not mistaken; Sheila was already seated by the tea-table, eating a chocolate biscuit.

"I had a lovely ride," she called out excitedly as Doreen entered. "Billy and I galloped all the way down to Barnleigh Common and came back over the hills. It was fun."

"I am so glad, darling," Doreen answered. "You aren't tired, are you?"

"Not in the slightest," Sheila replied. "Is Daddy coming to tea?"

"I have no idea," Doreen said. "He usually has tea in the laboratory, why should you think that he might?"

"I see Walter has put three extra cups."

Doreen looked and saw that she was right.

"Then we can expect him," she said reflectively. "That will be nice, won't it?"

Sheila made a tiny grimace.

"I don't know," she answered. "I would just as soon have tea alone with you. You never know what sort of mood Daddy is going to be in, although he was terribly nice last night when I was in bed."

"Did he come up and see you?" Doreen asked in surprise.

Sheila nodded.

"He said he was sorry he was cross at luncheon, in fact he was so sorry that he wasn't a bit like himself. Between ourselves, I think some of the guinea pigs must have died."

With the greatest difficulty Doreen prevented herself from laughing. It was so typical of a child to find a practical, matter-of-fact explanation for any unusual action on the part of a grown-up.

She thought it best to leave things as they were, not to try and exaggerate the importance of yesterday's disagreement.

"I expect that you are right," she said. "Men take their work very seriously and if things go wrong, it upsets them altogether."

"I don't like men much," Sheila said ingenuously. "I much prefer women. Not all women, of course, but women like you. They are much easier to understand."

"Thank you, darling," Doreen replied.

She watched the child help herself to a slice of cake

and something in the grace of her head and downcast eyes told her for the first time, that one day Sheila would be very lovely.

"What a responsibility for Michael!" she thought and remembered the bitterness in his voice when he had said "Sheila is not my child!"

How would he ever be able to guide, help and protect her?

A tenderness for the child linked with the man she loved, made Doreen want at that moment to sacrifice herself for both their sakes.

She would do anything, anything within her power, to bring them happiness, to keep them from the agony of loneliness and frustration which must, if things continued as they were now, be waiting ultimately for both of them.

"Help me, help me!" she whispered within herself.

And in a startled moment realised that she had said her first real prayer.

Tea was finished and there was no sign of Michael or his helpers. Reluctantly Doreen was forced to take Sheila upstairs to change.

After tea it had become a self-imposed task for them both to go and play with the evacuated children in the big central courtyard of the Castle, which had been given over to them as a playground.

Doreen and Sheila organised games for the older ones and kept the babies amused with toys and books, which already were in a very tattered condition.

"I must get them some more," Doreen thought as she looked at armless dolls, eyeless teddy bears and broken trains.

She wondered if she ought to ask Michael for money, or if she should order them on her own responsibility. She knew the answer, indeed there was no need for the question. He would be content as long as he was not troubled.

Yet the temptation to make some excuse to seek his advice, or force his attention, was to beset her at every turn.

She had not realised until this moment, that it was possible to yearn so terribly for somebody.

She wanted to see him, if only for a moment, to be reassured by his presence, to know that he was beside her, whatever his mood, even if it were one of anger.

A small child running towards another fell headlong at her feet and started screaming, more in fright than agony. She picked it up, soothing away its frightened tears.

"Let's find a nice picture book to look at, shall we?" she suggested in consolation.

She walked into the games room in search of one, still holding the child in her arms.

As she entered by the long window, she saw Michael at the far end of the room.

Her heart leapt at the sight of him, her pulse beat quicker, and her breath came sharply between parted lips.

She stood still, holding the child in her arms, clutching it closely to her, as though an instinctive protection against her own feelings.

"Miss Marston." Michael's voice was sharp. "You are wanted on the telephone. A Mr. Dale wishes to speak to you."

His words were like a sudden plunge into cold water. Doreen put down the child who, shy at Michael's presence, ran away from him into a corner of the room.

"I am sorry you had the trouble of coming to tell me," she faltered.

"I was having my tea," he answered, "and the call came through directly to the library."

"I am sorry," Doreen said again. "Walter is out this afternoon and the new footman doesn't understand the house exchange."

She turned and ran towards the pantry, conscious that Michael was angry and embarrassed because for that reason she herself was not far from tears.

She switched the line through to the pantry, and after a moment she heart John's voice.

"Anne?" he questioned.

"Is anything wrong?" she asked.

"I am half way back to London," he replied. "I stopped for a cup of tea at a village pub and thought I would give you a ring. You haven't changed your mind, have you?"

Doreen hesitated. She thought of Michael's angry voice and the agonising thought went through her that he might have considered it an impertinence for her private life to be so intrusive. She was only a governess—a servant in the house.

This was her second chance of escape, a second opportunity to alter her whole status.

Just for a moment she imagined herself saying goodbye to Michael and assuring him in light tones that should he ever come to South Africa, he could be sure of a welcome from herself and her husband.

John was waiting.

"Well, Anne, what about it? Weren't you just a little sorry when you saw me go? Shall I turn round and come back?"

There was some insidious note in his pleading. His voice divorced from his bodily presence attracted her and for one fleeting second she was tempted to say "yes."

Then she knew it was impossible. As her old self—as Doreen Wallis—she might have done it, might have taken the risk, might have grabbed what she could while it was still possible.

But for the person she had become, the new Anne Marston, a character into which she had forced herself more firmly than she knew, such a course was beyond her.

She must follow this new love, follow the truth, wherever it might lead her, whatever the future might hold.

With a sigh which was one of relief rather than regret, Doreen said:

"No, John, I haven't changed my mind."

TWENTY-FIVE

"It doesn't seem possible that the war started nearly five weeks ago," Doreen said.

"And such a queer war too," Edith Wickham answered.

Mrs. Wickham, at the top of the table, laughed.

"Edith is disappointed—she believes that her A.R.P. arrangements are so excellent that if she were honest, she would admit that she is longing for an air raid so as to be able to test them."

Edith flushed.

"What an awful thing to say, Mother," she expostulated.

Doreen knew that as usual there was a grain of truth in Mrs. Wickham's taunt, and that she was now enjoying her daughter's discomfiture.

"I don't believe our dug-out is nearly big enough to hold everyone in the Castle," Sheila announced.

"You'll have to squeeze yourself into a rabbit hole," Richard teased.

Doreen had brought Sheila over to luncheon at the Manor. This was not the first occasion, for she had thought it good for Sheila to see other households and other people and what had in conception been a tentative experiment, had proved very successful.

Sheila was welcomed at the Manor and she herself enjoyed exceedingly the time she spent there.

She was a great favourite with Richard and daily she made all sorts of excuses to go down to the Estate Office in the hopes that he would be there.

It was amazing to Doreen to see the difference in her uncle. He was working hard, but was ready to take on even more responsibility and to extend his energies in other directions.

Already she had handed over to him the household accounts at the Castle, as she had found them too complicated to manage alone with such a large number of people to cater for.

The local council, too, had approached Richard to take George Johnstone's place on committees and to everyone's surprise, he had accepted.

"I might as well do it all while I am about it," he explained. "If I am going to be an agent, I shall try to be a good one."

Doreen had not uttered the warning words about his health which had sprung to her lips.

Instinctively she realised that this might prove a better cure for Richard's ailments than any of the more expensive and elaborate treatments suggested by doctors.

There was no possibility, of course, of him ever becoming normally healthy and active.

Yet, at the same time, there was the chance that some part at any rate of his disability might be mental.

Faith had proved itself very often in the past and if Richard wished to undertake his work, it was far better after years of lassitude to let him have his own way, even though he might, for a short period, over-tax his strength.

There was, however, no sign of it at the moment.

At the opposite end of the table to Mrs. Wickham, he had been in an animated and conversational mood all through luncheon.

"Are you coming to see my roses?" Richard asked Doreen as they finished the meal.

Doreen shook her head.

"I am sorry," she said regretfully, "but Sheila and I have to rush back to the Castle—she is riding this afternoon and I have got several letters I must write before the post goes. I didn't have a moment yesterday to order the supplies from London that you and I decided on."

"I wish you would come and ride with me," Sheila said. "You promised that you would."

"I know," Doreen answered. "But that was before the war started. When peace comes I will ride with you every day. That's a promise."

"William is going tomorrow," Richard said. "I had to give him time to get out of his cottage. I hear that he and his wife are moving to the other side of Cheltenham—I'm glad that he is leaving the neighbourhood. The more I learn about that man's character, the more unfortunate I think it is that he has stayed as long as he has."

"Are you getting anyone else to replace him?" Doreen asked.

"Not at the moment," Richard replied. "I have raised Billy's wages and the boy assures me that he can look after both horses, at any rate for the duration of the war. He's a good lad and reliable and the only doubt I have in my mind is that he's too young for the responsibility. However, we can but try and give him a chance to prove himself."

"Billy told me that you were a sportsman, Uncle Richard," Sheila said.

"I expect that was after he heard about his rise," Richard said laughing.

But Doreen knew he was both gratified and pleased at the compliment.

"If you have finished, Sheila, we had better be going," she said, looking out of the window as she spoke. "I hope it is not going to rain before we get back. It was so fine this morning that I never thought to bring our mackintoshes."

The dark clouds were looming up over the distant hills and the sky was overcast. Doreen shivered. She had woken up that morning with a headache, and a feeling of thickness in her throat.

Now she felt chilled.

"I must be over-tired," she told herself, afraid to voice an inner suspicion that she might be going to have an attack of fever.

It had been fine weather for the time of year, but the warmth of the sun was lessening; there were heavy dews at night and a damp foggy mist surrounded the Castle in the early mornings.

It would be foolish not to expect that after living for years in the East, she would not be subject to all sorts of ailments during the first English winter she had ever experienced.

"Good-bye, Anne's Grandmother," Sheila said to Mrs. Wickham, holding up her face to be kissed.

She had already adopted Doreen's relatives as her own. Richard and Edith she called "Uncle" and "Aunt", but as if she felt that "Grandmother" was too familiar for her rather austere hostess, she invariably addressed her as "Anne's Grandmother."

"Good-bye, dear child," Mrs. Wickham said. "Come again soon."

"I am coming next Monday," Sheila replied, "and what do you think I am bringing you?"

"I have no idea," Mrs. Wickham answered. "A present?"

"Walnuts!" Sheila exclaimed with glee. "We have picked nearly a basketful. We couldn't bring them today because they weren't quite dry."

"That will be nice," Mrs. Wickham said. "How kind of you to think of it."

"I did think of it myself, didn't I?" Sheila said turning to Doreen.

"Yes," was the answer. "It was entirely your idea."

With many more good-byes, Doreen and Sheila at last got off and started pedalling with all speed towards the Castle.

They had not gone far before a sharp shower of rain forced them to dismount and shelter under a big oak tree by the side of the road. Sheila was wearing a tweed coat, but Doreen, in a thin wool jumper and skirt, was soaked through to the skin.

The shower did not last long and with the vaguery of autumn weather, immediately it had passed the sun came out again, to glitter on wet leaves and in the puddles by the roadside.

"I shall never again leave the house without our mackintoshes," Doreen vowed.

"Oh, a little rain won't hurt us," Sheila said scornfully. "Sometimes I have been nearly drowned in the rain, but it has never done me any harm."

Doreen felt that this was very likely true. The child

was strong and wiry, and in spite of her luxurious home had, through her own wildness, avoided being coddled or pampered unnecessarily.

When they got back to the Castle she sent Sheila up to change.

"Hurry," she said. "I will put away the bicycles. I don't want you to get cold."

"I'm not cold," Sheila said, "and anyway, I shall soon get hot riding."

She was half dressed in her breeches and boots by the time Doreen came, somewhat wearily, up the stairs and into the room next door.

"You have got plenty of time," Doreen said. "I didn't order the horses until half-past two."

"Billy is always punctual, so I don't want to keep him waiting."

Doreen tried to smile at this statement. Punctuality was a very new virtue as far as Sheila was concerned, and she had spent much energy in trying to instil it into the child.

The smile, however, was a wan one, for she was shivering and her head was aching almost unbearably.

Slowly she took off her damp clothes, put on another dress and changed her shoes and stockings. By the time she was ready Sheila was jumping about with impatience.

"Let's go down," she kept saying. "I am sure the horses are here."

She ran to the top of the stairs and gave a cry of greeting.

"Hullo, Daddy," she said. "I am just going riding. Come and see me on my pony. I am awfully good now, I am really. I jumped a perfectly enormous hedge last time."

"You will come a perfectly enormous fall if you aren't careful," Doreen heard in reply and instinctively felt that quick leap of her heart and the throbbing of her pulses.

She should have grown used to Michael's voice by this time and also to the sight of him.

Yet every time she encountered him unexpectedly,

she felt this same sensation of startled excitement, a sensation half pleasure, half pain.

Every day she told herself that she must grow used to his indifference, to the polite, but distant manner in which he had treated her ever since his one unreserved confidence many weeks ago.

But always she hoped for something more—always to be disappointed. It seemed to her as though he was deliberately avoiding being alone with her, or of finding a bond of intimacy, even in their conversations about the child.

His gravity seemed to have increased, and while she told herself it was absurd, there was, nevertheless, in Doreen's mind, the strong conviction that he had deliberately erected new barriers between them.

She had never believed that it was possible for her, Doreen Wallis, to feel as she did about Michael. Every night before she slept she prayed, not only for herself, but for him.

It was as though he brought forth within her some extraordinary depth of unselfishness which she had never realised was there before. She was unhappy, but she knew without need of confirmation that he was unhappy too.

Her life lacked fulfilment, lacked security, but he had suffered so much more in that he was frustrated and hampered by the knowledge of things that he had once had.

In thinking of the man she loved, a new understanding of human nature came to Doreen.

She saw that in the case of someone as sensitive as Michael, the old adage "It is better to have loved and lost, than never to have loved at all," was not applicable.

He had been hurt, wounded and scarred so vitally, that it was doubtful whether he would ever be whole again, while for her, there was only an emptiness and a yearning, which did not preclude the definite hope that one day things might be different.

It is hope which keeps the spark of life glowing within a human being and Doreen understood that Michael was as a man damned to eternal perdition because he believed himself to be without hope.

"Help him," she prayed in the darkness of her little room. "Help him to find happiness, if not with me, at least with someone else. Let him forget the past and look forward to the future."

It was difficult now to believe that she had ever been angry with him, had ever turned in scorn and fury upon him that day when he had been unkind to Sheila.

She knew now that whatever he said, whatever he did, she would be unable to force herself into battle with him.

Nevertheless, he had, since that occasion, been far nicer and far more sympathetic towards the child.

As Doreen came down the stairs behind Sheila, she saw him put out his arm in greeting, slip it round the little girl's shoulder and thus linked, walk with her towards the door.

"Where have you been?" he asked. "I missed you at luncheon."

"We have been to Anne's grandmother," Sheila answered. "And we bicycled home."

"You seem to be a pretty frequent guest at the Manor, nowadays," he said. "I hope they don't find you a nuisance."

He turned and just for a moment his eyes met Doreen's. Then he looked away.

"My grandmother loves having Sheila," Doreen said quietly, "and is delighted to see her any time."

"That is all right then," Michael replied, opening the front door.

The horses were waiting outside and Sheila ran towards them.

"Isn't Billy coming with me?" she asked sharply.

Doreen, coming to the top of the steps, saw that it was William who stood holding the horses' heads, not Billy as they had expected.

"No, he ain't," William said surlily to the child.

Sheila turned an anguished face towards Doreen.

"I think it would be better for Billy to take Miss Sheila, William," she said quietly to the groom. "He has been out with her for the last dozen times and she is used to him."

"I am taking the horses this afternoon," William answered insolently.

"I am sorry, William," Doreen replied firmly, "but I think it would be better if you let Billy go. Miss Sheila has been jumping with him lately. I know he understands exactly how much she can do."

"I am in charge of the stables until tomorrow, and I take out the horses or they don't go."

"You heard what Miss Marston said!"

Michael spoke from the top of the steps and until that moment William had been unaware of his presence. He swung round and as he did so, Doreen realised that the man had been drinking.

"Oh, it is you, Mr. Gillespie, is it," he ejaculated. "I was hoping to see you before I left."

"That still doesn't settle this point of who takes Miss Sheila riding," Michael answered. "Perhaps you had better ride one of the horses back to the stables and fetch Billy. Miss Sheila will wait here."

"So you're giving orders now, are you?" William said. "I thought you had abdicated in favour of your lady governess."

He spoke furiously, his face crimson, big veins beginning to stand out at the sides of his temples and down his thin neck. Doreen put out her hand to touch Sheila's.

Michael came slowly down the steps and without looking at William, walked up to the horses and took hold of their bridles.

"Do as I tell you," he said. "Fetch Billy. I will speak to you afterwards."

For one agonised moment Doreen thought that William would lose all control of himself. He had stepped back as Michael had taken the bridles from his hand.

Now he came forward again and she saw his hands were clenched tightly, so that the knuckles showed white.

"I am leaving this place tomorrow," William said hoarsely, "and before I go, I would like to speak my mind."

"This is neither the time nor the place for that," Michael answered. "Will you do as you are told?"

He straightened himself and something in his bearing, in the note of command in his voice, forced William to obedience.

The man turned furiously away, walking towards the stables.

You are splendid! Doreen's heart cried within her.

Why don't you assert yourself more often? Why don't you at other times remember your manhood?

The battle, however, was not finished. About fifteen yards away from where they stood, William stopped.

"I will just say this," he shouted. "I am glad to be leaving! Don't think you are turning me out. I should have gone anyway. When a man like you has a fancy woman running the place, it is time for respectable people to pack their boxes."

Doreen gave a little gasp. She saw Michael's jaw tighten, a sudden glint of anger in his eyes. He didn't even turn his head in William's direction.

Instead he said abruptly to Sheila:

"Get on your pony, and walk him slowly down the drive. I will see that Billy catches you up."

Awed into silence by what had occurred, Sheila did as she was told. As she moved off on her pony, Michael still holding the other horse, started to walk in the direction of the stables.

"What are you going to do?" Doreen asked urgently.

"Don't worry," he answered.

"Stop," she said. "Please don't go after him. There is no point in it. He is leaving tomorrow and he has had too much to drink."

Michael looked merely obstinate.

"It is quite all right, Miss Marston," he said soothingly. "You go into the house and wait there for me."

"No, please!" Doreen interrupted. "Please don't do

anything now, it won't do any good and it will only upset you. I will go back and telephone for Billy, if you will wait here. Please, Michael!"

She had no idea that she had used his Christian name. It slipped out in the earnestness of her desire that there should be no disturbance or upset.

She was afraid too, afraid of what this strange Michael, with a steely anger in his grey eyes and firm-set jaw, might do.

It would be so easy to start a scandal, to have the servants and the countryside talking of a fight between a drunken groom and his master, over an insult to the governess. Once again she spoke urgently.

"Please! Don't do anything."

She saw that she had succeeded in altering his intention.

"I will telephone Billy," she said quickly. "He won't be a moment or two. I am sure he is ready."

She ran through the hall and towards the pantry. The garage telephone stood on a small table by the house exchange.

She picked up the receiver and almost immediately Billy's voice said "Hullo". She guessed that he had been anxiously waiting the call.

"Will you come up to the house at once, Billy?" she said. "Mr. Gillespie is waiting with the horse outside the front door. Miss Sheila has ridden on down the drive."

"Very good, miss," Billy replied.

Doreen looked at the receiver and saw that her hand was trembling. For a moment she felt quite faint. Then she forced herself to walk steadily down the passage and back to the hall.

She did not go to the front door, but with a sense of deep relief, she heard the horse move outside and heard Michael's voice speak soothingly.

He had listened to her after all, she was thankful that she had been able to control him. But as relief eased her tension, Doreen wondered for the first time what was Michael's reaction to William's words.

She had been too frightened of what he might do

to worry over his thoughts. Yet now the full implication of them came to her.

So that was what some people were saying: "Michael's fancy woman!"

How she wished it was true. With sudden weakness she found the tears start to her eyes. Blindly she turned towards the stairs and started to climb them.

She had just reached the top when the front door slammed and she saw her employer come into the hall.

He looked up and saw her.

"Oh, Miss Marston!" he said. "I want to speak to you. Will you come into the library?"

For a second she hesitated, and a sudden agonising fear made her almost incapable of obeying him. What did this mean?

Was he going to dismiss her because of the evil implications of a drunken and discharged servant?

Michael was waiting.

Doreen turned and forcing with an almost superhuman effort her body to obey her, came slowly down the stairs.

TWENTY-SIX

Doreen walked into the library feeling unaccountably afraid.

Her knees were shaking and her whole body, already icy cold, was trembling. The big room seemed dark and comfortless.

There was no fire in the grate, but Michael was standing in front of the empty fireplace.

She drew near to him. He did not watch her approach, but when finally she stopped at the edge of the hearthrug facing him, he looked up.

He stared at her with an extraordinary and quite unfathomable expression in his eyes.

It seemed to Doreen as if he was looking at her for the first time, as though he was taking in every inch of her face, seeking for something she could not name. He did not speak.

At last, because she could bear the tension no longer, she broke the silence.

"What is it?" she asked in a voice hardly above a whisper.

"You know what it is," he answered.

His voice was low and hoarse, but his gaze did not falter, his eyes still on her face.

"No, what?" she questioned. "I don't understand."

In bewilderment she clasped her hands together, making the strength of her fingers grip and subdue the trembling which she could not control.

Swiftly Michael stepped forward and laid his ungloved hand on hers.

"Why are you afraid?" he asked. "Why?"

"I don't know," Doreen faltered. "I don't think I am really, it is just . . ."

Her voice trailed away into silence, the words died on her lips. She was looking into Michael's eyes, looking into them closely and intimately as she had never done before.

She had no idea that they were so grey, or they could hold in their depths such tenderness, such a gentle yearning, and another expression which she dared not name, even to herself.

"You know what I want to ask you, Anne," he said, his hand still holding both of hers. "I want to ask you to marry me."

The whole room swayed about her. Quickly the thought came to her that she was mad or dreaming; it couldn't be true that she was hearing Michael—Michael of all people—speaking those words.

"Oh my dear," he went on, "I had no idea that this could be such a surprise to you. I thought you must have known, must have guessed all that has been in my heart these past weeks.

"Now I have frightened you, I have made you tremble. But I understand. I too have been afraid, so terribly afraid of rushing things, of speaking before the right moment, of finding all that I hoped and longed for was impossible.

"But now I can keep silent no longer. I have got to tell you. I have got to know the truth and for God's sake, don't hurt me more than you must."

He took his hand from hers in an abrupt gesture. Doreen swayed and might have fallen had he not put out his arms and steadied her.

He noticed her pallor.

"This has been a shock," he said. "Sit down, my darling, and let me talk to you. There is so much that I want to say."

As though she moved hardly of her own volition, she obeyed him. He helped her to a chair and when she was seated in it, suddenly knelt beside her.

"Listen, Anne," he said, "before you answer me, before you make me either the happiest man in all the world or send me back to the purgatory in which I existed before you came into my life, I must explain.

"Since you have been here you have thought me cruel, hard and, at times, bestial, both to Sheila and yourself.

"You were right—I have been all those things, but you don't know what it is like for a man to live year after year in anguish and in loneliness, torturing himself because he cannot escape from his past.

"Only in work did I find a solace—a drug which numbed the pain a little, which made the passing of time a trifle easier. I grew used to thinking of myself as old, without a future, without any hope of happiness.

"Then suddenly you came here.

"At first I thought the sight of you irritated me. I had been so long without the society of women, that I thought the feelings I had about you, almost from the very first moment of our meeting, were ones of antipathy, dislike and abhorrence.

"Then gradually after a few days I began to be afraid. I knew that some alteration was taking place within me, that my misery was changing.

"Something was occurring; some emotional disturbance which could not be accounted for, and which was intensified by introspection.

"I fought against it; I fought against it desperately, fighting as a man who has long been a prisoner will cling to his cell and to his chains, rather than face an unknown freedom outside.

"I tried to drown myself in my work, to make it all absorbing as it had been for many years. But it was impossible.

"Always I could see your face. A smile, a gesture, the tone of your voice, the movement of one of your hands would haunt me.

"Slowly, so slowly, that when finally I faced the truth it seemed as though it must always have been there, I came to the knowledge of the truth, to the realisation that I loved you.

"It is a love, Anne, which is quite unlike anything I have ever known. Everything in the past has paled and become dim beside the glory of what I feel now.

"And I see how ridiculous I have been; how unbalanced and absurd to let the years drift by in vain regrettings, in suffering, in the torture of pride and bitterness.

"Today it seems like a bad dream. Now I am awake, but I am afraid, as I have never been afraid before, that I might lose you."

He bent his head suddenly and pressed his lips against Doreen's hands as they lay in her lap. She felt the touch of his mouth and looked down on his dark head. She felt a sudden horror creep over her.

It dispelled the almost paralysed silence in which she had listened to his words.

Yet she could not for the moment move, could not speak, could not even obey the impulse within her which made her want to run away.

Michael raised his face to hers. She saw an expression of awe and of adoration in his face.

"You don't know what you have done to me," he said. "You have given back my belief in goodness, my belief in all that is holy, wonderful and sacred, indeed my faith in God."

It was then Doreen moved. She pushed him from her with both hands and got to her feet.

"I must go away," she said desperately. "I want to think. I can't talk to you now."

He stood up and made a wide gesture with his arms as though he released her.

"I understand! I have spoken too quickly. I meant to wait, to wait until gradually, slowly, you came to love me. But I couldn't stand anyone speaking of you in a disparaging way. I couldn't bear that you should be abused, even by a drunken swine, when I know you as you are . . . my perfect woman!"

"Don't, please!" Doreen repeated.

"I will wait," Michael said softly. "I will wait for ever, if I must. But my darling, don't let it be too long."

As though he could not control himself he stepped forward and would have taken her in his arms. Doreen turned and fled from him.

She ran the length of the library, opened the door, and left him without a backward glance.

She did not stop to think or consider. She ran swiftly through the big hall and out through the front door into the drive.

She was in a panic which drove her without logic and without thought.

She only knew she must escape; that she could not stay in the Castle another moment; she could not face Michael; she dared not listen or believe what he had told her.

A humiliation and horror of herself, so intense that it felt like a burning flame within her body, consumed her. It forced her away from the man she loved.

She saw now how impossible her love had been, a love rooted in hypocrisy and deception which in the contrariness of life, had raised from the one man she respected and adored, a faith which she could not justify.

How could she turn to him with a lie on her lips?

How could she allow him to touch her where she knew that if he knew the truth, he would turn from her in loathing and disgust?

This indeed was a just retribution for the sins she had committed. It lay within her grasp, but she dared not take, dared not accept supreme happiness.

She was conscious of a throbbing head, of breath that came brokenly from her throat.

Yet she forced herself on, sometimes running, sometimes walking, her one idea to get away from the Castle and from Michael.

After a time she began to cry. The tears overflowed from her eyes and ran down her cheeks.

She made no attempt to wipe them away. She knew the taste of them, salt and bitter, as still she went on, moving automatically down the country lanes which were familiar, until she found herself nearing the Manor.

It must have been instinct which made her feet follow the road she knew so well, rather than take a strange path, for at no moment had she willingly sought her direction.

It was then, as she came in sight of the old grey stone house, that what she must do came distinctly to her mind as though someone had given her a command.

She must tell the truth; she must confess to her grandmother the part she had played to obtain their kindness and their generosity.

Then when they turned from her, she must go away into a wilderness of her own making, into a desert of loneliness and isolation.

What happened afterwards was unimportant.

She knew nothing could ever at any time console her for the loss of Michael, could dim the agonising pain which she already felt within her at the thought of never seeing him again.

He must never know, she told herself wildly, she must disappear, vanish, die—anything rather than he should once again know disillusionment, should find that all women were deceitful.

What was Elsie's deceit and infidelity, Doreen asked herself, compared with her own perfidy?

She had entered his house under false pretences, and she had loved him with her tawdry and well-worn emotions, unprepared for the fact that she might rouse in him a love that was almost divine in its sanctity.

As she stumbled up the drive of the Manor, her self-condemnation made her cover her face with her hands.

She was utterly weary, yet so detached from physical things that she was quite unaware that it had been raining for some time and that she was very wet.

Along the last hundred yards she forced herself forward with the greatest effort, and determination, to fulfil the task she had set herself.

She opened the front door and walked into the hall.

There was no one about; she knew that she would find her grandmother, and in all likelihood Edith and Richard, in the drawing-room.

Now that the moment was upon her, a strange lightness possessed her whole being; she felt as though she was very small and was watching herself from far away—a midget moving across a great table of space.

She was so weak that it required all her strength to turn the handle of the drawing-room door.

She stumbled into the room.

She saw her grandmother sitting at the writing desk.

For a moment she did not turn. Doreen stood just within the doorway, gripping the back of a chair, feeling a sudden dreadful lassitude sweep over her.

"Anne! What is it?"

From a long distance away her grandmother's voice came to her ears.

Then like the roar of a gun, Doreen heard her own voice reply.

"I have come back, Grandmother," she said, "to tell you the truth. I am not Anne. I am Doreen. Anne is dead."

She heard her voice die away. The silence became deeper and deeper and the room darkened. She fought against a great cloud which threatened to encompass her.

"Do you hear me?" she cried. "I am not dead, I am alive. I am here! . . ."

Her voice trailed away into a little gasp of pain. She slipped forward to the floor and into unconsciousness. . . .

There were hands lifting her and something cool on her forehead . . . she heard the murmur of low voices, then they were gone again and a deep almost dreamless slumber swallowed her up . . .

There were dreams, sometimes vivid, sometimes just figments of people and places, so shadowy that she knew, even while they passed before her, that they were not real, only creatures of her own imagination . . .

Always she came back to those brief hazy moments of consciousness, when there was the murmur of low voices and the feeling of something cool on her forehead . . . she opened her eyes to see a strange man standing by the bed . . .

She was aware of him and that it was a bed she was lying on, then she drifted away again into dreams . . . to the burning sunshine of deserts where she lay gasping for air . . . to rivers wide as the Nile, green-edged with palm trees, down which she could float for ever and ever. . . .

Doreen opened her eyes.

The blinds in her room were lowered, but the sun was piercing its way through, creating a golden haze against which she blinked, dazzled and bemused.

A gentle movement at the other side of the bed made her turn her head.

She saw her grandmother. For a moment she was glad.

She smiled faintly and in a voice so weak that she hardly recognised it as her own, she heard herself speak.

"Hullo, Grandmother. Have I been ill?"

Even as she spoke she remembered—remembered the words she had cried out in the drawing-room, the darkness that had swallowed her up.

She gave a little whimper, half of fear, half of pain.

Instantly Mrs. Wickham rose to her feet and taking a glass from the side of the bed, held it to her lips.

"Drink this," she said quietly.

Doreen did as she was told. She felt a liquid warm and vivifying pass down her throat.

Almost immediately after she had swallowed it, she felt her brain clear, felt stronger in voice and body.

"What is it?"

"The doctor said you could have it when you were conscious," Mrs. Wickham replied, putting the glass down.

"Have I been ill long?"

"Three days."

Doreen looked at her grandmother.

"I am sorry," she said quietly and they both knew that she did not refer to her illness.

"I wanted to talk to you," Mrs. Wickham said. "That is why I am here, why I have been waiting while you have been delirious with fever, until you were sensible again."

Doreen's lips twisted into what was almost a wry smile.

"I am going away as soon as I can."

She closed her eyes wearily. What was the point of talking, she wondered?

What could her grandmother say to hurt her now? Recriminations, reproaches, were all as useless as her own regrets.

It had happened; she had played the part and nothing could alter that fact, nothing could at this moment take away the agony of the loss of Michael.

Even in her delirium, she knew that her love for him had been growing, anguished and desolate, because of that sense of desolation.

"Listen to me!" Mrs. Wickham's voice was sharp. It drew Doreen, in spite of herself, to alertness. She opened her eyes. "I was alone when you came and spoke to me the other evening. I was the only person who heard what you had to say."

"Then you will have to tell Aunt Edith and Uncle Richard," Doreen answered. "They had better know. There is no question, now, of keeping up pretences. As soon as I am well enough, I will leave here and none of you need worry about me again."

"They don't know and they are never going to know," Mrs. Wickham said vigorously.

Doreen stared at her grandmother.

"What do you mean?" she asked.

Mrs. Wickham bent forward, her clear penetrating eyes fixed on her grand-daughter.

"The task you have undertaken," she said distinctly, "cannot be abandoned half-way."

Just for a moment her words brought a glow of hope to Doreen. Then she shook her head.

"You don't understand," she said.

"Downstairs," Mrs. Wickham went on as though she had not been interrupted, "Michael Gillespie is waiting—waiting to see you."

Her words made Doreen shrink back against her pillows in horror.

"He can't see me!" she cried. "I can't see him! Don't you understand, Grandmother?"

"I do understand and that is what I am trying to tell you," Mrs. Wickham replied. "Michael loves you—he has told me a great deal these last three days about himself and about his love for you. You cannot fail him."

"You mean?" Doreen whispered.

"That you are going to marry him. You love him—I am quite certain of that—and you must tell him so."

"How can I?" Doreen asked despairingly. "I have lied, I have deceived you all."

"That is not quite true."

Doreen glanced sharply at her grandmother.

"You knew?" she asked.

"The very first day you arrived," Mrs. Wickham answered. "Don't look so surprised, my dear, I didn't have to be a Sherlock Holmes, it was far easier than that. My daughter Martha wrote to me continually and there was very little she omitted from her letters.

"Three years ago she told me that her daughter Anne was suffering a great deal with her teeth and she was taking her down to Nairobi to have them seen to.

"All the front ones were to be replaced by a false set."

Doreen laughed weakly, she couldn't help it.

It was so farcical, so utterly unexpected—the one thing she had never suspected, the one clue to Anne's identity she had overlooked.

"Why didn't you turn me out?" she asked soberly.

"I was interested," Mrs. Wickham answered. "Above all things I like courage."

"And because of that you let me go on?"

"Not exactly," her grandmother replied. "I am going to say to you what I have never said to another woman in the whole of my life. I admire you."

"But, Grandmother!" Doreen ejaculated.

"As I have already said," Mrs. Wickham said, "it was courageous of you to take Anne's place, but it required something more than courage to keep up the deception of being a heroine and, as you believed, a saint.

"Anne was nothing of the sort, but because of what people expected of you, you gave the best that was in yourself, indeed the best of which you were capable.

"You have made my son Richard into a different man; you have given him hope and you have found him the one thing in life that can save him from himself—work.

"I didn't realise that, I who have loved him more dearly than anyone else since my husband died.

"You have brought happiness also to a young child who was running wild and growing up without discipline or understanding.

"You have given to her father, Michael Gillespie, a new life. Dare you in a few words destroy, not yourself, but them?"

"But I daren't go on," Doreen murmured.

"You have got to," Mrs. Wickham insisted. "That, if you like, is your punishment, your retribution, that you must never relax, that you can never take back what you have given, but must for ever give more and more.

"Your life is not going to be easy in the future.

"You will often be afraid, you will often lack confidence in yourself, but for the sake of those people who you love and who love you, you must go on.

"I am an old woman, I cannot help you—no one can

help you. You have got to stand alone, you have got to work out your own salvation.

"Whatever you have done, however much you are ashamed of your actions, that can be no excuse now for the weakness of a confession which can bring little comfort to yourself and only chaos into the lives of those who trust you.

"You have created faith in them and for that faith you have got to live, and if needs be, to suffer."

Doreen hardly dared to breathe. She could only lie still and tense, every nerve in her body strained to listen, to comprehend.

Only as her grandmother finished did she stretch out both her hands in supplication and entreaty.

"You are quite, sure?" she asked.

"There is nothing else you can do," Mrs. Wickham said with a note of finality, turning towards the door. "I am going to send Michael up to see you. He must only stay a moment because you are tired."

Then with a softness of expression which few people had ever seen on her face, she added, "God bless you, my dear."

Doreen heard the door close behind her. She shut her eyes and pressed both her hands against her breasts.

She was conscious that her heart was beating quickly, that there was a sudden throbbing of ecstasy, of thrilling wonder creeping through her whole body.

"Michael," she whispered to herself.

She knew for the first time in her life a happiness that was beyond expression.

She shut her eyes, and when she opened them again he was standing beside her.

She looked up into his face and saw there the dawning of a hope so poignant, so fearful and yet so rapturous that she could only stare at him wordlessly, unable to move, hardly able to breathe.

"Anne, oh my darling, you are better?"

He dropped down on his knees beside the bed so that his face was level with hers.

"I've been so worried about you."

"Is everything . . . all right . . . at the Castle?" Her

voice was low and she was trembling because of the nearness of him.

"It's empty—completely empty without you."

She knew he was not only speaking of the Castle but of his life. The emptiness and loneliness of the past would be nothing to the loneliness he would know now if she failed him.

"I'll be . . . back . . . soon."

"You don't know what hell it is without you."

She heard the pain in his voice and she knew she must help him, sustain him, give him back his manhood.

"How soon . . . could we . . . be married?"

Her words were only a whisper and for a moment Michael felt he could not have heard them right.

Then his face was transfigured.

"Do you mean that? Oh, my dearest, my little love, I love you more than life itself. I'll make you happy—I swear it."

The wonder of his words and the expression on his face made the tears start to her eyes and run weakly down her cheeks.

"I've made you cry!" Michael exclaimed. "This is too much for you when you've been so ill. I must leave you to rest, but my heart is yours, you know that—my darling, my wonderful, perfect woman."

His lips touched hers gently and tenderly, but she felt an ecstasy and joy within herself which was like a flame.

"I . . . love . . . you," she whispered.

And knew as she dedicated herself to him for all time that love would show her the way.